Plaudits For Author DAVID FULMER

- BEST FIRST NOVEL – 2002 SHAMUS AWARDS
- BEST OF 2003 LIST – BORDERS BOOKS
- BEST NEW SERIES – BOOKLIST
- NOMINEE – 2002 LA TIMES BOOK PRIZES
- NOMINEE – 2002 BARRY AWARDS
- NOMINEE – 2005 FALCON AWARD
- BEST OF 2005 LIST – THE ST. LOUIS POST-DISPATCH
- BEST OF 2005 LIST – LIBRARY JOURNAL
- BEST OF 2005 LIST – DEADLY PLEASURES MAGAZINE
- 2007 BENJAMIN FRANKLIN AWARD – ADULT FICTION AUDIO
- 2008 BEST OF THE SHELF – ATLANTA MAGAZINE
- BEST NOVELS YOU'VE NEVER READ – NEW YORK MAGAZINE
- NOMINEE – 2009 SHAMUS AWARD – BEST NOVEL

"Fulmer is both a fine plotter and a marvelously evocative writer, with an eye for character."

—*The Washington Post Book World*

"The atmosphere Fulmer creates is rich, nuanced, and authentic."

—*Minneapolis Star-Tribune*

"Shamus-winner Fulmer excels at capturing the feel and textures of earlier decades, even as he moves forward in time with each successive novel. Drawn in by the immensely likable characters and rich, realistic story lines, readers will be eager to see where Fulmer goes next."

—*Publishers Weekly*

"If you love a mystery with some punch, David Fulmer delivers."

—*Southern Living*

"The alchemy of Fulmer's fusion of history, music and literature makes it play like a paean to an era's corruption and human struggle against the whim of powerful force and injustice."

— *The Critical Mystery Tour*

"Fulmer brings us a novel dripping with detail, environment, and character."

—*Crime Spree Magazine*

"If there's any crime writer whose work should come with soundtrack CDs, it's David Fulmer."

— *The Thrilling Detective*

"David Fulmer is a fine writer."

—*Nelson Demille*

www.davidfulmer.com

The Fall

Also by David Fulmer

Lost River
The Blue Door
The Dying Crapshooter's Blues
Rampart Street
Jass
Chasing the Devil's Tail

The Fall

David Fulmer

FIVE STONES PRESS
Atlanta
2010

First Edition

www.FiveStonesllc.com

Publisher-Supplied Cataloging-in-Publication Data
Fulmer, David.
The fall / David Fulmer.—1st ed.
p. cm.
1. Actors—Fiction. I. Title.

PS3606.U56F35 2010
813'.6—dc22

Library of Congress Control Number: 2009941200

ISBN-10: 0-9776729-3-X
ISBN-13: 978-0-9776729-3-6

Book design by Susan Archie

Printed in the United States of America

To those friends who lent trust and spirit
to carry this dream along.
You are all guilty as charged.
— df

You say you'd never compromise
With the mystery tramp, but now you realize
He's not selling any alibis
As you stare into the vacuum of his eyes
And say, "Do you want to make a deal?"

—Bob Dylan, "Like a Rolling Stone"

1.

Later, after it was all over, I spent some time thinking about how it was for him at the end.

In the dark of night, the shadows between the trees would have been full of ghosts. He would have dreamed of his faces, of music and laughter, of sweet smoke and red wine. The valley, spread out below, would have twinkled with gentle lights as the moon, out from heaven and making the rounds, floated on the river.

Realizing what was happening, he would have held fast to this vision as he went over the edge. Knowing Joey, and how brave he was, he might have shouted *I'm flying* as he left all the weight behind, escaping, leaving those on the ground with a final *fuck you* salute to their sick and bitter little souls, as he kept rising.

He started to fall, but I want to believe that before he came down for the last time, some merciful angel draped him in a shroud of darkness that held blades of kind light on its horizon.

2.

Isabel stepped into the kitchen and brushed gentle fingers over my shoulder on her way to the coffeemaker. I could hear my daughters arguing as they got ready for school, a bit of busy music from their bedroom down the hall. The sun was butter melting over the rooftops as a start one to those glorious days that arrive to testify that even a wounded Manhattan is a marvelous place to live.

My wife brought her cup to the table just as the girls came in twittering like sparrows, their dispute resolved. I sat momentarily dazzled by their beauty, their small oval faces and round black eyes so full of light and life. They kissed the mom to whom they owed their looks and then me, and clattered out the door and into the elevator, miniature humpbacks under packs that threatened to topple them.

In the sudden silence, Isabel left me to my paper and went to stand by the window to watch them emerge onto the sidewalk and clamber onto the waiting bus. It was an even day, her turn.

I noticed the way her face was cast in the morning light, the green eyes set off by the tawny flesh and curly black hair of her Latin viejos, and then back to the Irish side of the tree for a sprinkle of dark freckles. Her lips were full and her nose held the slightest Indian curve. She looked so pretty and I felt so lucky.

The horn tootled merry notes and the bus pulled away from the curb. Her gaze was wistful as she released her babies to the world once more. After a sweet sigh, she shifted into career gear, stuffing sketches, photographs, notes, and the other paraphernalia of the designer's trade into her portfolio, launching her own busy Monday.

Our routine ended when I turned a page and saw the item that was wedged into the bottom corner. I said, "Oh, my God."

The note in my voice caused Isabel to stop and stare. "What's wrong?"

"Goddamn. I don't believe it."

She was starting to look alarmed. "What? What?"

"They sold the rights to 'She Loves You' for a TV spot."

Her brow stitched. "Sold what for what?"

" 'She Loves You,'" I said. "The Beatles' song. They sold the rights. They're going to use it in a TV spot."

"Oh." She shrugged and went back to organizing her case. She must have felt my frown over the top of the page, because she turned back around and said, "What?"

"Oh? That's all?"

"They do it all the time."

"It's not a –"

"And you bitch about it all the time." She snapped her portfolio closed and smiled at me. "Such drama."

"I know, but this is not just any song. It's different. To me, I mean."

She eyed me for a bemused moment. "Oh? How so?"

I pushed the paper aside. "I remember the very first time I heard it," I said. "Exactly where I was, who I was with, all of it. How often does that happen?"

Something in my tone caught her and she took a sip from her cup and cocked her head to one side, waiting for more.

"Don't you have to get to work?" I said.

"I'll go in a minute," she said. "I want to hear this. Go ahead. Tell me your story."

We were in my room in our half-double on Royal Street. I was sitting at my desk and Joey was sprawled on my bed, his arms folded behind his head as he gazed up at the ceiling. We were doing nothing, talking about nothing, lazing away a Saturday afternoon. It was too cold to go outside and there was really nothing to do in a little town like Wyanossing, anyway. We were gangly twelve-year-old twerps with bad haircuts. Even in those days, I was the serious one and Joey the clown.

The music trickling from my little Philco AM was so bland that it faded into the beige walls of my room, a hypnotic saccharine drone that pitched us into our private musings Through the window, I could make out the profile of Nock Hill, the ridge of blue Appalachian granite that ran along the other side of the river, a dull mount save for the jutting promontory of Council Rock. Winter clouds were hanging dark and low and the three radio towers atop the hill blinked in melancholy rhythm, lonely beacons in the gray afternoon.

Some time went by and I sensed the DJ's voice swoop in sudden urgency. I heard the words "new combo" and "the British Isles." By the time he reached a staccato "Liverpool," "screaming girls," and "huge!" he was almost shrieking.

Joey sprung upright and began flailing his hands at the radio and yelling, "Turn it up! Turn it up!"

I jerked to attention and fumbled to twirl the plastic knob just in time to catch the roll of a tom-tom, and the sudden rush of music that gushed from the speaker, jangling guitars, voices in harmony, and a driven rhythm, so much and so fast, and strange and familiar at the same time. It was every great song I had ever heard, distilled into the one that crackled with an energy that caused the tiny speaker to quake.

I lurched from my chair, gaping at the radio as if God himself had taken over the broadcast.

Joey was jumping up and down on my bed, his eyes popping out of his red face as he threw his arms around at crazy angles. Two minutes and twenty seconds later, it was over.

Joey was trembling as if he had some kind of condition. He said, "Oh, my God, oh, my God, oh, my God, did you hear that?"

I heard. We heard. Joey and I.

Isabel had propped her chin on her hand to listen. Her dark eyes remained fixed on mine as I finished.

"It was a H-bomb," I told her. "In that one moment, my whole world got knocked sideways." I sat back. "I can remember maybe a half-dozen times in my life when that has happened. When something just broke open and my whole life changed." I said, "One of them was that first time I met you."

She blinked and said, "Oh, honey," and in a small daze, laid her hands over mine. I guess work would wait if I was going to go on like this.

"And when the girls were born," I said. She knew that one far better than I ever would, and nodded.

"Anyway, for a twelve-year-old, it was big," I said, tapping a finger on the paper. "That one song in that one moment and my world was never the same again. It was that important." I paused. "You must have had things happen like that."

She shifted in the chair and the cast of her gaze turned dreamy. "I told you I went to Madrid one summer during college. Well, we were at the Prado and I got separated from my friends and wandered into one of the rooms, and there on the wall was the whole triptych of 'The Garden of Earthly Delights.' I sat on the bench for hours and just stared. They had to drag me out. When we got back on the street, it was like a different world." She rubbed her arms as if she had a chill.

"That's it," I said. "And that's the way I feel when I first heard 'Like a Rolling Stone' and 'Good Lovin' and –"

"– and the beginning of 'At Last,'" she said. "Those strings. And then her voice..."

I jabbed the *Times* with my index finger. "Well, this was one of those for me, times ten," I said. "I remember it so well it could have happened yesterday. About as close to a perfect memory as I'll ever have." I lifted my hand. "And now they're going to use it to sell cat food."

Isabel mused for a few more absent seconds, took another sip of coffee, and stood up. Her day was calling.

"I wonder what he's up to now," I said.

"Who?"

"Joey. My friend. The one who was there that day."

Her gaze was blank.

"Joey Sesto," I said. "I told you about him. He was my running partner all the time we were kids. And then after I left home, we hung out, stayed in touch. At least for a while."

She grabbed her keys off the hook. "I don't think you ever mentioned him."

Was that possible? "Wait, a minute," I said. "You're telling me we've been married eight years and I –"

"Nine."

"Okay, nine years, and I never once mentioned Joey Sesto?"

"Maybe you did," she said, kindly declining to add that her memory was better than mine. "It's still a good story."

I picked up the paper again, cast a baleful eye at the headline, then slapped it back down on the table. "You know, the day will come when they get every song, down to the last one."

She slung her bag over her shoulder and said, "Tell me again what it is you do for a living?"

I gave her a look.

"Sorry. Cheap shot." She stepped around the table to kiss my forehead. "I'm sorry about your song." As she went out the door, she said, "You're cooking dinner tonight."

After she left, I sat there, mulling the article some more. She was right all the way around. Who cared anymore? Half the spots on TV worked to ram something down viewers' throats to the tune of a blast from the past. Most of the time, the songs had no connection to whatever was being shilled. It was a cool song and that's all that mattered. The agencies that committed this fraud were sodomizing their consumers' best memories in order to get into their fat wallets. Though lazy and uninspired, it was not a criminal offense. Too bad about that.

Meanwhile, Isabel had nailed me on a shameful truth: that I was an active soldier in the army that was employing this musical scorched-earth policy. For the past two decades plus, I had worked as an actor and voice talent in the New York commercial world. *That's* what I did for a living.

I stood up to peer out the window just as my wife hit the sidewalk and headed off on the twelve-block walk to her office. I left my coffee, went into the living room, and thumbed through the CDs.

It was the last cut. I cranked it as loud as the neighbors would tolerate. After the final "Yeah!" had faded, I wandered into the bedroom to dress for my day.

I had a late morning meeting with my agent at a joint on 27th Street called Harper's.

Sondra James is a rare creature in our business, a mama lion who will defend a loyal client to the death. She hates liars and sneaks and bullies. She has been put on the shit list at various times by producers and ad directors who did not like the way she stood up to them. This rarely lasted long, because the problem was never with her. She was too much of a pro. An erring account exec, producer, or director would get spanked, the actor would be back on the shoot, and the production would move forward. Likewise, any client who tried to run something on her would be advised to leave town or make another career choice, because that person would be finished in the Five Boroughs, and Bergen County, too.

She was a direct, no-nonsense woman whose parents had migrated from Trinidad to Brooklyn. She was beautiful to my eyes, and had put me in my place when, early on, I tried to add something personal to our business relationship. Specifically, I got drunk and tried to jump her. She was going through a divorce at the time, and I sensed a chance for a vacation on her lush island body. Like no one had tried that before.

Fortunately, her good sense overcame my wild impulse, and I ended up with a fine agent and later a wife whom I adore. Though I admit that I still get jealous pangs whenever I see Sondra with a man.

She made it all the harder for me by always looking great. On this day, she was wearing a tan skirt, knee-high boots and a black sweater that followed her curves. A headband held back her curls and shades masked her pretty gray eyes. She was some picture, and most of the heads in the place turned as she passed. With those looks and her radiant energy, a lot of people in the business thought she was crazy for not staying in front of the camera. But she knew what she was doing. Pretty faces came a dime a dozen and she didn't want to play that game.

She sat down and Sam, her regular waiter, materialized at her elbow with an Absolüt bloody mary, no salt. It was a late morning ritual and she never drank more than one. She would follow it with coffee and a good brunch that would hold her until dinnertime. She placed business lunches on the same level with most meetings as major wastes of time.

She took a sip of her drink and flipped open the folio she used to keep track of all the details of running a successful talent agency.

My mind didn't often drift when I was with her, but some minutes went by and I felt a fingernail tapping the back of my hand. "Richard? Hello, sir?" I stared at her. "What about the spot?" She waved some papers in the air. "The Relusite spot. The reason we're sitting here." When I didn't answer, she said, "Were you not *listening* to me?" I knew she was irritated, because her Brooklyn accent blossomed.

I said, "I was, uh..."

"You were what?"

I shook my head, trying to dispel the mood. "It's nothing.

What was it, again?"

"We were discussing the Relusite spot. At least I was. Are you on board?"

I thought about it for a moment, then smacked my hand on the table, rattling the silver. She gave me a startled look.

"Of course I am!" I said. "I'll sell any damn thing they want. That's what I *do*, right? Stand in front of a camera and pretend to be someone else in order to convince people to buy crap they don't want or need."

My voice had gone up, drawing looks from the diners at the next table. Sondra gaped at me in vexation. I folded my hands before me in a gesture of contrition and said, "Sorry. I read something in the paper this morning that kind of took the wind out of me."

"Did somebody die?"

"Something did."

I hesitated to tell her. I had grumbled over what the agencies were doing with music man times before, causing people around me to roll their eyes. I repeated what I'd read in the *Times*, and then said, "I know I complain about it..."

"All the time."

"...but this is different."

"Why?"

"Because this one really mattered to me. Personally, I mean."

"So what do you want to do?" Sondra said. "Quit the business? Get a law passed to forbid the use of songs that you love in spots?"

I said, "That's an idea." But she was right. What could I do? No one cared and everything was for sale. I sighed and shook my head. "What were we talking about? Before, I mean."

"Relusite."

"Ah, yes...Relusite..." I clasped my hands and they turned fervent white. "Who wouldn't be happy to use his or her talents to sell products that enhance the elimination of body wastes?"

She gave me an arch look. "So is that a yes?"

I raised my hand and asked Sam for a bloody mary of my own.

We didn't discuss the Beatles or the criminal use of songs in commercials or any of the other things about the world that disappointed me. We just left all of it alone and instead went over the projects that were coming along. There was a time when I would have spent a few minutes bugging her about a movie role or theater work. Not anymore; my face had become too recognizable. No one wanted to hire the funny guy in the Kia commercial.

After we finished, I grabbed a cab to the studio on the Lower East Side where we were doing reaction shots for a spot for... What was it this time? A lawn treatment guaranteed to grow greener grass. That was it. Something about the grass being greener on the other side. How clever.

All through the day, I kept flashing back on the *Times* article, and hearing "She Loves You," thinking about the afternoon so long ago, and wondering what Joey would say if he could see me now.

3.

Though I'm a decent cook and enjoy my turn at the stove, I wasn't in the mood that night, so I picked up take-out from HoHo. The girls liked the pot-stickers and moo-shu. They also got root beer, which delighted them. Afterward, they carried bowls of chocolate ice cream off to their room to do whatever little girls do in their school night universe.

I put the leftovers in the fridge and came back to the couch. Isabel had started a DVD and I sat down with her to watch the images flicker back and forth across the screen. Some time passed and I was aware that she was speaking to me.

I looked at her. "What's that?"

She said, "Are you with us this evening?"

"Sorry. I'm stuck on that thing about the song. I know it sounds stupid. But it's just such a crime." I turned to face her. "Do you remember when they sold the rights to 'The Times They Are A-Changin'' to that accounting firm?"

She shook her head.

"It was before we met," I said. "Anyway, they sold the rights to that... that anthem. That was one of the last times I talked to Joey. I told him about it, and he went bonkers." I smiled at the memory. "He kept on saying, 'And you work for these people?' He was going nuts." I paused for a few seconds. "And you know what? He was right. Pretty soon, there's not going to be anything left."

Isabel placed a wifely hand on my arm. "I believe 'these people' have paid you a lot of money over the years," she said. "That's biting the hand that feeds you, *vato.*"

"I'd bite it right the fuck off if I could," I said.

It came out with so much heat that she laughed. She gave me a consoling pat and returned her attention to *Elmer Gantry*.

Halfway through the movie, I got up and walked down the hall. The girls were on the computer, so I doubled back to the kitchen, where I picked up the telephone and dialed Information. Responding to the recorded voice, I asked for Wyanossing, PA, the last name Sesto, first name Joseph. Information had no Joseph Sesto. No last name "J. Sesto" either. I held for a live operator, who came on the line to tell me that all they had was an "A" Sesto. That stopped me.

"Sir?" the woman said. "Would you like that number?"

I said, "Yes, please."

I jotted it on the pad, then stood around being a chicken a few minutes. I picked up the phone again and dialed. It rang three times.

The voice was familiar.

"Angela?" I said. "This is Richard Zale. I mean Richie. Zaleski."

"Richie." She sounded stunned. "My God..."

"I know. It's been a while, huh?"

There was a silence from the other end that went on so long that I thought she had hung up on me.

"How are you?" I said.

"I'm all right. How are you?"

I caught a strange, strained, shaky note in her voice. Something was wrong. Maybe it had been a mistake calling her out of the blue.

"I'm good," I said, doing my best to sound breezy. "The reason I called, I wanted to see if I could get Joey's phone number from you. It's not in the book. And Directory Assistance didn't have it."

"No, they wouldn't," she said, sounding as if she was far away. "He always kept it unlisted."

After another strained pause, I heard her voice break into a small sob.

"Angela?" I said. "What's wrong?"

"I thought you were calling about..."

"About what? What?"

"You don't know."

I felt a chill start up my spine. "Don't know what?"

"Joey had an accident."

"What kind of accident?"

She drew a jagged breath.

"Angela?"

"Joey died, Richie."

My vision blurred and I felt a hard blow to my chest. "Jesus.' I said. "What happened?"

From the front room, Isabel said, "Richard?"

Angela was talking. "You remember Council Rock, right? Up on Nock Hill? He was up there, and somehow he fell off. He fell all the way to the bottom, down to the railroad tracks. They didn't find him until the morning. There was nothing anyone could do. He fell too far." She started to weep again.

I said, "Angela, God, I'm so sorry."

Another few seconds and she calmed. The sobs ceased and she drew a long breath.

"When was this?" I asked her.

"Three weeks ago."

Three weeks. My life had gone on as if nothing had happened and all that time, Joey had been dead. I caught a numb breath. "How are you holding up?"

She sniffed. "All right. Better, I guess."

I gave it a few moments, then said, "I don't understand. This happened at night? What was he doing up there?"

"I don't know. Wandering around. I guess. And he just… It's all been too much… all the – the…" She was stuttering as she tried to bite down on her weeping. She said, "I need to hang up now."

"Okay, I understand."

"Thank you for calling. Maybe we can talk again in a few days, if you want."

"Sure, sure." I started to repeat how sorry I was when I heard a click and then the dial tone.

Isabel took one look at me and sat up, her eyes getting wide. She put the movie on pause. "What is it?" I sat down on the couch. "Richard?"

"That guy I was telling you about? Joey?"

"Your friend."

"Yeah. Well, I just called to try to find him, and..." The words stuck in my throat for a second. "He had an accident. And he died."

"Oh, no. When?"

"Three weeks ago."

"A car accident?"

"No, he fell. Off this steep cliff. It's near where we grew up. It's a real long drop. He fell and it killed him."

Isabel watched me for a moment. "I'm so sorry, honey."

I looked at her kind face and said, "Joey's dead." The words sounded odd to my ear, as if spoken by a stranger.

I spent the rest of the evening in a vague and baffled place. It wasn't like Joey and I had been close. Not like before. It had been a long time since I had even seen or talked to him and much longer since we had shared wild days and nights. So I couldn't put a finger on my emotions. There was the repeated shock over the terrible way his life had ended. With this came the gut-sinking realization that I would never get to laugh over our crazy memories, never get to resume the friendship, never see him again. And this led me to a more general sorrow for all that the years had taken away.

There were no tears, only a sighing sadness. Every few moments, Isabel would touch my arm and murmur something to let me know she was sorry. When she did that, I smiled, understanding how much the years had given back.

It didn't change the sad fact that Joey was gone.

I pitched around so much that my wife went from sympathetic to exasperated. She had to get up for work in the morning. I finally rolled out of bed and padded into the kitchen to pour a short glass of wine, which I carried to the living room window.

I stared down at a few lonely taxicabs rolling along the street and thought about how Joey had been a touchstone, one of those few people who I could rightly say had a hand in defining the path of my life. He played a role in my movie, one that couldn't be erased or discounted. While time had stolen some of the history, much remained.

We had grown up on opposite ends of our small town, but once we stumbled onto each other, we were connected at the hip. He was in the vicinity when I got and gave my first real kiss. And the first time I laid a hand on hidden female flesh. Also the first time I got stoned and ate mushrooms. From the time we were fourteen until I turned twenty and left for the Army, we were a two-man wrecking machine. With him leading the way.

Lisa Strockman whispered in my ear, took my hand, and led me into the dark alley. Joey ducked away with Cheryl Casey and they disappeared behind the Penney's store, closed for the night.

I followed Lisa to the narrow space between two garages. She leaned against the cinder blocks and, with a wicked light in her eyes, guided me, taking one of my hands and directing it against her stomach and then up under her brassiere.

Thirty-five years later, I remembered that first touch, the way the cotton and elastic yielded, the mound of her breast, soft and firm at the same time, a perfect fit for my hand, the nipple stiff at the tip of my fingers.

Lisa giggled at my clumsiness, but it was a sweet laugh all the same. She put her lips to my ear and took my other hand. "Now," she whispered. "Down here..."

I fell into a delirious spin that didn't stop until Cheryl came to the end of the alley and hissed that it was time to go. Lisa put herself back together. When we stepped out into the light, Joey was grinning drunkenly. Lisa kissed me in a rush and the girls hurried home before someone's dad came looking.

Joey and I stood under the streetlight. He slapped my giddy face with a light hand and said, "Welcome to heaven."

—

Time passed and we weren't kids anymore. Our teenage delinquency ran its course. I left Wyanossing while he stayed. We held it together for another ten years, but eventually the strings that tied us stretched and broke and I never again had a friend who was that close, who intertwined with the arc of my life.

When I saw him on my rare visits back home, he would come up with snide asides that told me he resented my leaving and hinting that I had somehow betrayed him. So there was always a faint tinge of wounded feelings lurking. And yet he was as happy a man as I have ever met. Nothing got in the way of his good time. That's what I wanted to remember.

Numbed by the wine, I finally felt weariness overtake me. I padded down the hall to the girls' room and watched my angels drift through their sweet dreams before creeping back to crawl into bed with my wife. It was warm under the blanket and I was worn out. Sleep pulled a shade.

I was standing at the tip of Council Rock, throbbing with the thrill of perching with nothing but air and a few stunted trees for almost six hundred feet straight down. The river was slow-moving, the surface like glass, the reflections of the clouds drifting on the current.

Two short steps and I would be off. At thirty-two-feet-per-second-squared, I'd be dead not long after. The notion brought on a wild, terrifying rush.

Joey was keeping far back, watching me as I turned around and spread my arms wide.

"This is too cool," I said. "You gotta come out. C'mon, man..."

He shook his head. "No fucking way." He actually began shuffling in reverse.

"Oh, come on," I said, and did a little jig to tease him. I saw the look on his face, realized that I had gone too far, and then I was going over the edge, falling, down, down, into a dizzying blackness, my heart rising into my throat.

"Richard!"

I opened my eyes to the gray light of predawn.

"What?" I heard the croak of my voice. "What's wrong?"

"You let out a yell." Isabel was sitting up. "You scared me half to death."

My breath was coming short and I could feel sweat on my face as I broke from the dream and the endless fall. My wife was blinking at me, her mouth open a little, still bleary with sleep. I was in my bedroom, in my apartment, safe with my family. As my heart slowed, pieces of the nightmare came back, and a thought intruded, sudden and sharp.

"He never went out there," I said.

"Who?" Isabel frowned groggily. "Never went out where?"

"Joey," I said. "He wouldn't go out on Council Rock. It was a hell of a drop and he never went anywhere near the edge. He was afraid of heights. Terrified."

"Oh." She thought for a few seconds, then put her head on the pillow and pulled the covers over her brown shoulders. "Well, maybe he got over it."

"Yeah," I said after a moment. "Maybe he did."

I laid there with my eyes open, staring up at the ceiling. Isabel, sensing my unease, put her arm across my chest, defending me from the shadows.

4.

It wasn't long after I opened my eyes that I thought about Joey and he stayed on my mind while Isabel and the girls got up, ate breakfast, and trundled away in two shifts. I could tell by the puzzled looks they kept giving me that I was out of it that morning. And there were the exchanges:

"Dad?" Silence. "Daddy?"

"What?"

Or: "Richard? Richard!"

"What?"

"Did you hear me?"

They gave up and left me alone. Joey had nothing to do with them. He was a ghost that had traveled through a time and a place that had passed into history. Long before there was *Daddy*, before there was Isabel's husband, before there was Richard Zale, New York actor, there was Richie Zaleski, racing through endless ecstatic days and magical nights in the little American hamlet of Wyanossing, Pennsylvania with his pal Joey Sesto. And they could never understand what that meant to me.

I spent an hour reading the *Times* and checking out the theater auditions section in the *Voice*. Though I hadn't auditioned for a play in years, I still read the notices. Sometimes I would imagine the monologue I would prepare for this part or that, and then imagine myself nailing it.

Though on that morning, my mind drifted away from the words

on the page. Jesus and Mary and all the Saints, Joey was dead and gone. Because, his sister had said, he had wandered onto Council Rock and taken a wrong step. How could it be?

Sometimes things collect and they did that morning. Outside, I flagged a cab to carry me to the pre-production meeting for Relusite. I couldn't wait to sink my teeth into that one.

The driver was a young Arab. He was polite but wouldn't quite meet my eyes. I had been catching this same kind of reaction since that day the past September, a faint mix of shame and fear. Would I be one of those who would glare at him with hatred? Would I take a single look and ruin his whole day by climbing back out in a red-faced huff and slamming the door behind me?

That wasn't me. I didn't blame this fellow. What happened was not his doing. I preferred to think of him as an immigrant, like my grandparents, trying to build a life in a new land. Anyway, my thoughts were about to take a small, odd turn away.

We had just started the creeping drive uptown when I glanced out the window and saw the kid slouching in a doorway. The guitar case in his hand looked to be one of those old clapboard pieces. I imagined a blonde, age-worn Gibson B-25 tucked inside, one like my first real guitar, now long lost. I made the mistake of lending it to a friend who managed to leave it on the side of some two-lane.

The kid was nineteen or twenty, scruffy in a leather coat that had worn through the finish, dark scarf that draped from his neck, and driving cap turned backwards. His face was still round with lingering youth, framed with a dark tangle of hair. For a moment, I was looking at a photograph from 1964.

He saw me watching him and gazed back, his eyes cool and blank. The traffic broke and we rolled away. When I turned to peer out the rear window, I couldn't see him anymore.

The cab swung to the curb at 40th Street and the driver waited patiently while I stared at the door to the building. On the other side of it was a set of stairs and at the top of the stairs was a room and inside the room a producer, director, a selection of agency people, and several other actors were waiting. A table would be laid out with coffee, tea, bottled water, fruit, bagels, and danish. The chatter would be light: talk of vacations, hot restaurants, funky new stores.

At some point, the creative director would clap her hands and we would all get down to the business of planning a television commercial that would run nationally to hype the merits of a bowel medication. I would be the face and voice of this campaign.

Since they sometimes shot tests on a digicam, true professional that I am, I had brought along my bag with a change of clothes. In other words, I was ready to go to work with those same vampires whom I had just the day before cursed for the way they exploited things I cared about. It was at best simple laziness and at worst something far more cynical.

Hey, remember this cool song? Good, now go buy this crap!

Joey had always railed against these and assorted other villains. He had been right.

Isabel was right, too; I was one of the willing executioners, a good soldier in the huckster army. Though I had appeared in spots that used songs from the past, the songs had no meaning for me. I knew one day it would happen. Some creative type would pluck out a tune that had some magical connection. That day had arrived.

Maybe I'd be offered the cat food spot. I let out a cold laugh at the thought. The patient driver glanced in the mirror.

And then what? "No, I'm sorry, I can't take the eight grand because I object to your choice of music."

I could just see the baffled looks; they'd think I'd lost my mind. There were a thousand actors in New York waiting to step into my shoes. If the spot turned into a campaign, I would be blowing off a down payment on the girls' college tuitions. Isabel would kill me.

The image of her furious face dissolved into Joey's, angry at me for making the "right" choice. I heard his voice as he called me a sellout or worse. *He'd* never cave in like that. Though as far as I knew, he'd never had to make the choice. And everything came down to choices.

I sat with my hand on the door handle until the driver said, "Sir? Somet'ing wrong?"

With a last glance at the façade of the building, I told him that I had made a mistake and I needed to go downtown again. He shrugged, put the car in gear, and pulled into the street. As we turned the corner, I told myself I was not doing this. At every intersection, I thought about saying *sorry, take me back*. I had a job to do. I had made a commitment. People were depending on me.

I got on my cell phone to call Sondra.

Forty-five minutes later, I was putting the key into the ignition of a new Chevy Lumina. I drove it off the Avis lot on 76th Street and traveled north for two blocks before turning east, then south, then west, then north again. This random tour went on for about another half-hour, varying the cross streets and avenues.

Finally, I gave up. "Okay, Joey," I said, and headed for the bridge.

She picked up on the second ring, sounding busy. "Isabel Zale."

"I called to tell you I'm leaving you."

She said, "I hope it's for a woman this time."

"Ha-ha. I'm… I'm going to P.A."

"When?"

"Now. I'm in Jersey. About to get on I-80."

"How did you get there?"

"I rented a car."

"You —" She was quiet for a cool second. "What is this?"

"I'm going to Wyanossing."

Someone spoke in the background and she said something in return that sounded a little bit snappish. "I thought you had a production meeting this morning."

"I bailed on it."

"Oh? And what did Sondra have to say about that?"

"She wasn't happy," I said. "But there are other actors in Manhattan. And I've never done it before. Never."

Another pause. "Does this have to do with your friend?"

"It does, yeah."

"He died two weeks ago."

"Three."

"So why are you going now?"

"I don't know," I said. "To pay my respects. To visit his grave. To say good-bye. I just need to go. I just..." I just what? I didn't know how to explain it. "It's not that far. This is the least I can do for him." She was quiet, listening. "I want to do it."

She said, "This is strange, Richard."

I said, "You know that no one in Wyanossing ever called me that."

"Called you what?"

"Richard."

"Oh, yeah? So what did they call you? Captain Douchebag who leaves town without consulting his wife?"

That was my Isabel. "It was 'Richie,'" I said.

"I see. Well, is there anything else you're not telling me, *Richie*?"

"No," I said. "Actually, yes. Except for you, he's the best friend I ever had."

It worked. She didn't have any comeback and before she could think of one, I said, "I'll call when I get there, okay?"

"Okay," she said. It was grudging.

"I love you," I said.

"I know you do, and that's the only reason I'm not arguing about this," she said. "Be careful." She clicked off.

There was only one gas station at the Delaware Water Gap exit and I drove up to it in mist of spring rain.

When I got out to top-up the tank, I saw two kids walking along the access road that led back onto the interstate. They looked like college students, stoners, or grungers. Who could tell anymore? They had packs strapped on their backs and the girl held a cardboard sign that read "80-West." I stuck the nozzle in and started pumping.

Joey and I had been standing on the side of the road for hours. There hadn't been a car in a while and we looked too weird for the few that did pass to even think about stopping. We were stoned, too, and I'm sure that didn't help at all. The spot was next to a pasture and Joey was goofing on the cows that were grazing on the other side of the fence. The cows observed his antics with their blank, stupid eyes. He couldn't get a rise out of them.

"I'm gonna ride one," he said.

"Do what?"

"I'm gonna ride one. Like in a rodeo."

"Those aren't rodeo cows."

"So I'll break some new ground. I'm going to straddle me some beef, man."

"I don't think they're that kind, either."

He wasn't listening. "You know anybody who's ever done it?"

"Done what?"

"Rode on a fucking cow. What the hell are we talking about?"

I had to think about it. "No."

He was halfway over the fence when a rumble erupted in the distance. The car rolled up with a snarl of glass-packs, a '55 Chevy, midnight blue sporting Cragar mags, a low-slung jungle cat with a motor that meant business. Joey glanced regretfully at the nearest heifer, then climbed back over the barbed-wire and hopped down the bank. We really needed to get out of there.

At the wheel of the car was a bony greaser, maybe twenty, with a dice tattoo on his biceps and a Lucky dangling from his lips. He was as sharp-faced as a river rat and sporting a DA that was black and sleek with Vaseline hair oil and set off with razor-cut sideburns.

"Where you guys headin'?" he yelled over the throaty rumble of the V-8.

As we climbed in, he said he could take us as far as the turnpike. I said, "That's cool."

We pulled away. The driver looked over at me, then glanced at Joey in the mirror. "Guess you guys have a fuck of a time getting rides with that hair and all." He nodded, then sliced a dismissive hand through the air. "Hey, man, I don't give a shit. Look at me. I like my hair like this. You wanna grow yours long, what's the fucking problem, huh? Ain't nobody's goddamn business, is it? Fuckin' right, it ain't. You know what I say? I say, live and let live. You know what I mean?"

We all mulled that for a few seconds. I was about to comment on this benign sentiment when the greaser smacked his fist down on the dashboard. His face pinched up in anger. "But what I can't stand is these goddamn niggers!" he yelled. "Every time I look at TV, there's another one on! Jesus Christ Almighty! What the hell is goin' on in this country?"

He dropped us at the side of the road and drove off. We waved a fond good-bye.

Joey said, "Peace, brother."

I stepped inside the store to pay for my gas and grab a ginger ale and a snack for the road. I decided I was going to pick up the kids and carry them as far as I could. But when I laid my purchase on the counter and looked out the window, they were gone from sight.

"Somebody pick them up?" I said.

He glanced at me. "What?"

"Those hitchhikers."

"Hitchhikers?" He turned to the window.

"They were right out there. You didn't see them?"

"I didn't see no hitchhikers." He laughed a little. "I ain't seen any hitchhikers in pro'bly, I don't know, ten years."

"They were standing right out there."

He shrugged. "I didn't see nobody," he said. "That's eleven on the gas and a two-twenty-five for the drink and the crackers."

I didn't encounter the pair farther down the line, either. The misty drizzle turned into a steady rain and by the time I passed the Hazelton exit, it was pouring. The traffic was light and slow. I turned on the radio and found a station I could stand, playing jazz and blues. It was down low on the dial, probably a college station, and when I lost it, I hopped to another, this one playing anguished young musical poets. When I got tired of them, I tried some higher frequencies. As I expected, there was nothing worthwhile and so I tuned in to public radio stations and listened to Bach and the rain on the roof and the tires planing over the wet road. There were enough big trucks throwing up clouds of water to keep my mind fixed on driving. I didn't really think about Joey and Angela and Wyanossing. There would be too much time for that soon.

5.

It was early afternoon when I drove onto the long bridge over the Susquehanna and crossed the borough line on the other side. The rain had passed and the sun was out in swatches. I had stored a photograph of my hometown in my head for the ten years since I had last visited and the thirty since I had lived there.

From what I could see along the first blocks, the quaint charm that I remembered hadn't been glassed or paved over. The buildings were for the most part stately and of classic construction. Many of them were decades old and the most regal went back a century or more. These homes sat properly in the dappled shade of the tall boughs of hardwood trees.

It was all very familiar, locked in time. But as I drove on, I saw that some parts of the town were changing. The stores that lined the two blocks of downtown had been gussied-up but had still managed to avoid the strip-mall sameness that had blanched the nation from one coast to the other.

I spied a café in the space once occupied by the five-and-dime with the name "Charlotte's" across the faux façade. I parked up the street and put a quarter into the meter for an hour's time.

I stepped into a small and neat room that was painted in calm pastels with a dozen round and square tables and a counter faced by six high stools. It was late lunch and only two of the tables and one of the stools was occupied. Still, every eye in the room shifted my way as I sat down at round with a view of the street. A waitress, plump and smiling, followed me with a glass of water and a menu. "Sandy" was printed on her name tag.

She said, "Good afternoon," and then stared. "Hey, you know who you look like? That guy on that commercial. It's for… oh, what is it…"

"Maxwell House." It came from a man at the counter.

The waitress blinked and her smile widened. "That's it. Is that you? It is. I heard about you. You're from here, right?"

The man at the counter said, "His name's Richie Zaleski. Except he doesn't go by that any more." He glanced my way and said, "You probably don't remember me, do you?"

"Actually, I do," I said. "John Miller." It was an easy call. Squat-bodied, with large teeth planted in a thick and florid face, he had always reminded me of a Halloween pumpkin. Now it was one that had been sitting out too long after the holiday. His gray hair was so short I could see the pink gleam of his skull.

"Oh, I'm sorry," the waitress said. "Would you like something else to drink?"

I told her the water was fine. She was treating me to a dizzy smile, so I took a quick glance at the menu. "I'll have a tuna on wheat. Toasted. A side salad with ranch dressing."

She nodded, looking pleased, and moved off. Miller was regarding me with blank eyes.

"So what brings you back to the old burg?" he asked. "I thought you were gone for good." Before I could answer, he said, "Guess you heard about Sesto."

I turned in my chair. "I did, yeah."

He said, "That was a hell of thing, all right. You two, you used to be tight, didn't you?" He called back over his shoulder for the benefit of the waitresses. "You believe it, this here TV star and Sesto?" He entwined two fingers "They used to be like that. A couple of street punks. Way back when."

His tone had gone brittle and his smile wasn't pleasant. He stood up and chugged down what was left of a Coke. He set the glass on the counter. "So how long you in town for?" he said without looking at me.

"Not long." A cool silence followed.

"Well, I have the three stores now. One here in town. One out on Route 22. One over in Greensburg. Stop by if you need anything. In the way of an appliance, I mean."

I had not inquired about his stores and the chances I'd be interested in purchasing a large appliance from him or anyone else while I was in town seemed not have crossed his mind. I wanted nothing to do with him anyway. I hadn't liked him before and saw no reason to make a change.

His name marked him as a member of one of the clans that had roots in town going back deep into the 1800s. These same families, extended throughout the valley, had never quite adjusted to the latecomers who had invaded their quiet Anglo-Saxon haven. My tribe – Joey, me, a guy named Leo, and a few other coconuts – were the immigrant rabble and later the stoners and crazies who didn't respect their exalted places in the community. Though that had all happened a long time ago, I sensed from John Miller's little act that some of the grudges remained. It didn't matter; I hadn't come back to fight stupid thirty-year old spats. I just wanted to enjoy my sandwich and salad and say goodbye to my friend.

As I gazed out the window, musing on old enmities, I sensed someone hovering. First came a scent, a sweet spice, then a soft motion in the corner of my eye. I turned to see a young woman, posing carefully with one plate in each hand. She placed the sandwich in front of me and arranged the salad to the side, as if they were precious gifts.

She was pretty, blonde and tan, with green eyes and the pertly-freckled nose of an ingénue. The tag on her blouse said "Crystal" and happened to adorn the slope of her left breast. A nice picture; and yet there was something just a little off about her, a light in her gaze that hinted at a whole other train rolling down the tracks.

She had delivered my lunch with deft precision, arranging it just so, and I thanked her as I picked up my fork. She didn't move and I looked at her again. Wearing a giddy smile, she pulled an order pad and pen from the back pocket of her denim skirt and slid them onto the table in next to my placemat.

"Can I have your autograph?" She sounded breathless. Everyone else in the room was quiet, watching.

I shook my head, doing a modest turn. "You don't really want my autograph."

"Yes, I do," she said with an earnest nod.

"Give her your autograph, Richie." John had moved to the doorway and was wearing the same hard smile. "You'll make her day." The little bell over the door tinkled as he made his exit.

Crystal was waiting. I glanced at her nametag again, making sure my gaze didn't rest too long, then wrote, "To Crystal, with best wishes, Richard Zale," on her pad.

She snatched up the pad, read the inscription, and said, "This is so *cool*."

It had been a long time since anyone had called me that. She whispered a thank you and flitted away. I felt her eyes tracking me from behind the counter as I ate my lunch. After I left, I realized that without thinking, I had left her a New York-sized tip.

Angela Sesto's house was a renovated Victorian on the corner of two quiet residential streets, sitting high on the gentle slope that rose from the Susquehanna. The bricks were egg white with red edges and the trim around the door and tall windows was an old blue. Hanging baskets of flowers and plants adorned a front porch fitted with gingerbread moldings. The front yard stretched around a trio of sugar maples and was bordered by beds of stunning red tulips. In winter, when the oaks and maples were bare, there'd be a view from the upstairs windows of the river as it wound down the valley. It was a storybook house, the kind that most New Yorkers only dream about.

I parked the car and was halfway up the walk when the front door opened and Angela emerged from the shadows of the porch. I stopped, entertaining the sensation of meeting a stranger. When she stepped into the full light, I saw her face and she wasn't a stranger anymore.

She had been a dark-haired, dark-eyed wisp of a girl who was mostly in the way. The first time I really noticed her was one summer morning when I was sitting at Sesto's kitchen table, waiting for Joey to finish his breakfast so we could get on with our juvenile delinquency. I was sixteen, and had my own wheels, a 1959 Chevy four-door that I had bought with the money I'd earned pumping gas.

Angela walked in and stepped into the lemony morning light that was pouring through the window. I noticed in that sudden moment how pretty she was, with her black hair, deep green eyes and olive skin. She had a full mouth and a gentle bow of a nose. My eyes went roaming and landed on the place where her blouse had gone unbuttoned and I caught sight of the nubile rise of her –

"Hey!" I was stung by a sudden smack to the side of my head. Joey was frowning at me. "What the hell's wrong with you? Let's go."

I followed him out the door. I glanced back as I closed it behind me and saw Angela watching with a knowing look in her eyes.

A second picture, this one from two years later, and wrapped in blue shadow. I had spread a ratty old blanket at the edge of the clearing at Nock Hill State Park that came to a point at Council Rock. It was her first time. As I undressed her, she tried to look into my eyes and kept whispering, "Richie, wait... please, wait... Richie..."

"Richie?" She descended the steps to greet me.

Some women are just lucky that their beauty changes from one phase to another, from young and heartbreakingly gorgeous to middle-aged and sweetly handsome. It wasn't common. Time too often took its toll. But it just worked out that way for a random few. My wife was one. And Angela was another.

"Or am I supposed to call you 'Richard?'" She came up with a kind smile. "Did you forget where you were?"

"I did," I said. "And Richie's fine."

She didn't look surprised to find me on her doorstep and I told her so.

She said, "Well, it's all over town."

"I've been here..." I looked at my watch. "What, an hour?"

"Wyanossing, Pennsylvania. Population four thousand, two hundred and seven." She laughed lightly. "I got a phone call from someone who got a phone call from someone who saw you. *Richie Zaleski's in town*. That's how it works here. You don't remember?"

"It's been a while," I said.

"About twenty years, right?"

"You look great."

She paused to give me a dubious gaze, then said "Would you like to come in?"

"I was wondering if we could go see Joey first."

She hesitated only for a moment. "Okay, if that's what you want."

When we were young, the far edge of the cemetery was bordered by thick woods, with glades that went on for miles, all the way over the Mahoning Ridge and into the next county. My little gang would disappear at nine o'clock on a summer morning, carrying paper bag lunches, and would not emerge again until the shadows fell all the way in the other direction. Older kids tried to spook us with stories about a crazy man who ran naked and dirty through the trees, and if we waited long enough in one spot, he'd appear. But who had that kind of patience? We were little boys.

One scene that stuck in my memory was coming to a clearing and finding a deer carcass. The eyes were open and solid black. Flies were swarming and it smelled gagging awful. We stood a little ways back and stared at it for long minutes.

I discovered that the cemetery had claimed an additional half-mile and most of what had been our enchanted forest had been cleared. The trees were gone and paths that we had roamed had been replaced by half-acre lots for ranches and split-levels. There were scant woods for kids or madmen to roam.

I was glad to have that to ponder, rather than dwelling on my jumble of thoughts at riding with Angela to visit the grave of her brother, my one-time best friend. She poked into my thoughts only to give the occasional direction.

"You can stop," she said at last. She pointed a finger. "It's right over there."

We were on the little road that bordered the new section. I pulled over and she led me fifty paces down the incline. It was early afternoon and very quiet.

She said, "He's not actually here, you know." I told her I understood. She said, "No, I mean not even his body. He was cremated. This is a memorial marker."

The inscription on the stone read "Sesto" at the top. Then "Joseph Anthony, 1952-2002, At Rest."

It was the proof, carved in marble. I would never see him again. I heard Angela sigh. She stepped closer, knelt down and put a hand on the marker.

"Joey, honey," she murmured. "Richie came back to see you."

"You think he can hear you?" I said to her back. The words sounded stupid as soon as they left my mouth.

She straightened and moved off. "I'll leave you alone."

After she walked off, I said, "Joey?" twice and then nothing. What did I have to offer him? What would he want to hear from me? A speech about all the great memories? That my childhood, my life, would not have been the same if he hadn't been there? That I had come back because I had recalled a moment of magic from forty years in the past?

Talk about a day late and a dollar short. I had no true right to be there. He had deserved better from me. I stood up and turned away.

I found Angela leaning on the fender, her arms crossed, staring at the ground. She studied my face for a moment, then opened her door and got in the rental car without a word.

Riding away from that field of lonely stones, I felt the ache in my gut deepen and I wondered if it had been a mistake to come there. If I had made the trip for nothing save my own guilty conscience, I didn't feel one bit better. And if I had been expecting to settle something, that hadn't happened. All I had done was to open a wound.

"How long has it been?"

I looked over at her. Her window was down and she was wafting her outstretched hand through the air.

"What's that?"

"How long has it been since you've been back?" she said.

"Four or five years ago. And that was just for a day. Some stuff with my parents' house."

"How long since you saw Joey?"

I shifted in the seat, hedging. "A while," I said at last. "Ten years." She didn't ask for an explanation. I drove for another block and then said, "Did he ever get married? Have kids?"

"Joey?" She shook her head, bemused. "No. That would have been too responsible. He lived with a few women. I think he cared for them, but they all ended up leaving him. And of course, he ran through the local hussies. He was some tomcat. Or so he thought." She laughed a little. I saw her eyes begin to mist and changed the subject.

"And what about you?" I said.

"What about me?"

"Married? Kids?"

"I was married, yeah," she said. "Pretty young. Nobody you know. I have a son and a daughter. Joey's nephew and niece. Twenty and twenty-two. Both in college."

"College," I said. "Good God. What about your husband?"

"Oh, the usual," she said. "He had other interests. I don't remember their names. It's a small town and when he ran through them, he moved on. And that was that."

"And your work?"

"I'm an attorney," she said.

She saw the surprise on my face and said, "Yeah, how about it? I went to Penn State. Law School. I have a quiet little practice here."

She asked about my family and she seemed pleased that I had become a father, though a late bloomer. The subject shifted briefly to New York. I told her the city was still in aftershock, but that we were carrying on in spite of our public and private griefs. We returned to talking about our kids until we pulled up to her house.

I realized that my business there was finished and I could say good-bye to her and go home. I also noticed that I wasn't making any moves in that direction.

She saved me. "You want to come sit on the porch? I'll make coffee."

"Yeah, that'd be nice."

She opened her door. "You can tell me all about Broadway," she said as she got out.

"No, I can't," I said, but she didn't hear me.

"And about Joey." She stopped to regard me with intent. "I need to hear some stories, Richie. I need to hear some good stories about my brother. You got any of those?"

It was our first day and our foreman, whose name was Duane, was explaining the job. He was a thin, twitchy sort with a weird, too-narrow face. He had us captive in a small room, paneled in cheap hardboard with a shiny white surface. A conveyor belt entered through a square opening in one wall and exited from the other.

Duane hitched his pants, telegraphing that this was going to be serious.

"What ya got here is pro'bly the most important job in the whole friggin' plant." He grabbed one of the plucked, headless chickens that were laying on the conveyor. "This fucker's gotta go outta here without no more hair than a friggin' cue ball, y'understand?" He pulled something invisible from the skin of the bird and held it between a grimy thumb and index finger. "Some old snatch gets one of these friggin' pin feathers stuck in her craw and chokes to death, they'll throw ya's in the state pen for the rest of your friggin' lives. Ya understand?"

Joey had been staring at Duane with a glazed look, as if he had been speaking Urdu. Abruptly, he guffawed.

Duane glared at him. "I say somethin' funny, Sesto?"

"What's so funny?"

Angela set a tray with two cups on the little wicker table.

"I was remembering this job I worked with Joey."

She sat down, her eyes brightening.

"You remember Poultry Pride?" I said. "They processed chickens for restaurants and hospitals and whatever all over the state. They had a plant on Route 12." She nodded. "Well, Joey and I got jobs there. We were in this little room and we were supposed to check to make sure there were no feathers left on the chickens. All day, every day, we just sat there and watched dead chickens roll by. Thousands of them." I snickered. "And we stayed stoned the whole time."

Joey and I were sitting on boxes on either side of the door. He was toking away. Duane walked in and smacked his hand on the wall.

"It's a break, not a friggin' vacation," he said. "Let's hit it, you two." If he noticed the joint, he didn't comment. The reek of rotting poultry was so strong that toxic waste wouldn't have made a dent in it. He ducked back outside.

Joey rose to his feet. I punched the switch and the conveyor motor cranked up to its mechanical racket as the endless train of white flesh resumed. Joey hit the button for the rickety ventilator fan and the five three-foot blades started rattling away. I ambled over to the creaking belt and shoved the roach into the ass of a chicken.

"Something for Granny come Easter," I explained.

Joey stared at the advancing parade of dead birds with an inflamed eye and muttered something I didn't catch.

"Say what?"

He raised his voice. "I said can't stand this place no more."

"Motherfuckin' chicken-pluckin'!" I sang out.

He wasn't having any of it. "I hate this shit!" he yelled. He glared for another moment and then grabbed hold of the closest hen, stepped up as if he was Terry Bradshaw in the pocket, and hurled it into the whirring fan. The blades slowed for a second, like a buzz saw meeting lumber, then went back to speed. The chicken disappeared.

I said, "Whoa, look at that."

Joey yelled "You hear me? I can't take it no goddamn more!" He grabbed another chicken and sent it flying into the blades.

He winged a third bird and I heard the voices outside. Number four brought shouts and fists pounding on the door.

Joey was grabbing chickens and firing them into the fan at a faster pace. The motor noise would dip with every new entry, then roar back to speed. Like a fighter switching to southpaw, he started throwing with his left. Then he was whipping them with both hands. His face flushed pink with the effort.

I heard Duane's muffled bellow. "Sesto! Zaleski!"

The door flew open and our foreman stood there, splattered with chicken bits, paralyzed as he gazed upon Joey fast-balling the company profits into those greasy blades. He opened his mouth to scream again, but nothing came out. He turned and jabbed a wild finger at me. "You! Hit the goddamn switch!"

I cocked my head. "Excuse me?"

"Hit the goddamn switch!" Spittle sprayed from his mouth.

"You didn't say plea –"

He shoved me aside and in a furious rush slammed the red button on the wall with one hand and the switch on the junction box with the other. The conveyor stopped rolling and the fan wound down. The last bird Joey had thrown bounced off a blade and dropped to the floor with a fat plop.

Our co-workers crowded outside the door, marveling at the carnage. Some of them were sporting raw chicken bits on their clothes, on their faces and arms and in their hairnets. Duane was sputtering like a busted hose. I thought he was going to have a stroke.

Joey said, "Duane, I'd like to tender my resignation, effective immediately."

Angela's laugh was a lovely thing to hear. She clapped her hands and her dark eyes were merry.

"By lunch-time, I was out of there, too," I said.

She touched a knuckle to her wet cheek. "That was Joey, all right," she said. She sipped her coffee, then sighed, her mood turning melancholy. "I loved him," she said. "But he was such a pain in the ass. Always making trouble for somebody."

"Yeah? Like what?"

"Oh, if it wasn't the borough council and zoning or what Zelecon was dumping into the river, he was going after the right-wing guy who does the talk radio show over in Radley. He never stopped. He used to drive me nuts with his ranting. Now I could listen to him all night."

She rose from her chair to stand at the railing and gaze down at her lawn.

"Can we talk about his accident?" I said.

"What about it?" she said without turning.

"What was he was doing up there in the middle of the night?"

"Oh, now and then he'd go over and wander around after they closed the gates," she said. "It was one of his places. Speaking of smoking pot, he still did that, you know. After all these years. So he'd got up there and sit down and have a smoke and look out over the valley."

"At night?"

"Especially at night."

"Seems a little strange."

She turned around. "A man of fifty sneaking into a state park in the dead of night to smoke a joint and stare into space? You find that strange?"

I paused for a few seconds. "And so he was up there wandering around and fell? That doesn't make sense."

"Why not?"

"What I remember is that Council Rock always scared the hell out of him. Because of the drop. He used to be afraid of heights."

"Yeah, I know," Angela said. "He always was. But they said they couldn't tell if he was out on the rock or fell from some other place. It gets so dark up there. There's no light at all once they close the gates. He got turned around somehow and..." Her voice quivered. "...and off he went."

She took a sip of her coffee, collecting herself before she sat down again. The creak of the rocking chair was the only sound for the next minute or so.

"So, how long are you staying?" she asked.

"I was going to drive back this afternoon," I said. "It's getting late, though. I might just stay over and go in the morning."

"Stay where?"

"I'll get a room at one of those motels down on Route 12."

She considered for a second, then said, "I can put you up here."

There was nothing untoward about the invitation. In fact, I was surprised that it was so breezy, given that she and I had history, too. Though as yet it hadn't come up. Maybe she had decided to leave it buried.

"That might not be such a good idea," I said. "You don't want to get a reputation as a wanton woman."

"Oh, I think I could live with that," she said. "Anyway, I don't give a damn what these people think. Your reputation is the one we need to worry about. You're a married man. And you're famous."

"I am married. I'm not famous."

"Whatever you say. You're welcome to stay. I have three empty bedrooms."

I gave it some more thought. Now I felt like she'd be a little disappointed if I turned her down. "Okay, if you're sure."

"I am. It's empty here with the kids gone. You can go ahead, get your bag if you want."

"I think I'll take a walk first. Have a look around town. I haven't seen anything except the inside of Charlotte's. And I haven't seen anyone except John Miller."

She grimaced at the mention of his name.

"Him, and a waitress named Crystal."

"Oh, you met *Crystal*." She grinned. "Let me guess. She asked for your autograph."

I nodded. "Yeah, she did."

"That's our girl." She started picking up the coffee cups. "I'm going to my office. There's a key under the doormat if I'm not around when you come back. I'll make dinner. We'll eat around seven."

She watched me go down her walk and stop to lock the car doors. "You know you don't have to do that here," she said. "It's safe."

—

It had been a long time since I had enjoyed an afternoon in such silence. That would have been during the previous summer when we went to visit my parents on the Gulf Coast. Even then, the relentless wash of the surf filled the days and nights.

Wyanossing nestled in the still and quiet common to small towns, moving in gentle rhythm, with none of the shrieking, racing chaos that animated New York from dawn until midnight. Except for teenagers in their cars, no one seemed in any big hurry. I was surrounded by rich shades of green and the daylight was even, with high, thin clouds like gauze over the sun.

I walked down Fourth Street and turned the corner onto Ashland, encountering small remnants of my past along the way. Some of the homes had been on the paper route I'd had when I was eleven. I saw the rundown house that people once said was inhabited by a witch. Except for a flitting profile, no one had ever seen the occupant. Another house was the home of a former high school baseball star and A-student who had been involved in a horrible crash that left him crippled, disfigured, and insane, and so he dwelt there like a fairytale ogre, attended by a mother and sister who came and went in dark silence. Yet another was the home of a family headed by a drunken swine of a father, his scraggly wife and three dirty kids. Then one day there was a gunshot. One of the dirty kids had accidentally shot another. I remembered that they marched us from our elementary school to the funeral home to view the body, a trauma that I never forgot. The little boy wore a blue suit in his coffin.

I passed another house that was the home of a girl named Corinne Wiley who was known as the town slut. She had a reputation for a willingness to do anything with anyone. She offered group entertainment. The older guys talked about her as they slouched on the corner of First and Front, smoking their Luckies and spitting into the gutter. I wondered what had happened to her, too.

Finally, I arrived at 669 Royal Street, our house when I was a kid. I walked up one side of the street and down the other. Not too much had changed. Everything was smaller. The older houses where the poor people lived had been refurbished. The brick alleys that had been there for almost a hundred years remained.

I wandered for a good while, wondering if I would encounter any ghosts. Or at least an echo of something. I saw not a shade, heard not a whisper. Of course, it was the middle of a pretty spring day. Perhaps the haunting would begin after dark.

Before I left, I strolled along the alley that split the block and reached a vantage point where I could look up and see the window of the bedroom that had once been mine. It was the same room where Joey and I had spent a hundred winter afternoons dreaming out loud. The room where we first heard "She Loves You" on my Philco.

We were smart, he and I, but we didn't have a dime bag of common sense between us. I went to college, hated it except for the girls and dropped out.

The rumor was that the draft was finished, and even if it did go on, they wouldn't go higher than 50, 60 max. I was wrong. The letter arrived while I was at a music festival in Canada and was sitting on the dining room table when I came home. They had stopped at 85, and my number, swear to God, was 84. And it was the last time in the 20th century that the U.S. government would employ the Selective Service system. Lucky me.

I considered refusing and going to jail. I thought about turning around and heading back north. After some thought, I decided to see the other side. I had caved in. Joey was right about that, too, though he never accused me. The weeks passed and it was time for me to go. The night before I left, he and I climbed Nock Hill to look at the stars. He brought along some weed that he had grown in a tray on his windowsill.

"You're going into the goddamn Army," he said in a voice filled with wonder. He studied me for a few pensive seconds. Then he broke the stare and shrugged. I had a feeling that he wanted to say that he was going to miss me. If he did, he never got it out.

"Make sure you get sent somewhere they got good weed," he said with his giddy grin. "And don't forget my address."

I crashed in his apartment. He was still sacked out when I woke up. When I looked in his bathroom mirror, I saw the kid for the last time and I did whisper a good-bye. I crept out the front door, into the cool spring dawn, to meet the bus that would carry me away.

Before I turned the corner onto Market Street, I looked back and saw Joey's silhouette in the window. He raised a hand in farewell.

It was a little before six when I got back to find Angela puttering in her kitchen. I had stopped at the State Store, which was still in the same location, too, and showed her the pinot grigio I'd found.

She was sipping a tall vodka and soda and offered me something. I opted for a gimlet. I got the impression that cocktail hour was not something she did as a habit, as the bottle of Stöly she took down from the cabinet carried a light patina of dust. Then I wondered if she needed to brace herself. Maybe she was having second thoughts about her invitation, as I was having about accepting. It occurred to me that I was going to have to make a phone call to explain to my wife. If I had not mentioned Joey, I definitely hadn't mentioned his little sister and what had gone on between this little sister and me.

I stopped to muse on this. Was it possible that he never knew that I was the one who had deflowered her? And then took her dozens of times more? She and I became master thieves of the night, stealing moments in the darkness, inventing excuses and stories, coming together for what were sometimes fierce and feverish seconds and other times languid hours entwined in bliss.

To my shame, I sometimes used our secret pact to run off to something or someone else. All the while, she never looked at another boy. She clung to me until the draft snatched me away. I wrote and then I didn't write anymore. The last time I had seen her was the week after my discharge. She was seeing someone else but came to me in a carnal instant. And then I was out of there for good. Time took care of the rest.

Still, the memories had never faded: the look of her as she lay naked and open to the night and to me; the earth-ripe smell of her body; the urgent words and frantic sounds she poured in my ear. Decades had passed, we were other people now, and yet I knew now that I would never forget any of it.

—

She led me on a tour of the house. She had done it up nicely, with light oak trimmings, good artwork on the walls, and plenty of light from all those tall windows. There were four bedrooms upstairs, one of which was now her study. She showed me to the one I'd be taking. It was at the other end of the hallway from hers and overlooked the street.

Downstairs, we stepped onto her back patio to finish our drinks as night fell.

I told her about my walk around the borough and asked for an update on some of the legendary figures from the past. It turned out the old witch, Miss Mary Franklin by name, had owned property all over town. With no family close by, she left a small fortune to a distant nephew who had shown up from Maryland and left stunned by the check that reached seven figures. Angela had done the probate on the old woman's estate.

William Kaye, the accident victim, had died years ago. Corinne Wiley, the most popular girl in town, at least at night, had moved away. Angela said she'd heard of a marriage and children, though she couldn't be sure. She mentioned some other folks, but then the weight of nostalgia dragged the recitation to a halt.

When she got up to check on dinner, I took out my cell phone and dialed Isabel. She answered on the second ring from the taxi on her way to pick up the girls from their after-school.

"Where are you?" she asked directly.

"I'm still in Wyanossing," I said, already feeling my cheeks beginning to burn. "The time got away from me. So I'm going to stay overnight."

She said, "Stay where?"

"At Joey's sister's house."

"Joey's sister..."

"Angela. She invited me. "

"So, what, then? You'll head back in the morning?"

"That's the plan."

She didn't say anything, so I offered to drive back that night.

"No, it's late," she said. "We'll see you tomorrow. Don't forget to buy something for the girls. What do they have out there?"

"I could find some Amish dolls."

"I guess that would be all right." She sounded vague and I could tell she was a little bothered. I didn't blame her. I had left the city without telling her in advance and now was back in my hometown staying overnight in the house of a strange woman.

"What about you?" I said.

"What about me?"

"What do you want me to bring for you?"

"My husband," she said, and before I could think of a reply, she said, "All right, we'll see you tomorrow." She clicked off to my children's happy voices in the background.

As I dropped the phone back in my pocket, I noticed that there was no sound coming from the kitchen.

Angela prepared a nice dinner, roasted chicken, steamed vegetables, and salad, nothing fancy, but she had a touch. I opened the wine. It went well with the rosemary and lemon seasoning.

It was her turn to ask about my life and career. I took her through the thirty years, getting myself to New York and jumping into the old struggle to be seen. I had a decent voice and a good face for commercials, not handsome or pretty, just unusual enough to catch the eye. Or so the casting directors said. Whatever I had worked. I had stayed busy and made decent money.

"What about plays or movies?" she asked. "Haven't you done any of that? I thought I heard something."

I refilled the wine and then explained that I had done some theater and minor roles in a couple small films. I kept getting called for spots, though, and as the years went by, I found myself booked almost solid. I told her about Sondra and blamed my superb agent for much of this success.

She asked me about movie stars and I told her about meeting this one and that. The truth was I was more likely to run into Al Pacino at D'Agostino's than on a set or stage. She seemed just a bit disappointed that I didn't have any better tales to tell.

"I'm just a hack actor," I explained.

She regarded me steadily, her dark eyebrows stitching. "And is that okay with you?"

"That's what I am," I said. "Every time I start to bitch about it, I remind myself that there are a thousand guys in New York who would kill to trade places with me."

"I guess that's true," she said.

"It is." The words came out harder than I'd intended.

She gave me a quizzical look and said, "We don't know much about that kind of thing around here."

We switched to my wife and kids and I took their pictures out of my wallet.

"They're all beautiful," she said. "The boys are going to be knocking down your door."

"Don't remind me." I poured the last bit of wine into her glass. "I keep on thinking that there will be a day of reckoning. It's going to be payback time for all the screwing around I did."

A second later, I was wishing I hadn't said it. I wondered if we were going to open the book to that chapter, because Angela was staring intently into the shimmering liquid in her glass. The moment passed and she just smiled in an offhand way.

"Do you want anything for dessert?" she said presently. "I've got some ice cream and –"

"No, nothing. I'll help you clean up and then call it a night."

We carried the plates into the kitchen and loaded the dishwasher. Brushing by each other as we moved around, I caught her scent, something light and natural. She didn't seem to notice that our bodies had touched. She seemed distracted, and I got a sense from her brooding expression that she was thinking about Joey again.

When we finished, I said, "Well, then..."

She gave me a wan smile. "Good night, Richie." Her face turned mock serious. "I mean, *Richard*."

"Really, Richie's fine," I said and waved goodnight to her.

It was dark and quiet. Even as I tumbled into a deep sleep, I was aware of her steps padding to the door of the room. After a moment, they moved off again. Or maybe not; I could have been dreaming.

6.

It was full light when I came awake and looked at my watch. 8:10.

In New York, my ears would be filled with the early strains of the day-long jazz of the streets, winding up, winding down, and never stopping, even in the deep hours of the night. Now, from beyond the window, I heard a random car pass on the street, the slow metallic clanks of someone working off the back of a truck, voices crossing a fence in a lazy rhythm. All followed by great gaps of quiet. I told myself to get out of that soft bed right that second. Instead, I drowsed a while longer.

After a few guilty minutes, I rolled out in gradual moves, letting my bones un-kink, and stepped down the hall to the bathroom. The house was empty, so I descended the narrow stairwell in my t-shirt and boxers.

A note from Angela was propped on the kitchen table like a little tent: "Help yourself to whatever you want. My work number is 477-9881." She had left coffee on and I drank a cup as I stood by a window gazing out at her tidy backyard and small garden of spring flowers. It was a curious moment. Had I not wandered away, would I be there at that same moment, though by a different road?

If I turned my head just a few degrees, would I find that the life I knew had been a dream and that my children were not Juliette and Annabelle but, I don't know, Samantha and Justin? Our kids – Angela's and mine. And would Joey still be alive? Would we have somehow altered his path so that he did not arrive at Council Rock in the dark of night and take the errant steps that sent him plunging over the edge? I played with this until the construction collapsed. My life was my life, Angela's was hers. Joey's was over, and there was no changing any of that.

Carrying my cup back upstairs, I took a shower and put on my one change of clothes, all in slow motion. The sense of unreality was hanging around. What was I doing? Why was I idling in the home of my best friend's little sister, the one whose maidenhead and heart I had broken almost thirty years back?

Before these thoughts twisted me into a knot, I made the bed and got moving. In the kitchen, I poured a second cup of coffee, telling myself that what I needed to do now was get in the rental car and drive back to New York, to my home and career, and most importantly, to my wife and daughters. And yet I couldn't summon the gumption to make the first move in that direction, and so I drank my coffee and stared out the window at Angela's tiny, tidy, flower-laden yard.

After another quarter hour of idling, I roused myself to a decision to grab some breakfast, have a last look around town, say goodbye to Angela, and then leave in time to make it home for dinner.

As I stepped outside, it occurred to me that once I finally pulled away and started the drive east, there would be no more reason to come back.

Crystal must have caught sight of me through the window, because she pounced the moment I stepped over the threshold.

"Good *morning*!" It was a trill of delight, and the heads that hadn't already turned now came around. Ten pairs of eyes fastened on me and I had an urge to crack a joke. *Good morning, ladies and germs! Two midgets are walking down the street and a hooker falls out a window...*

I thought better of it; something told me that these folks would not take kindly to a stand-up routine.

Anyway, there wasn't time. Crystal was herding me to a table near the front window with whispers and nudges. She gave the street outside the once-over before she would allow me to sit. I got the feeling that she wanted maximum exposure should anyone happen by. Crystal the waitress had a prize, the New York actor ("He's on TV and *everything*!") at one of her tables.

I took my seat, feeling foolish. If only she knew. I wondered what she would do if a real movie star ever happened by. I imagined her going into an orgasmic spasm before winding up and exploding, splattering voluptuous little Crystal droplets all over the walls, while the locals looked on with slack-jawed awe.

Damn, Howard, there's somethin' you don't see every day.

I smelled sandalwood and felt warm breath and looked up. She had placed one hand palm down on the table and the other on her hip as she gazed intently at my face. I knew the signs of a practiced pose and she wasn't doing it very well. Still, she was some sight, with her pelvis at an angle and her little waitress dress unbuttoned as far down as she could get away with on a Tuesday morning in Wyanossing, PA. I could see a silver crucifix dangling on a thin chain. I could see the shadow of her cleavage and the swell of one of her breasts. And of course she knew I could see all this.

I felt her smile as I dropped my eyes back to the menu. "What's good?" I asked her.

"What looks good to you?" she said and let out a wicked little laugh.

I didn't dare raise my head. I was a married man with two children, all of whom I loved desperately. I was a successful New York actor. And I was feeling a tingle at having a woman young enough to be a daughter standing so close, her lush little body broadcasting in stereo while her sultry whisper set the hook.

For those few seconds, she had me. Then I flipped on the mask and said, "Two scrambled eggs. Canadian bacon. Wheat toast. Coffee, half-decaf." Now I did look up. She was studying me archly, as if I had muffed my lines in a scene for the tenth time. She plucked the menu from between my fingers. The part of her smile that returned was cool. She turned away.

I peered out at the street and reminded myself I should be ashamed. After a few seconds, I noticed her reflection in the glass. Our eyes met there and her smile returned.

"So how do you like it?" The voice was sharp. I came off Crystal's mirrored image and looked around.

A policeman was standing at the table behind me and to my right, twiddling the brim of his hat in his fingers. His eyes roamed from me, over his shoulder to Crystal, then back to me, where they settled. His mouth was a level line. The little silver nametag over his pocket identified him as "Dewitt," and he looked like guys I had known in the Army who took all the chickenshit parts of the military seriously.

"What's that?" I said.

"I asked how you like Wyanossing. Since you grew up here and all. Isn't that correct?"

"I did, yes." I couldn't think of anything clever and so said, "It's, uh, quiet."

"Yes," Officer Dewitt said. "I suppose for somebody lives in New York City, it is quiet. I guess that would be right."

He nodded sagely as I tried to figure out how he knew this information about me. *Small town*, I thought.

Crystal came sashaying back with my coffee. She maneuvered past the officer with a look that was so purposefully blank that I knew instantly there was something between them. I got the rest of it, too. She had cornered the stranger in her little corral and was now in major flirt mode, torturing the policeman and rushing on the power. Meanwhile, he was doing his best to play the staunch lawman who could not be swayed by the wiles of a female, no matter how much a temptress.

She put my coffee on the table, blessed me with a smile that was too familiar, and turned away. Out of the corner of my eye, I saw Dewitt fuss with his hat a little more, then take a step closer to the window and my table, poking a little deeper into my personal space. He still didn't look at me, but gazed outward, cutting the profile of the vigilant peace officer keeping watch over the townsfolk. Though the hunch of his shoulders and jut of his jaw told me that at that moment, Bumfuck, PA's own Gary Cooper was more interested in staking out his territory indoors.

"You have family here, Mr. Zaleski?" So he knew my name, too.

I said, "Not anymore. My parents moved away when my father retired. I've got a brother in New Mexico and a sister in Philly." Like it was any of his business.

"So you came to visit friends?" he went on. Even as he tried for casual courtesy, I picked up an edge that hinted at another kind of interest.

"Actually, an old friend of mine passed away," I said. "I came to pay my respects."

He kept his gaze on the street. "That would be Joseph Sesto." His gave the slightest shake of his head. "Very unfortunate what happened to him."

I nodded and waited.

"That was some fall he took," Officer Dewitt added.

Since he seemed so inclined to chat, I said, "Did anyone find out exactly what happened to him?"

"What happened?" He considered the question for a moment. "Well, we have a pretty good idea. That's been a hang-out up there for years." His eyes shifted to me for a half-second and one side of his mouth curved upward, a bare hint of a smile. "But you know that. Since you grew up here and all. Probably spent some time up there yourself."

"That's right, I did," I said, and wanted to bite my tongue.

Sonofabitch, I thought, he *is* grilling me.

He said, "As nearly as we can ascertain, Mr. Sesto was trespassing up there, roaming around in the dark. He was on Council Rock and stumbled and went over the edge. Very unfortunate. Yes, sir." There was a pause and then he took an abrupt step backward and said, "You enjoy your visit." He could not have meant it less.

He headed for the door, nodding to the other breakfast diners. Except for two brief glances, he hadn't actually looked at me. I guess he felt he had adequately pissed his little line on the floor, because he went out the door without a glance back at Crystal or me.

I watched as he crossed the street to a patrol car. Maybe I was too quick to judge, but he seemed to be a type I'd encountered before.

The sort that worshipped at the far right end of the political spectrum and spent a lot of energy frowning and nodding when the nuts and bullies on the radio went after those evil creatures who were assaulting their holy white majority, growing more frightened and angry the more the world changed. The type who would fight to stay on top. Some of them would kill for it. They were —

I stopped. What the hell was I doing? The ranting voice in my head sounded like Joey's. Just that quickly, I had fallen back into the posture of the old battle, us against them. But I wasn't a homegrown radical anymore, if I ever had been one. I didn't care about screeching partisans, as long as they left me alone. So Officer Dewitt was not my enemy. Though maybe I was his, since it appeared to have claims on Crystal.

She hadn't missed the exchange. When she stepped up and put my plates on the table, she said, "And what was that all about?"

"The officer and I were talking about Joey Sesto." At the mention of the name, I saw her face cloud. "Friend of yours, right?"

She blinked in confusion. "Friend... who?" she said.

"Officer Dewitt," I said. Now I was playing word games, too.

"Oh. Yeah, I guess so." Her troubled look lingered for a few seconds. Then she brightened again, eager to return to the subject of what she really wanted.

Ignoring her other customers, she said, "So, hey, what I want to know is, can you tell me how you got from here to being on TV and all? I mean, God! From Wyanossing? Who'd ever imagine that?"

I picked up my fork. "It's not much of a story. I just –"

She waved a hand to silence me and bent close again, her blouse falling open at the top like a blooming flower. In a whisper, she said, "No, actually, I mean could you tell me later on? I get off at two o'clock. Maybe we could have lunch. You could tell me then. 'Cause I'm interested. I mean, I'd really like to do it. I just need to know how."

"Do what?" It came out before I could catch it.

She gave me a pert smile. "Act. Or sing. Or dance. Or whatever would get me out of here." She giggled. "What did you think I meant?"

I raised my eyes past her cleavage, saw the invitation in her expression, and reverted to the old actor's trick of staring at the point between her eyes.

"Well, the problem is, I'm going to be leaving," I said. "Probably around one. I'm going home to New York."

She straightened, her lips pursing. She didn't like that at all.

"But I can give you the short course," I murmured quickly. "First, get out of here and go to New York or Philly or some other city. Find yourself a good drama class. And then it's just a matter of working at it. Hanging on. Not giving up." I saw that she wasn't listening; her gaze was blank. "That's really it," I offered, winding down. "It's not like there's a magic formula or anything."

"Well, I know *that*." Now she sounded petulant. "It's something to think about, all right." Her eyes shifted away from me. "You have a nice trip back," she said and moved to the next table over.

For the next half-hour, she treated me to the big chill except to refill my coffee, and I finished my breakfast in peace. Two elderly women stopped to ask for autographs. One of them remembered my mom. Both had seen me in the Maxwell House spot.

I stepped up to the counter with my check. Crystal tried for blasé as she rang it up, but there was an accusing light in her eyes. She could definitely use the acting lessons.

"Did you know him at all?" I said.

She didn't look at me. "Know who?"

"Joey Sesto."

She dropped one of the coins, then scooped it up again. She said, "Sure, I used to see him around." She made a half-shrug. "It's a small town. You meet everybody sooner or later."

There didn't seem to be anything else to say. She put on a smile that didn't reach beyond her lower lip. As I walked out the door, I wondered if she had fucked my old friend. I hoped it had happened on the day he died, so that he carried the sweet memory over that ledge and into the darkness.

—

It was the start of a beautiful day, with all the green brilliance of spring bursting from the gray lock of winter. I had a memory of getting out of church on mornings just like this one and tearing home to throw off my clothes and hit the sidewalk in my new Red Ball Jets, with that feeling of being able to run so fast and jump so high that I was just short of flying. I thought about it some more and realized that had been almost forty years in the past. I looked up and down the street. Forty years, and not much had changed, including the Sunoco sign that had been a fixture on the corner of River and Front Streets forever.

When Leo saw me ambling across the concrete, he clapped his hands, did a little hop, and said, "Holy fucking *shit*! Richie! Somebody said you were around." He held his hands wide, gave me a quick hug, and then stepped back. "Damn, man. What brings you to town?"

"I heard about Joey and I decided to drive out."

His grin dipped. "Yeah, what a drag that was." A sedan pulled off the street and rolled up to the pumps. Leo threw the driver a vile look. When the car didn't drive off, Leo said, "Hey, hang out for a minute, okay? I got to pump this old bitch's gas and then we can shoot the shit."

I said, "Sure."

He jerked a thumb over his shoulder. "There's coffee there on the counter," he said and went to pump the old bitch's gas.

I watched through the plate glass as he filled the tank and then went under the hood to check the fluids. The woman was ordering him around like a servant and the way he glared at her made me laugh.

I had known Leo Kowicki all through grade school, but we didn't hook up as friends until I was thirteen and discovered cars. His dad owned the garage and let all the hoodlums gather there, as they spent so much of their cash on gas, oil, and parts. I spent about a month hanging around across the street, watching those gorgeous Chevys, Fords, and Mercs ripping in and out of the parking lot with their pipes blatting and metal flake finishes shimmering under the lights. One night Leo noticed me lurking and waved me over. From then on, we were pals.

Later, he was one of the gang of stoners that included Joey and a half dozen other local guys. We had smoked a lot of weed. He became a charter member of the inner circle that gathered at Council Rock. He had stayed in Wyanossing and remained a good friend to Joey. Unlike me.

He hadn't changed much. His hair was still long, parted in the middle and hanging straight down on either side, the pale blond now streaked with gray. He reminded me of Iggy Pop and he was always bright and funny, an all-around good guy. He was also a person with little ambition, which was why he was happy to take over the garage when the old man retired. It was the path of least resistance. Though the hoodlums and their rods were long gone, it appeared that he was doing well in a modest way.

The Buick crept off towards the street and Leo walked towards me, smiling his crooked smile.

"You remember her? Mrs. Donaldson? She was already like a hundred years old when we were kids. You hit a ball into her yard, she kept it. Now she stays alive just to give me grief."

I laughed. Leo hadn't changed much, either.

"Fuckin-A, Richie," he was saying. "It's good to see you." He gestured to a tube metal chair with torn vinyl upholstery. "G'head, siddown."

I sat. He perched on a stool at his register. "How's Angela doing?" he said. I looked at him in surprise and he shrugged. "Hey, man, I got the only place in town people can buy gas. Ain't much goes on I don't hear about. So, how's she doing?"

"She seems to be holding up okay," I said.

He picked up a coffee cup and stared at its contents for a long moment. "Joey's dead. You believe that shit?"

"I didn't even know about it," I said. "I just happened to call up here and I got a hold of her and she told me. I was just floored."

Leo thought about it for another moment and then said, "Yeah, but y'know, it was *Joey*, man. He wasn't gonna go out some old man lying in bed." He paused. "Unless he was there getting laid, of course."

Something had been on my mind. I looked at Leo and said, "You don't think there's any chance that he...uh..."

Leo's brow arched and I made a gesture with my hand plummeting downward.

He said, "You mean jump? No way. Not him. Never." He smiled. "He was still the same guy, Richie. Except that he got crazier as he got older." He laughed a little. "He was always a wild man. The revolutionary, you remember? He never gave that up. Never changed, except to crank it up over the last few years." He stopped again. "When's the last time you saw him, anyway?"

Again I felt my face flushing. "It was, I guess, almost ten years." It wasn't almost ten years; it was that many and then some.

"Yeah?" Leo said. "Ten years?" He gave me a knowing look and said, "What, you guys have some kind of fight?"

"Why? Did he say something?"

"Naw, but he made a career out of tangling with people." He grinned. "Even his friends. I can't count the number of times he got pissed off at me over something. He wouldn't talk to me for like six months, went around bad-mouthing me to everybody in town, and then one day he'd just drive in like nothing had happened." He came up with a lopsided grin. "Usually that was when he was short on cash and needed some work done on his car. That was Joey."

"He didn't have any serious problems with anybody, did he?"

"Serious how?"

"Serious like making someone so mad that they'd want to hurt him."

Leo gave me a dubious look that said I watched too many movies. "Well, you know, there were people around who couldn't stand him. Mostly the business people and those assholes on the borough council. He was always raising hell about something. He kept his eye on those greedy fucks and they despised his ass. But hurt him? No way. First of all, he could handle himself." He grinned. "And he was one fucking charming guy. Even the people that hated him liked him." He shook his head. "People don't generally get into the rough stuff around here. That's more your neck of the woods."

"But there's something that doesn't make sense," I said. "Why the hell was he still hanging around up there? After all these years, I mean."

Leo shrugged. "I don't know. He would go up and sit and wonder why it wasn't just like the old days."

"Angela told me that," I said. "I'm talking about Council Rock. Don't you remember? He always stayed way back when we went up there. He was scared of heights. We used to ride his ass about it all the time. You don't remember that?"

Leo pondered for a few seconds. "Y'know, I do. But, hell, it was dark. He probably just took a wrong turn. And down he went."

There was a finality about the way he said it that kept both of us quiet for a few moments. We watched through the glass as another customer pulled up, pumped gas and paid with a card at the island.

Leo said, "So, what's been goin' on with you? Except for being a big TV star?"

I told him a little bit about work and showed him a picture of my daughters. He studied it closely. "So, their mom's a black lady?

"She's half Puerto Rican and half Irish."

Leo glanced at the picture again and shook his head. "Y'know, I don't care what those racist motherfuckers say. If God didn't want people mixing, he wouldn't make their kids look like this." He handed the photo back.

It was a touching sentiment coming from a small town moke and I said, "Thanks, Leo," meaning it.

I asked him about some old friends. He mentioned this person and that. Most had either gone away and never looked back or had settled into staid local lives. Some of the hottest girls had become frumps who went through husbands one after another, trading them off like baseball cards. The shits were now lording over the town. No surprise. Everything he told me was predictable and dull, until I asked about Louie Zag.

"Oh, right, you don't know about him." He grimaced in dismay and I thought he was going to tell me that Louie was dead, too.

Instead, he said, "He finally snapped, man. He was in Danville for a long time and then they let him out. Now he just wanders around town, bouncing a basketball."

"Doing what?"

Leo made the motion of dribbling. "He just walks up and down the sidewalk bouncing a goddamn basketball. Sometimes he talks to himself, sometimes he sings. Sometimes you can carry on a half-way normal conversation with him. Sometimes he's nowhere to be found."

"When did this all happen?"

"I guess about six months ago. He got some bad medicine, if you know what I mean."

I was stunned. We were all smart kids, and of course if you smoke enough, everything's hilarious, but Louie Zagarelli was the real deal, a natural-born comedian, and in terms of raw talent, the funniest person I'd ever known. Some of his lines and escapades were local legends. He could have killed doing stand-up. Now I was hearing that he was the village idiot. Though in a way, it didn't surprise me. As long as I had known him he maintained an insatiable appetite for herbs and chemicals. From what Leo was telling me, it had finally caught up with him.

"You'll run into him if you hang around," he said.

"I'm going back to New York this afternoon."

"It's just as well," Leo said. "It'd bum you to see him like that. But I'll tell him you said hello."

"You think he'd remember me?"

"Yeah, he's still pretty sharp that way. He's just nutty as a fucking fruitcake, is all."

I sat there for a moment, thinking about Louie back when, then got up out of the chair. I extended a hand. "Listen, I'll come by, fill the tank before I take off."

Leo said, "I do got gas, bro."

We stepped outside into the bright morning light. I walked away a few steps, then stopped and said, "Oh, hey, what's with that girl in the café?"

"Who, Crystal?" he snickered. "She's some piece, huh? She's like the most recent edition of Judy Fisher," he said, recalling a turbo-charged nineteen-year-old fuck machine who had made every one of us very happy at one time or another. And where was Judy Fisher now, I wondered for a second, with her bursting breasts and her luscious pelvis and the arms and legs that had wrapped me in such wet ecstasy one spring night that I still remembered every moment of it decades later? I almost asked Leo, but after hearing about Joey and Louie Zag, I decided that didn't really want to know.

"What about her?" Leo said. "She zoom you?"

I nodded. "She seems a little... hungry for attention."

"That's putting it mildly," Leo agreed. "Yeah, she'd consider you a trophy. Being on TV and all."

"She's a bit too young for my blood."

"But you ain't too old for her."

"And she's got something going on with that cop Dewitt?"

"Him and some others, from what I heard. But not me." He patted his groin. "I don't trot out the golden pole for just any little piece of tail, you know." His grin went comically sober. "Plus it'd probably kill me."

"How about Joey? She have anything going with him?"

Leo laughed again. "I don't know. Maybe. Wouldn't surprise me." He shook his head. "I used to tell him, we can't be doing all that crazy shit anymore. Those days are over." He got a sadly whimsical look on his face. "But you know how he was, if he could get it, he'd take it." He sighed. "That's what he did. Right to the end."

I left Leo brooding and wandered back through town, making my way along Front Street. I saw an appliance store, one of those that John Miller had mentioned that he owned, and remembered that it had once been a movie theater. It was there that I had seen my first show and became enamored by the magic of performance. Now the only theater was a multiplex at the mall and the space was dedicated to hawking microwaves and refrigerators.

There were other businesses lodged in the converted storefronts: an insurance office, a real estate agency, and a CVS store. Business was slow. Like other small towns, most of the commerce had gone to the Wal-Mart up on the four-lane.

Keystone Hardware occupied the next corner. With its dirty bricks and yellowed windows, the store had been there since before time, the kind of place that would be standing when everything else was gone. From what I could see, it was the one edifice that had not changed a bit.

I was curious for a look at the place. This was a mistake. As I stepped closer, I saw a thin billow of smoke wafting from the doorway and then caught sight of Elmer Smalley, standing in the entranceway and rocking on his heels as he puffed on a pipe. I wondered for a second if it was a joke. Who smokes a pipe anymore?

There was no mistaking this particular hometown character. Composed of circles and ovals, now as before he spent his days stuffed like a sausage into clothes that were never loose enough to accommodate the girth. Along with the pipe, a thick spike of a nose jutted from his face and his eyes were almost lost in folds of fat.

He was talking to John Miller, who stood next to him with his arms crossed. It was too late to run; they had spied me. They stopped their chat and a short laugh passed between them. I intended to amble by with hello and a polite nod. But then Elmer drew the stem of the briar from between his teeth and jabbed it forward as he leaned into my path.

"Mister Zaleski," he said, then chortled. "Sorry, I mean *Zale*. What brings you back to the old borough after all these years?" The question was deliberate; he knew what I was doing there.

I said, "Hello, Elmer."

"What's it been?" he said. "Ten, fifteen years?"

"Something like that." I stopped to glance past him into the store. "You're the hardware man?"

"That I am," he said, planting the pipe in his mouth again. "That I am." He had always been a pompous ass, and the passing of time had only bottled his act in bond. In those few seconds, I'd sampled enough of him to last me another decade.

Miller stood aside listening and studying me with his bulbous gaze, ready to jump in somewhere with some more of his snide wit. After all this time, I could tell that these two still despised me and I was happy to return the sentiment.

Elmer had fixed me with a haughty look that made me want to smack the pipe right out of his mouth.

"You look well," he observed dryly.

"And you haven't changed a bit," I replied. I hoped he would take it to mean that I thought he was still a fat asshole prick. Though I didn't necessarily mean that in a bad way.

"In town for long?" he inquired.

"No, not long."

He took the pipe out of his mouth again, tamped the bowl in his palm, and shook a shower of ashes down onto the pavement.

"Well, it's nice to see you," he said. "In person, I mean. We do catch you on the television now and then. Always a treat when a local boy makes good." This was delivered in a rounded, considered tone that dripped with derision. John, meanwhile, continued with his cold smirk. I guess real men didn't do things like act. Real mean sold nuts and bolts and toasters.

I shrugged and said, "I guess that's right," and started away. I could feel their hard eyes on my back.

"Too bad what happened to Sesto," Elmer opined.

I turned around. He had spoken these words without a shred of regret and now regarded me as if he had said something about my mother and was waiting to see if I would start something. I wasn't about to give him the satisfaction.

"Well, he lived a good life," I said. "For this place, I mean." I left them to chew on that.

But as I made my way through the streets to Angela's house and my car, I entertained the creepy feeling of being sucked into an old spat, the Wyanossing version of the Hatfields and McCoys. That's what you get, I told myself, when you come back to a place you left far behind.

To shake off my foul mood, I sat on Angela's porch steps and spent a few minutes drinking in some more of the lovely morning.

There wasn't any reason for me to linger there. I had told Isabel I'd get on the road. If I started moving at that moment, grabbed my bag, and drove to Leo's to fill the tank, I could be in Manhattan and pulling my life back on like an old sweatshirt by mid-afternoon. Tomorrow, I would be hard at work hawking product, a cable-ready carnival barker.

Instead, I slouched for another half an hour, musing on everything and nothing, watching the slow ebbs of a quiet day in my little hometown. Joey crossed my mind a dozen times and most of the memories were tinged with sadness, though not all. He wouldn't be the type to abide grieving. I owed him some joy. He deserved someone remembering some of his greatest hits.

I spent more moments telling myself it was time to leave. But as I thought over Joey's life, and how it had intertwined with mine, I realized there was something to finish before I could put a period on my sad little pilgrimage.

I left the borough and crossed the river bridge, then drove a half-mile along the two-lane that wound along the Susquehanna at the base of Nock Hill.

Running down the west edge of the river, it was the last rough jut in a small finger of the Appalachian range. The coalfields began up the valley to the north and stretched to the Poconos. The blue ridge that formed the opposite wall of the valley rose in a gentler slope several miles distant. To the east and south stretched the rich, rolling farmland of Pennsylvania Dutch country.

The state park at the summit of Nock Hill drew travelers who wanted to enjoy the grand view of the valley, picnicking families, and lovers looking for a clandestine place to meet. Nature trails meandered deep into the woods for the pleasure of hikers. Parts of the crest had been cleared to accommodate visitors and their cars. Three hundred years ago, the Susquehannock tribes of the Iroquois Nation – hence the *Nock* - had held their councils on these heights, which was why the rock from which Joey had fallen carried that name.

A narrow asphalt road twisted and turned up its steep slope. I passed through the gate that bore a sign announcing that the park closed at sundown. As kids, we had figured various ways around this obstacle. A clearing along the road led to a path that switch-backed in a steep grade all the way to the top. The climb was worth it, because Nock Hill was such a great location at night.

Once the park rangers made their last sweep, it had become our playground. The officials must have known what was going on, and yet it was rare that anyone was chased out. We weren't doing any harm. The rude drunks had their own hangouts. Our crowd of misfits began to disassemble after high school, drifting off to college, jobs, marriages, grander adventures or lesser fates. While it lasted, Nock Hill had been some garden of delights. Joey had stayed to go back again and again, and then spend the last moments of his life on those heights.

I steered onto the narrow road, snaking my way upward for a quarter mile. Through gaps in the trees, I could see the other side of the valley laid out like a shallow bowl. Once at the summit, I passed the pavilions and picnic tables to reach the gravel parking lot.

Only one other vehicle sat idling at that early hour and as soon as my tires hit gravel, the sedan's engine cranked to life. Two young men averted their faces as I drove past. Times had changed, even in this part of the world.

I drove to the far side of the lot, leaving the couple in peace. I climbed out of the car to stroll along the four-foot chain link fence that was intended to keep the careless from tumbling down the slope and plummeting sixty stories over the steep and jagged face to the old railroad bed below. As Joey Sesto had managed to do.

This footpath rose and fell over rocks and the roots of stunted trees. As soon as I was out of sight of the paramours, I grabbed the top rail of the fence and clambered over and landed on another path, barely discernible in the long grass and following the face of the hill. Fifty feet further on, I stepped between two bent scrub trees and, for the first time in twenty-five years, stood upon Council Rock.

The outcropping had grown in stature as a process of fading memory. It was still impressive, a solid chunk of granite, fifteen feet wide at the base and jutting some twelve feet at a slight upward angle, roughly in the shape of a hand outstretched with the palm up and fingers closed. We used to sit at its brink with legs dangling over nothing but air. It was a seventy-five-foot drop to a meager rounded rock shelf, then another six hundred feet almost straight down to the railroad tracks.

I took a moment to scan the valley, once again dazzled by its sweep and beauty, then I turned my attention to closer geography. Where the rock attached was a clearing of gravel, moss and wild grasses, a thirty-foot-wide indent in the face of the hill like a tiny amphitheater. This was the spot the Susquehannocks once held their councils and surveyed their domain. That was before white settlers joined with rival tribes to drive them westward and away forever.

This piece of ground had always been a good place to slouch and enjoy displays of stars. And it was as far Joey would ever go, sometimes all but clinging to the rockface like a stoned barnacle.

I looked around for a few moments, picking out spots that held small memories. Here and there, I saw faded initials scratched into the granite. None of them rang any bells.

With careful steps, I edged onto the slab of granite and sat down, dropping my legs over the side as I had so many times as a teenager. In the daylight, it was some gorgeous view. The valley floor on the other side of the river was dappled into a patchwork of farm fields, narrow roads, houses and barns, painted into the pale blue distance. It was not hard to understand why first the Indians and then the English, Scots-Irish, and German settlers had chosen it. The river offered water, food, trade, and transportation. The hills around were a barrier against the worst of the weather. For hundreds of years, it had been a barge port and a river crossing. A boat could float all the way to the Delaware Bay.

Later came the immigrants to work the fields and the mines in the mountains further up the valley: Italians, Slavs, and my own Polish forbears. A busy rail junction had kept Wyanossing on the map for a while. Now that was gone, too, though I could still see a lone freight engine dragging cars on a single track that ran through a deserted yard.

It was quiet. The rumbling of an occasional semi passing on the two-lane below faded into the sound of the breeze through the trees. It didn't seem a perilous place.

Closing my eyes, I tried to imagine Joey wandering in the dark, stepping onto the rock and then stumbling and falling, just like in my dream, with violent shadows and sharp curses and the frozen moment as he went over the edge.

When I opened my eyes again, my heart was drumming. I pushed the wild images aside and got to my feet. Standing so high above the valley, a door opened in a corner of my memory and I recalled the last time that Joey and I had been up there. It was the night before I went off to the Army.

I shuffled out while he hugged the hard concave in the side of the hill. He was so freaked that he wouldn't even look at me as I stood at the end of the rock.

This was in the wake of one of his rants. I remembered him saying something like "You think it's nothing? It ain't nothing. They're coming for us."

"Who is?"

"Whoever!" he barked. "Whoever wants to sell our souls to the devil. They already sold theirs. We're next."

On that perch high above the river, I laughed at yet another of his melodramatic prophesies. I didn't want to engage in an argument, not on that night. In eight hours, my life was going to change forever. So I stood on the end of the rock and stretched my arms as if I was about to launch into a swan dive. It would be one way to get out of the Army.

Joey did shut his mouth then, horrified. "Don't do that, man!"

For a brief instant, his fear snagged me. It was a hell of a long way down and I was very buzzed. A hard clutch of fright had me backpedaling to join Joey in the embrace of the mountain.

A small echo of that same terror made a visit as I stood high on the promontory. I backed up and plodded around for a little while. With no more memories to interest me, I climbed the path, hopped the fence, and ambled to the parking lot, as innocent as could be. Two more vehicles had arrived, a second sedan and a pickup truck. The cab of the truck was empty. When I reached my car, the passenger in the sedan, a middle-aged woman, glanced at me, and then stared.

"Maxwell House," I said.

I drove down the winding road, through the gate, then onto the highway. A few hundred yards along, I pulled onto the berm, got out, and climbed the embankment to the railroad bed that followed the base of the hill. The rails had been hauled away years ago and only the corners of rotting ties protruded from the black dirt at odd places.

I could lean back and gaze straight upward at the outcroppings of boulders, stunted trees, low brush and wild grasses, all profiled at stark angles against the light sky. Tilting my head farther, I could see Council Rock jutting like a spearhead.

I walked along the bed for a hundred feet to stand directly beneath the rock. I traced a line downward that ended at a point a few yards away, somewhere near the point where Joey would have landed. On his back, with his eyes open, he could have taken one last look at the stars over the river. More likely he was dead or unconscious by the time he hit the track bed, and saw nothing except a last darkness descending.

I walked around in an aimless circle, pondering. What worse for a person with acrophobia than to take a lurching fall? What horror would have shot through his bones when he slipped and began to tumble. The kind of fear that would have shut down his mind and send him into —

I jerked back at a sudden clatter of stones. A dozen rocks of different sizes were rolling to a rest near the very spot I had been studying. I stepped back a few paces and looked up. Nothing moved on the granite face of the hill. The falling rocks and the wisps of black railroad dust they had kicked up were nothing but random punctuation on an epitaph.

Joseph Sesto. Dead and gone.

I saw him lying there, his body crumpled like a bag of broken sticks and bloody rags and found myself asking him to solve the mystery.

How did you come off that rock, Joey? That place that you feared so much? How did you get from there to here? Was it really an accident? Did you take the last heartbroken step on your own? Is that why we didn't we get to say good-bye?

I caught myself, turned abruptly, and hurried back to the car.

Though it was about time to get gas and head out, I passed Leo's Sunoco sign and cruised aimlessly through town, with an eye out for any landmarks I had missed in my walks. I came up on Seventh Street Elementary School. I drove past Jimmy's Corner Store, our hangout in Junior High. The building was now vacant, the windows boarded. I circled the baseball field and located the place in the outfield where one summer night I had lost my virginity with Carol Ann Gary.

I pulled to a curb and let the car sit idling, telling myself that I had now completed the tour. I had paid my respects at Joey's grave. I had visited the spot where he died. I had seen pretty much all of Wyanossing there was to see. I could go now. That's what I was telling myself as I went back to cruising, my thoughts trailing back to the patch of black dirt where Joey had last been alive.

Driving down River Street, I spotted a pizza joint and parked in a lot where a gaggle of teenagers were hanging out, drinking Cokes and taking turns performing skateboard tricks. Dodging them, I went inside and bought bottled water. Back outside, I leaned against the building and thought about calling Isabel and telling her I was on my way.

I watched the kids for another minute. They were either too old for school or skipping and that brought me around to my teen years, too. One of them really was good, performing ballet on a piece of carbon fiber and four little wheels.

I dug into my pocket for Angela's work number. When her

secretary asked who was calling, I said, "Arnold Ziffel."

She said, "One moment, please, Mr. Ziffel."

Angela came on the line. "Very funny."

"I couldn't help myself," I said. "I think I'm regressing."

She laughed quietly. "Where are you?"

I glanced at the sign. "Tony G's Pizza."

"Good Lord. You are regressing. What are you doing there?"

"Just hanging with my peeps," I said.

"Uh-huh. So what's your plan? You heading out?"

"I figured I'd do that after lunch. If you can go with me. To lunch, I mean."

She said, "I've got an appointment."

"Oh. All right, then I'll –"

"But I can cancel it."

"Is that okay?"

"Yeah. These people won't be going anywhere. Ever."

"Where and when?"

"Definitely not Tony G's," she said. "Pick me up in a half-hour. We'll drive over to Middlebury. They have actual food there."

She gave me directions and then said, in a voice that was meant to be overheard, "No, thank *you*, Mr. Ziffel."

We drove south out of town on State Route 44 for a few miles and then crossed the river to Middlebury, the county seat, a quaint borough of 9,000 that hosted a small private college, St. John's, and so could sustain a decent restaurant or two. Angela directed me down a side street to an airy establishment called Lightfoot's.

She was dressed as if she was spending her day at the park rather than in a law office: jeans, a white shirt with a vest, hiking boots. I told her she looked like an L.L. Bean ad.

"Oh, I put on the uniform if I have to be in court or have a deposition or something like that," she said. "But if I'm just working around the office, I don't bother. I don't have to impress anyone."

"You said you had an appointment."

"The Shoemaker brothers. They're senile. I could show up buck naked and they wouldn't know the difference."

"Do you know that for a fact?"

She considered. "I'm guessing. Maybe I'll try it sometime."

"It would definitely give a new meaning to casual Fridays," I said.

We both smiled as we lapsed back into the kind of banter we used to share, the sparring that started out easy and then kicked into a high gear that was either funny or cruel, depending on the mood of the day. At times, the verbal duel got overheated and we ended up horizontal on the couch or floor. The memory seemed to take a shape and linger in the air between us. I enjoyed the moment. There was no harm done; I'd soon be on my way.

"So," she said, getting off the subject. "How was your morning in Wyanossing?"

I told her about breakfast at Charlotte's and my second encounter with Crystal. She snickered over that.

"Is she from around here?" I asked. "Someone's daughter? I mean someone I would know?"

She shook her head. "No, I think she's from out near State College or Bellefonte. She's only been here a little while." Her eyebrows arched. "Why? Do you like her?"

"She says she wants to be an actress," I said. "Or a singer. Or a dancer. Or whatever."

"'Or whatever.' I'll bet she does."

"I thought she was sincere," I said. "I mean, at least she's got some looks."

Now she laughed out loud. "God, you guys never change. Some little wench pushes her boobs in your face and gives you a fuck-me-daddy look and you're ready to take her to New York and launch her career."

My face got hot and I opened my mouth to protest. Laughing, Angela held up a hand. "It's a joke, Richie. She's dreaming out loud. I know that." She sipped her drink and eyed me. "Let me tell you what's going to happen to Miss Crystal. She's not going anywhere. She'll end up married to Roy Dewitt or some other boob and have a couple kids. They'll live in a crackerbox out on Fifteenth Street. She'll keep working at Charlotte's and get fat and never leave this place except to go the Shore for a week every summer."

"She'll be sorry to hear that," I said.

"It's what women in this town do."

"You didn't."

"Well, I'm different."

She looked at me, waiting to see where I'd go with that. As if cued, our server appeared, strictly college, skinny and pale in khakis and a white shirt. He moved away and Angela and I were back on safe ground.

"So, what else have you been doing?" she asked.

I told her I had seen Leo and she smiled. "I always loved that guy."

I recounted a couple stories about him and Joey and me, then asked her if it was true about Louie Zag.

Her smile dipped. "Yeah, it's true. You know he was always really nutty, but it was like one day he was okay and the next he was completely out of his mind."

"Leo said he got some bad drugs."

"That's what the doctors said. Joey was furious about it. He wanted to kill whoever had sold him that crap. Nothing to be done."

We left a moment of silence in memory of Louie's wasted brain. So many pieces of my past were breaking away.

I said, "I drove over to Nock Hill."

She had lifted her glass. She put it back down.

"I went out on Council Rock," I said. "And down below to the tracks, too."

"To where they found him."

I nodded. She got quiet. I took a sip of my water. The waiter returned with our salads.

"There's something I've been wanting to ask you," I said, after we had started eating. "Did he ever talk about me?"

She shrugged and said, "Yeah, now and then."

I waited. Then: "Well?" She looked a little uncomfortable and I said, "What?"

"You know he was hard on people. So..."

"So, what?"

"Do we really need to discuss this?"

"I would like to, yeah."

"All right, then. I think he felt that you kind of threw away your talent. By doing the commercials and things like that." Though ill at ease, she went on. I had asked for it. "I guess he thought that you should have acted in films or something. You guys were such good friends. He wanted you to be the most famous person who ever came from here."

I began to prickle a little. "You're saying he thought I was a sell-out?"

"He never used those words," she said. "I'm surmising. He –"

"And this was coming from a guy who spent his life smoking dope, chasing tail, and getting into pissing contests with dolts like John Miller and Elmer Smalley."

Her eyes flashed and her mouth cut a tight line.

I said, "I'm sorry I couldn't live up to his high standards."

"That's not fair," she said, glaring.

I glared back. "What's not?"

So we could still go at each other. I looked away from her and we both took a moment to let things cool down.

"It was something else," she said. "He never understood why you stopped coming back to see him. Why you stopped calling." She paused carefully, then said, "I wondered about that, too."

Now I couldn't tell if she was talking about Joey, her, or both of them. Cowardice compelled me to choose the first one.

I said, "I'm guilty, counselor. I got wrapped up in my life. New York is a different world. After my parents moved away, there didn't seem to be much reason for me to come back."

Her brow furrowed. "You guys were best friends, Richie."

"He didn't come visit me, either, you know. I was three hours away. And I don't ever remember him ever calling me in New York. Not once."

"More like brothers," she went on, as if she hadn't heard.

"Okay, I got it," I said, heating up again. "He was right. About all of it. I could have been an artist. Except that in my line, the chances are one in a thousand that you can even make a living. I have to live in Manhattan. I have children. I'm lucky to be getting any kind of work. So please pardon me for having a career that allows me to feed my family."

Though my voice had gotten louder and a couple people at nearby tables looked around,

Angela didn't try to shush me.

I said, "Christ, you're a goddamn *lawyer*. His own sister. He must have been really proud of you."

Angry as she was, she laughed and rolled her eyes. "Yeah, except for when he wanted to take one of his enemies to court."

I thought it might be could time to change the subject, but she wasn't finished.

"What about the other part?" she said. "You guys not seeing each other any more. Not talking."

I sat back in my seat. "That… that I've got no excuse for. I just drifted away. And eventually I pretty much forgot about him. And I figured he did the same."

"You hurt his feelings."

"I didn't know."

"Did you care?"

That was enough for me. "Look," I said. "Things change. Our lives went in different directions. New York is two hundred miles away. They have this newfangled device called a telephone. And this other crazy invention they call email. If he was so crushed, he could have told me. He would have told me. He never kept his mouth shut about anything else."

I half-expected her to start yelling back at me. Instead, her face fell into a sad and sweet repose. "Yeah, he never was one to hold back on his opinions." She sighed, then took a small bite of her salad.

We nibbled in silence for a half-minute. "Do you think I betrayed him?" I said presently.

She shook her head. "No. But I don't get a vote. That was between the two of you." I wondered if she thought I had betrayed her, too. How could she not? I was thinking that over when she touched my hand and said, "It's all right, Richie."

I nodded, but my thoughts had already started down a forgotten path. Sitting there with her, in that restaurant in that little town, with the April sun streaming through the windows, I realized some of what I had missed when I left.

To get past this, I asked her about her years living in Wyanossing. She spent the next half-hour filling in blanks: her kids growing up, her marriage and a couple relationships, her career, her big old house.

The conversation wound down and we finished our salads and the weight of my imminent departure was hanging in the air. Now I would carry her back to her office, get some gas from Leo and be off.

"So," she said. "Will you come back at all?"

I said, "I don't know. Probably not."

She nodded as if she had expected this. It was time to go.

I pulled to the curb in front of her building. She looked at me and said, "It was really good of you to come out here, Richie. Joey would have appreciated it. I know I do."

"I'm sorry about all of it," I said. "This and what happened before..."

She came up with her quiet smile and said, "My brother was a firecracker from the day he was born. I really loved him and admired him. Even though half the time he made me so angry I wanted to smack his face. But he lived his life the way he wanted to. How many people do you know who can say that? How many people do you know who haven't given up on their crazy dreams? Right or wrong?"

I didn't say anything. She wasn't really talking to me anyway. She stared out the windshield and in that moment, with her brow furrowed into a stubborn profile, she looked like Joey Sesto's little sister again. I saw a tear well at the corner of her eye.

"He was a relic," she said. "He wouldn't let go. He thought those old days, when he was just a gypsy, was paradise. And that it would never end. But it did."

"So why didn't he leave? He's not the only person who still feels that way. There are all kinds of little lost communities out there."

"He wanted it here. And I think he wanted to stay for me, too. After our parents passed away and I got divorced. He was being my big brother." She paused to gaze out the window. "Anyway, he kept on trying to get it back. He never gave up. He never gave up on anything." She sighed in a sweet way. "Listen to me. I sound like a character in some movie."

"It's a good speech," I said. "He'd like it."

"Yeah, well..." Her eyes were moist and she tilted the mirror to check her makeup, dabbing a finger here and there.

"You look fine," I said.

She smiled a sudden, wicked smile. "It's all right," she said. "If I go in there looking a little messy it'll make their day. They'll think we were at some motel out on 12. Fucking.

I coughed out a laugh. "Jesus, Angela!"

The mood in the car brightened. She gave me a sly look, lowered her voice, and said, "Hey, here's something really interesting. We're being watched."

I blinked. "Watched as in..."

"Watched as in surveilled, dummy. There's a car back at the corner. I saw it when I flipped down the mirror. And it was parked outside while we were eating lunch."

"Who is it?"

"I have no idea." Her eyes widened. "Maybe it's Crystal. Maybe she's stalking you."

"You're kidding, right?" I started to turn.

She snatched my forearm and said, "Don't."

"What the hell?" I said. "Who'd be watching us?"

"I don't know," she said. "I guess it could have something to do with one of my cases. I have a couple divorces going on. Usually, one party stalks another, though."

"So now what?"

"Now what? Now I get out of the car and go back to work. And you go back to New York."

"I'll walk you to the door."

'I'll walk you to the door.' You know how many times you said that to me? And then talked your way inside? And ended up –"

"Okay, okay," I said. "I won't walk you to the door."

She grinned at having flustered me, then leaned over to kiss my cheek. I caught a flower scent in her hair.

She leaned away and said, "I'm really glad you came. If you want to call or email me sometime, that would be fine. But I won't hold my breath. Fair enough?"

I said, "Fair enough." She got out and I watched her walk to her building and slip inside without looking back.

I started the car and pulled away from the curb. I had to look in the mirror to see my way clear and I spotted the car, a white Mercury Sable with a figure behind the wheel. I couldn't tell whether it was a man or woman. Whoever it was stayed put as I drove to River Street.

I pulled up to Leo's pumps and he came out of the office, wearing his goofy grin. We chatted while I filled my tank. I gave him a business card.

"You call me if you're coming to New York," I told him.

"I don't know about that, but I'll keep it in case you get really famous," he said. "Then I'll sell it to somebody."

I said, "Good luck with that, Leo." We shared a brief hug and I got in the car and headed for the highway. I was going home.

7.

In order to do that, I had to drive back through town. As I passed around the park, I spotted a landmark that caused me to drift to a stop and then pull to the curb.

The Wyanossing Public Library was housed in a narrow, three-story brick building that had been built in the mid-1700s. It had been a haven when I was a kid and well into my teens. I had discovered Shakespeare there when the librarian Mrs. Eldridge read me the Three Witches scene from *Macbeth* with high drama. She got me started on Sean O'Casey and Tennessee Williams. Also Malamud and the Japanese author Oe. She suggested William Campbell Gault and Henry Gregor Felsen for their tales of teenage hot rod angst. She had read them all.

One last stop, I promised myself and got out to cross the park. It would be a perfect farewell to my hometown, because I had nothing but great memories of this place. One of which popped into my head at that moment. It involved a girl and some clumsy groping in the stacks, and Mrs. Eldridge interrupting with a whispered admonition that the library was not the place for such *diversions*. Though the grand woman was furious with me, she didn't rat me out to my parents. Her disappointment was enough. I never tried that again. Okay, well, there was that one time…

I opened the doors and stepped back thirty-five years. On first glance, it had barely changed. Before the town had claimed the house for the library, it had been some prosperous burgher's domicile. The colonial design featured a foyer leading to a large main room with the other, smaller rooms branching off. The ceilings were high and every room retained the outline of a fireplace on one wall.

The young girl behind the desk looked up and smiled when I entered, then went back to checking in a stack of books. I noticed that instead of a date stamp, she handled a stylus that was connected to a new computer. So time had not stood still.

I made a slow tour of those familiar shelves and laid a hand on the long table where I used to sit and read while outside a gray Pennsylvania winter howled.

"Mr. Zaleski." The stentorian voice came from behind me.

I turned around. After a startled moment, I said "Mrs. Eldridge. You're —"

"Still alive." Her eyes danced. "And I'm as surprised as you are."

She looked well for her age. Remarkable, in fact. A small woman, she was even smaller, her back bent slightly. She appeared more frail, though her color was good and she stood sturdily, still a regal presence. The hazel eyes I remembered bearing down on me so unmercifully in that long ago moment remained just as bright, though they now shone kindly behind the lens of her tiny eyeglasses.

I held a chair at the table and she sat down. I took the seat opposite.

She was enjoying my shock. "Eighty-four," she said.

"You look wonderful."

"And you, as well," she said. "How long has it been since you visited last?"

"A long time," I said. "More than ten years."

"Well, I'm glad you thought to stop by," she said. "You're the only famous person this town has produced."

"People keep saying that, but I'm not famous, I'm just –"

She gave me arch look, so I broke off the disclaimer and said, simply, "Thanks."

"So, what do you think of Wyanossing these days?"

"Not much has changed."

"No, and not much will," she said. She paused for a moment. "You came back because of Joey Sesto?"

I nodded. "Yes, ma'am."

"Poor man," she murmured. "You and he were good friends."

I said, "Yeah, from the time we were kids."

"I remember. The two of you used to come in together. You read O'Neill and Ionesco while he pored over the pictures in the back of the *National Geographics*."

I laughed at the memory. Mrs. Eldridge folded her hands before her and said, "You know he was in here quite a lot just those last few months before he died."

"Who was?"

"Joseph. Joey." She spoke his name a gentle way. "He and I became friends. In a way. Do you believe it? After all these years?"

"You and Joey?" I smiled at the thought of this prim librarian and that lunatic taking tea and discussing Jane Austen.

"As it turned out, we shared a dislike for the more mercenary and reactionary elements in town. And he stayed on top of things."

"What things?"

"He kept raising his fist and complaining and getting in the way. And he was right. The developers were trying to cut down those gorgeous woods up along the ridge so they could build their subdivisions. Zeloco was dumping tons of chemicals into the river. And there was collusion to keep certain people out of the political process, the town council and county commission and what have you. He was right about all those things."

She composed her face in a stern look. "There were – there are – people willing to do damage to Wyanossing for their own gain. And others who wanted it run to suit their personal agendas. He poked a finger in their eyes. And I said, good for him."

A flush had risen to her cheeks. Now she stopped to regain her calm. "He was wrong about some things, too. There was room for improvement. For new businesses. That kind of thing. But he didn't know how to get what he wanted without insulting people. He did not know the meaning of tact. Or compromise. So he was always shooting himself in the foot." She shrugged her thin shoulders. "Still, I respected what he was doing. And then he started spending a lot of time here and we became friendly."

"A lot of time doing what?"

She tilted her head. "Reading in our Collections Room."

I remembered that what had been the kitchen of the original building had been used to shelve all the reference materials and to store newspapers, magazines, and books dating back to the 1700s, along with other obscure documents from three centuries of small town life.

"He was doing research," she said. "Homework on his adversaries, I believe."

At first she thought she was making an odd joke. Joey Sesto? Research? I couldn't imagine him sitting still for such tedious work. Or tedious anything.

Mrs. Eldridge said, "He was in there quite a bit. We also have a small legal section and he searched through the ordinances and laws he could use. He really learned his way around."

I shook my head over Joey the fledgling academic.

"It's true," the librarian went on. "Now and then I had to make him leave because he was still back there and it was closing time. Even more so in the weeks before his accident. I asked him why he was working so hard and he said, 'Looking for something.' I have no idea what he meant. He was digging through plat books and other papers on properties around town."

"He never said what he was looking for?"

"No," she said with a sigh. "And then he was gone."

It was a puzzle, but who knew what went through that crazy mind? We changed the subject. She was eager to hear what had happened in the years since I made my escape, the few plays I had been in, the fewer feature films, and my commercial career. She cooed over the photos of my wife and kids. It was so comfortable there, so comforting, and I felt like I was drifting back to a simpler an gentler time, when the books on these shelves and the games on the streets outside were all that mattered to me.

By the time I turned my head to look at the clock on the wall, it was 2:40.

"Uh-oh," I said.

She gave me a questioning look.

"I need to head back to New York."

"Oh, of course."

The girl at the desk stepped over to whisper something in Mrs. Eldridge's ear. She said, "Don't leave just yet," and rose to her feet.

I sat staring out the window at the trees swaying in the afternoon breeze, then at the books on the wooden shelves around me.

What Mrs. Eldridge recounted had me puzzled. Joey had spent long hours in the dustiest stacks of the library in the days leading up to his death. It didn't fit at all. Unless he had somehow remade himself as a scholar. I began to wonder if there was some connection to his "accident." Could that be? Or maybe being there had stirred up so many ghosts that I was creating things that weren't there.

Mrs. Eldridge was heading back to join me. I stood and said, "I'm going to step outside and make a call."

To which she replied, "Please, use my office."

She led me through the warren of rooms. When we reached her office, tidy save for multiple stacks of books, she patted the chair, oak with leather padding. "You can sit right there. I'll be out front." She left me alone.

When Angela picked up, I said, "I'm still in town."

"Oh?"

"I got held up," I said. "I stopped at the library. Mrs. Eldridge is still here."

Angela laughed. "Isn't she amazing?" she said. "You know she and Joey were pals."

"She told me. That's kind of the reason I'm still around."

"How's that?"

"She told me what he had been doing here."

"Which was what?"

"I want to talk to you about that. So I thought what I would do is just wait until later. Go home after dinner. If you'll go with me. To dinner."

She hesitated and I guessed she was wondering if I was playing some kind of game. Then she said, "I'd like that," and asked me to meet her back at her house. After we hung up, I braced myself and dialed Isabel at work.

"I think I'll come back late tonight." Then: "Or maybe tomorrow."

"*Maybe* tomorrow?" I could imagine the cool look on her face. "Do you want to tell me what's going on?"

"What's going on is I want to stay a little longer." Isabel said nothing. "Because something kind of came up."

"What kind of something?"

"Having to do with Joey. It's probably nothing. But I want to spend a little more time here."

"Doing what?"

"Talking to some people. Checking on some things. That's all."

"And you're coming back tonight or tomorrow?" She sounded dubious.

"That's my plan."

She was quiet for a few seconds. Then she said, "Have you spoken to Sondra? You know, your agent? The one you depend on for your livelihood?"

"I'll call her. I promise."

She took another moment and then said, "All right, here's what I'm going to do. I'll tell the girls not to count on you coming home tonight. And I'm not going to wait up, either."

"Isabel –"

"I don't know what's going on," she said. "Just please don't do anything you'll regret." Then in a calm and even voice, she said, "We love you, Richard."

She clicked off as I was saying, "And I –"

I closed the cover on my phone and spent a few seconds on the verge of rushing out the door, jumping in the car, and tearing back to the city. The urge passed.

I put in a call to Sondra and when I got her voicemail, explained I'd been held up and would be staying an extra day. Of course, she'd call back if there was anything important. I hoped there wasn't and she wouldn't. When I finished, I got up and wandered around until I found Mrs. Eldridge.

"Could you show me what Joey was looking at back there?"

She studied me for a vexed second, then said. "If you like."

With all the shelves loaded with books, bound folios, old newspapers, magazines and journals, the file cabinets, boxes stacked from floor to ceiling, and a table and chairs, it was a tight squeeze. Even with the air conditioner mounted in one small window and a ceiling fan turning lazily overhead, the must of age remained.

Mrs. Eldridge crossed the room to stand next to a bookshelf and lay her hand on an old folio, bound in black. "These are the plats of the houses and farms outside of town. Joseph spent a lot of time going through them."

"Could I see?" I said.

"All right. But before you start..." She stepped to what had once been a sideboard and went into a drawer to produce a pair of white cotton gloves. "These keep the oil on your hands from staining the pages. Please be careful. Some of these volumes are very fragile."

"I understand."

"It's all yours, then. I'll be in my office if you need me." She backed out of the room and closed the door.

I stood in that cramped silence, letting my eyes roam over shelves

that sagged under the weight of Wyanossing's history. Something there had drawn Joey's interest just before he died.

Whatever it was must have been important. He wasn't the type to sit poring over old pages.

But for me to find what he was digging for was a long shot at best and as I surveyed the shelves, I considered dropping the whole matter. It wasn't like I could bring him back to life.

I thought about that for a few moments, then pulled a folio from the closest shelf and carried it to the table.

—

The next time I looked at the clock it was almost five-thirty. I found Mrs. Eldridge at the front desk.

"Well?" she said. "Did you solve the puzzle?"

I shook my head. "I didn't, no."

"Well, perhaps you can visit again."

I thought about that and said, "You'll be open tomorrow, right?"

I stepped out into the end of the working day. Cars moved along the streets, though not so many that I didn't notice the white Sable parked at the next corner with a lone figure behind the wheel.

The sedan sat idling and after a few seconds, pulled out to disappear down Second Street. I leaned against the building and replayed my conversation with Isabel. She was trying to understand, but I wasn't doing a very good job of explaining. Because I didn't get it myself.

My phone rang. It was Sondra calling. I told her I had been held up in Wyanossing and would be back to work in another couple days.

"So I can schedule things for you?"

I thought about it and said, "Can we wait until I get back?"

She said, "How long have we been working together?"

"Thirteen years, I think."

"Then we'll wait," she said.

"I thought you were *leaving*."

I turned around to find Crystal in line to use the ATM. The only one in town, it was located inside the foyer of the National Bank. Which meant I was stuck in a six-by-ten foot glass cube with this busty vixen and an elderly woman who, from the way she cocked her ears and the rapid blinking of her eyes, had an intense interest in our conversation.

I crossed my arms, going for cool. Crystal hooked her fingers in the belt loops of her jeans and thrust her full frontal array in my direction. My peripheral vision told me that the fabric of her blouse was summer-thin and that she had only a t-shirt on underneath. I forced my gaze to roam between her face and the street beyond.

All the time, she was following my eyes, trying to gauge her effect on me. I caught the look of something like desperation that was swimming just below the surface, one I knew well. In my younger days, before Isabel, I had specialized in gorgeous wackos. A couple of whom had come close to wrecking my life. I remembered enough about those times and women to get right on top of the situation.

"I just couldn't tear myself away," I said quickly, treating her with the same whimsical smile I had once employed in a puppy food spot. The machine beeped and spewed a dozen bills and my card. I stepped out of the way of the older woman and moved to the glass doors. Crystal spun around as if mounted on a turret. It would have been rude to walk out, so I waited, my smile in place.

She offered up a forgiving look, announcing that though I had erred, she just couldn't bring herself to punish me. She opened her mouth to say something, then stopped when I waved a hand and tilted my head towards the third party. That brought a conspiratorial grin and she began to prattle on about nothing at all, the weather, the traffic, her work, until the woman collected her money and left.

She stepped to the machine, giggling like a munchkin, and fed it a card. Glancing back at me, she said, "So, how long *are* you staying?"

"I decided to leave that open for now," I told her with a lazy flip of one hand.

She liked that. She put a hand on her hip and her eyes flashed. "You better be careful. You could get stuck here and never get away."

"I guess that's true," I agreed, suddenly wondering why in the world I was still standing in that box with her. Like I didn't remember the pleasure of trading brainless chatter with a vixen. It was akin to eating Cheetos, a guilty pleasure, without the telltale orange residue left on fingertips.

She snatched up her cash and retrieved her card. I opened the door for her. We stepped onto the sidewalk and into the fading yellow light of the new evening. She was studying me, eyes narrowed, waiting for something.

"I guess I'll be seeing you," I offered.

"When?"

The switch from giggly shtick to flat ice was so abrupt that it caught me by surprise. I said, "When? Well, I don't –"

"I'm free tonight."

"Tonight… I have plans. Sorry."

She said, "Oh?" Her eyes followed mine, looking for a clue. "All right, then, later. After your thing, I mean."

"I don't think that'll work, either."

She drew back. "Are your plans with Angela Sesto?"

I wondered how she knew. Then I remembered: small town. Still, I didn't care for the scrutiny.

Her tan brow furrowed in petulance. "Okay, wait a minute. Does that mean you two are to –"

"No," I said. "It doesn't mean anything. We just go back. Her brother was my best friend."

"I knew that." She got a little loud in her annoyance and I took a small sideways step, ready to bolt. It seemed that half the people I'd met wanted to know my business, if they didn't already.

She must have noticed I wasn't pleased and retreated a few inches. "Look, all I want to do is talk to you," she said and now there an earnest plea in her tone that stopped me. "About New York and all that. About getting out of this place." She lowered her voice. "You know what I'm talking about. You did it."

"Yes," I said. "I did."

Now she smiled and threw out her arms as if she was on stage and greeting a round of applause. "Don't you think I could do something? Don't you think I should?"

She was some sight, and it occurred to me that it was taking place in the middle of the sidewalk in the middle of the main street of Wyanossing. So I quickly said, "Sure, yes, if you –"

"Well, then?" The arms came down. "Can you help or not?"

Again, something in those wide eyes was there and gone in an instant. She was making me dizzy.

I said, "Sure. We can talk about it. Before I leave. I promise."

Now she switched to an arch expression. "You *promise*? I've heard that before."

"Not from me, Crystal, I generally do what I say."

Her smile re-appeared, making her look young and happy again, the puppy from the commercial, ready to leap into my arms.

"I just *knew* that," she said. "I got a feeling as soon as I saw you." Her eyes shifted. "You're not like these people around here. Are you?"

Before I could fathom the question, she had dipped into the bag that was slung over her shoulder, and produced a card.

"You can call me," she said. "Anytime." She backed up, then waved merrily and turned to walk away.

I watched her cute ass switch down the sidewalk, then looked at the card she had handed me. "Crystal" was printed in florid script at the center with a phone number below it. That was all. I shoved it in my back pocket and strolled to the park, where I had left my car. Crossing Kane Street, I saw a white Sable parked a block away. I took a single step toward it and watched as it swung around the intersection and rolled off.

Angela showed up at six and I told her about catching sight of the Sable two more times.

She frowned. "Did you see who was driving?"

"Too far away."

"That's strange behavior. For this place, I mean."

"You think it was the same one? Those cars are pretty common."

She gave me a look over her shoulder. "What do you think?"

"So?"

"So, I don't know. Whoever it is is either the worst stalker on the planet or wants you to notice." She stuck her key in the door. "I still think it could have something to do with your little girlfriend."

"She's not my –"

"I'm kidding, Richie," she said. "Relax. Though it wouldn't surprise me if one of her guys was dogging you. She could make that happen. She's got that thing going on."

"What thing?"

"What thing." She gave me a bemused look as she opened the door. "You know what I'm talking about. You're not that old."

She saw the abashed look on my face and said, "What?"

"I ran into her. And she... she..."

Angela started to smile. "What? Buzzed you?"

"Kind of."

She unlocked the door. "Then no wonder someone's following you."

When we got inside, I said, "All I've done is talk to her."

She started up the stairs to change for dinner. "Don't worry about it," she said. "You're leaving, right? By this time tomorrow, whoever it is will be on whatever other guy she put her eye on. It's what she does." She looked down at me. "Do you remember Susan Daley?"

I did. Susan Daley had been one hot ticket. She wore her hair and makeup like a streetwalker, along with the shortest skirts and tightest, lowest-cut tops she could get away with. All on what one of my New York actor friends would call a "porn star body." She was like some jungle creature and she worked it all so well that even the buttoned-down boys went to fighting over her.

"What happened to her?" I asked.

"She was two-timing her husband. He caught her and the boyfriend in bed and shot them dead. He got life, but he might get out in fifteen. So ended the saga of Susan Daley."

She gave me a significant look and continued up the stairs.

She came down twenty minutes later wearing a dress of soft cotton. At the bottom of the steps, she snatched a black leather jacket off the post, slung it over her shoulder, and dropped ten years. For my part, I felt like an alley rat in my second shirt and trousers and old sport coat.

"So, where to?" I asked.

"The Riverside." She saw the look on my face and said, "It's not the place you remember."

I hoped so. During my childhood days, the bar at the Riverside Hotel had been the refuge of the refuse, those local drunks who weren't welcome at any of the hose companies – a scary thought. Later, there were whispers about that the dingy upstairs rooms being used by traveling prostitutes. Our parents commanded us to avoid the place, so of course we spent a lot of time lurking nearby, hoping for a look at a comical drunkard or a painted floozy. Now Angela and I were going there to sample what Angela swore was fine cuisine.

When we pulled up to the intersection of Fourth and Queen Streets, I saw that she'd been correct: it wasn't the same place. The bricks were painted in a white and red fade and the trim was rich blue. Plants and warm yellow lamps were framed in the windows. The sign over the door had been carved by someone who knew the craft.

We stepped through a heavy oak door that was inset with leaded glass. Inside, the smoky bricks had been acid-washed to a pale shade of red, part of an earthy décor that would have worked in SoHo.

While we waited to be seated, Angela explained that five years before two professors from Bucknell had bought and then renovated the hotel. They brought a real chef in from Philly to prepare a limited fare of New American cuisine. The six rooms upstairs were used for private events. I was impressed that the partners had managed to turn the dank, shadowy, beer-and-piss-smelling hole into a cozy upscale restaurant. The wait staff was varied, men and women in their twenties and thirties. They offered a nice wine list. I could imagine the old drunks spinning in their graves.

As it turned out, there were enough diners around the valley who were fed up with dough and grease and were willing to make the drive to Wyanossing. She said that while the Riverside was a favorite of the local professionals, the rich old guard still chose to dine at one of the country clubs, where they didn't have to worry about mingling with dagos like her or Polacks like me. That much hadn't changed.

We had a good meal, fresh seafood, pasta, and a nice chenin blanc. We didn't mention Joey or Leo or Crystal or Louie Zag. We didn't discuss Wyanossing or New York. At first, we didn't talk about anything important at all. As we worked our way through dinner, the conversation veered to filling in more of the blanks in the years that had passed.

I wondered why this bright woman had chosen to pass her life in that provincial village. Why hadn't she run for greener pastures, as I and so many others had done?

"I came close so many times," she said. "But it wasn't in the cards. Every time I got ready to take off, something would come along to keep me here. I came back after law school to take care of my parents. I met my ex-husband while that was going on. He wasn't about to move. Among his faults was a lack of interest in anything except his own good time. So we stayed. We had the kids. I was busy getting my practice going." She shrugged. "And before I knew it, twenty years had gone by."

"You really should have left," I said. "You believe what's out there."

She gave me a withering look, but it was too late to take it back.

"I know what's out there," she said. "I could have gone if I really wanted to. I didn't. I stayed. I like it here. And by the way, this is the real world, too. Just not to you." She watched my face for a few seconds. "You know, you have this snotty disapproval thing about this town that's very annoying."

"I think I earned the right," I said. "I did the time."

"Maybe," she said. "But nobody wants to hear that crap. You don't like it here, that's fine. Hit the road, Jack." She squared her shoulders and her eyes lit up in a familiar way. She wanted to do battle.

I obliged her. "Are you going to trot out that routine about how this is God's country? The heartland? And the people who live in cities are either elitist snobs or S&M junkie murderers?"

"Well, there's a –"

"The fact is, when it comes down to it, we're the ones doing all the heavy lifting," I said. "The rest of you are just along for the ride." I was exaggerating, knowing it would set her off.

It did. She almost hopped out of her chair. "*That's* what I'm talking about," she said. "You think you're just *it* and we're nothing but a bunch of dumb hicks sitting around our whole lives with our thumbs up our asses."

"And what are you doing?" I asked. "I mean while we're building the buildings and making the businesses run and writing the plays, and shooting the films, and creating the fashions, and printing the magazines and recording the music, and all the rest of it. How exactly are you spending your time while we're doing all that?"

"We're not –"

"Why, holding down the fort, that's what!"

Angela, who was all ready to lay into me, looked up at the same time I did. Elmer Smalley was standing a few feet from our table.

"Just happened to be passing by and I overheard," he said with a shrug that supposed to be casual. Just passing by. Sure he was.

I could tell that he wanted to jump into the fray; but then he caught Angela's cool gaze and raised his hands. He offered a smile of feigned benevolence and began backing away. "Yes, we're just holding down the fort for you good people." He turned around to make his way across the room.

Angela glared at the spot where he had stood, then turned to me in dumb wonder. "Do you believe that idiot speaking up for me?" she hissed. "What's he doing here? He runs the goddamn hardware store. You see what you started?"

"Now who's the snob?" I said.

"This is different," she said. "I really have earned the right. I've been living here. And it's guys like him who give good places like this a bad reputation. Greedy little, small-minded little piggies."

"You sound like your brother," I told her.

She thought about this for a moment and smiled as if she didn't mind the comparison at all.

After that, we managed to keep our conversation civil. A couple people came to the table to ask for autographs. I signed while Angela sipped her wine and enjoyed my discomfort.

"So tell me about the library," she said in the wake of one such moment.

"You know the Collections Room in back? That's where Joey

was hanging out. They've got all old newspapers and magazines and documents in binders." I held out my hands apart. "And these huge plat books that have drawings of all the old houses. Some of them are from the 1800s. The paper's like parchment."

Angela said, "Right. The county moves them to the borough libraries when they run out of room."

"Well, he was looking through those."

"Why?"

"I don't know, but something got him interested. I started to go through them, but I ran out of time. He didn't say anything about any of this to you?"

"Not a word," she said.

"Because unless he changed, he wasn't the type to spend a lot of time sitting still like that."

"He didn't," she said. "And, no, he wasn't."

"He was after something," I said. "And thought it was important enough to sit there and do that."

Angela said, "I wonder what it was."

Outside, I looked at my watch. It was almost nine o'clock. I'd done it again. We walked up the street to the rental car.

"So, now what?" Angela asked me.

"I don't know. It's already late."

"Well, do what you want," she said. "You're welcome with me."

Do what you want. Isabel had said it and now Angela. But I couldn't decide. I wanted to go and I wanted to stay. I missed my wife and kids. At the same time, something was holding me to his place, a dormant attraction to Angela surging back or some other connection that I wasn't yet ready to break.

We climbed into the car and I started driving, telling myself I'd make up my mind when we got to her house. Or maybe I wouldn't.

I said, "You up for a ride?"

She said, "Sure, that'd be fine."

We cruised, talking about the places we passed and over the next half hour, covered most of Wyanossing. It was clear that I wasn't going to be driving back to New York this night. I had dallied and it had gotten too late.

We finished our little tour and stopped at an intersection. I said, "So? What else?"

Angela had been quiet for some time. Now she turned to me and said, "I want to go up on Nock Hill. And see the Rock."

I studied her. "Are you sure?"

"I've got to do it sooner or later,' she said. "You're here. Let's get it over with."

A deep blue shroud had settled like a soft blanket along the west side of the valley, over the river and Nock Hill. The moon was hidden behind the rise and we drove into the kind of inky darkness I never encountered in the city.

We found the gate closed and padlocked, so I parked the car in the gravel space across the road, just as I had done so many times as a kid. Angela and I got out and started walking. As we made the climb, shadows came to life.

I had received the letter. It's my turn.

Joey and I are walking up the road with Leo some others in our crew. It's my going-away party. My girlfriend Julie is with me. She doesn't understand. She thinks I should do something, take a stand. I could run. I could refuse. But I already decided that I want to see if I can survive it, as my father and my uncles had. Now I wonder if she's too mad for a good-bye fuck, a roll on the leaves or a stand-up against a tree for now and forever. She's pretty angry.

Mad or not, she takes me into the woods and comes on with everything she's got. Her pelvis launches me into the treetops and then she has me in her mouth as if trying to swallow me whole. It's one for the books, but when it's over nothing has changed. I'm still going away.

Joey is waiting when she and I come out of the brush and he's wearing his cunning smile. Then Angela appears and she's staring at us with eyes that are black with hurt and anger.

It was a good hike, winding upward at a steep angle through the dark outlines of the groves of trees. After twenty huffing and puffing minutes, we reached the summit and crossed the deserted parking lot, now cast in dark silver from the crescent moon.

I hadn't traversed the top of the hill in the dark in thirty years. And yet I crossed the gravel lot as if guided by radar and found the footpath along the fence. With Angela following silently behind, I located the place where the extruding tree root offered a step up. I helped her over and then hoisted myself to the other side. We didn't exchange a word, thieves in the night.

The path was lost in the dark and I felt my way along for another forty feet, checking back every few steps to make sure she was with me.

Forty feet on, the path bottomed out and Angela stopped at my side. Council Rock jutted, a begging hand into the night. Across the river, the lights of Wyanossing twinkled like lonely stars and cars and trucks moved toy-like up along River Street. Joey had spent his final dizzy moments in that same place, and the valley below was the last thing he saw before he toppled over the edge.

Standing there, we continued our silence, thinking our own thoughts.

As before, I was baffled. I recalled sitting on the edge, my legs dangling as I grooved on that dizzying view, and turning to see Joey crouched down, shaking his head *no, no, no*, huddling against the side of the hill as if clinging for life. I couldn't remember him ever setting more than a foot on the Rock. And yet somehow he had tumbled from its point.

"When were you up here last?" Angela said. "Before today, I mean."

"It was... just after I got out of the military." I thought about that time, remembering. "And I was with Joey. I was just back and he and I partied for about three days straight. We came up the one night and watched the sunrise." I said, "What about you?"

"I've only been up a few times," she said. "Joey didn't want me tagging along, remember? And my dad thought you guys were a bad influence."

"That's right, he did," I said.

"Which you were."

I wasn't touching that, but something about the way she spoke the words told me that the same image was dawning on both of us. One of the few times she had come there had been with me. That was the night on the blanket on a moss-covered patch of ground not fifty feet about from where we stood when I had helped myself to her virginity. That moment, that event, had been hanging over us, and I decided it was time to break the silence.

I said, "Joey never found out?"

She took a moment and then laughed quietly in the darkness. "No. For all his radical noise, he was still a regular Italian male at heart. He wouldn't imagine his little sister could be anything but a virgin." I felt her eyes on my face. "And you never told him."

"Uh-uh. No way."

She laughed again. "He would have killed you if he had known."

"You were here, too," I reminded her.

"Yes, I was," she said. "I sure was."

She stepped ahead of me, gazed over the valley.

"God, I miss him," she said with an infinite sadness that brought a throb in my gut. I wanted to tell her that I felt the loss, too, but thought it would sound phony. How could I miss someone I hadn't seen in so long? I didn't know what to say. There weren't any words that fit.

I heard her sigh. She said, "Can we go now?"

"Yeah," I said. "Let's go."

I don't know if she hooked a finger in one of the belt loops on my jeans because she couldn't see her way or for the simple comfort. But I was glad she did it.

We reached the chain-link fence and she had just started over when a branch cracked, sharp in the dead silence. I peered up the slope.

"What was that?" she said.

"Probably… nothing," I said. "Just a –"

Now we heard footsteps on gravel, followed by something that could have been a hushed voice.

"Did you *hear* that?" she whispered. "There's somebody up there."

"It's probably just kids." I said. She didn't look convinced. "Let's go." I bent to hoist her. We both made it over the fence and started up the path to the parking lot when we heard the scrabble of running feet, followed by the sound of a car door slamming, an engine coughing to life, and the crunch of rolling tires.

I said, "Come on!" and we climbed up the path, tripping and sliding in the darkness. I reached the parking lot a few steps ahead of her. Peering through the trees, I saw a boxy shape moving through the trees and down the winding road. It was gone before I could get a fix on it.

Angela came up behind me, all out of breath. "What was it?"

"A car. Maybe a pickup truck."

"Somebody was up here?"

"Probably kids."

"The park's closed," she said. "The gate's down and locked. How'd they get in?"

"Well, maybe –"

"Maybe what?"

"Maybe they know a back way."

"Back way from where?"

I didn't have an answer. It might have been park rangers checking the grounds. Some local could have a key to the gate. Or maybe there was another entrance. I mentioned these scenarios to Angela as we walked to the rental car.

She didn't buy any of them. "Somebody followed us up there, Richie. Or knew we were here. And showed up to check on us."

"Why?"

"I don't know," she said. She paused, then glanced over at me. "Was whatever you saw white?"

"It could have been," I said. "I couldn't tell anything for sure. It was halfway out of sight when I saw it." It could have been taupe or aquamarine or coral. It could have been the Wienermobile or a flying saucer. And it could have been a mythical creature, a white whale swimming through my waters of my imagination.

"I'd lay money it was that damn Sable," Angela muttered. "Somebody's following you. Or me. Or both of us."

"I haven't done anything. Have you?"

"I'm guilty of practicing law," she said. "Does that count?"

When we reached the bottom, the gate was closed, the lock and chain in place. The rental car was where I had left it. We crossed the road and climbed in and I cranked the engine.

Angela said, "I wonder if it has something to do with Joey."

I glanced over at her. "Why do you say that?"

"You came here and started talking about him. Now there's someone following one or both of us around. And up here." She paused. "Where he died."

"But he's gone. It's over."

She thought about that and said, "Yeah, he's gone."

We drove back from Nock Hill with Angela watching out the rear window to see if we were being followed. We were both still plenty wired when we got to her house and she went directly to the kitchen and poured wine. She sat on the front porch swing, pushing herself back and forth in nervous arcs, while I stalked about in little circle, kids basking in the afterglow of a dangerous prank.

The merlot did its work. She slowed her frenetic motion and I stopped pacing to lean against the rail. Still, I could see there was something bothering her. I hope it didn't have to do with me.

"What's on your mind?" I said.

"Maybe I'm just being paranoid..."

I waited.

"You came back here and started talking about Joey. Asking questions. Poking around in the library."

"So?"

"So maybe somebody noticed," she said. "No, not maybe. Not in this town. Somebody would notice" She planted an elbow on the arm of the swing and put her chin in her hand. "Walk through everything you've done since you got in."

She had switched into attorney mode and was watching me with intent.

I said, "I got lunch at Charlotte's first thing."

"And met Crystal."

"Yeah. John Miller was there and I talked to him. After that, I came here and we went to Joey's grave. Then I went for a walk around town and came back. We had dinner and went to bed." I stopped, feeling my face flush. "I meant –"

"I know what you meant." She took a sip of her win. "And what about today?"

"I went to Charlotte's for breakfast. And talked to Crystal again." Angela produced a wry look and I said, "She started giving me the line about getting out of town, becoming an actress, all that."

"I can hear it now," she murmured. "Then what?"

"That cop, Dewitt, came in. He gave me the third degree, but I figured that was probably because of the girl."

"Maybe," she said. "Go on."

"I left Charlotte's and I walked down to see Leo. Talked to him about a half-hour. And on my way back I ran into Miller again, and Elmer, in front of the hardware store. I came here and hung out for a little while and then drove over to Nock Hill to look around. I drove back down to the bottom to see where they found him."

She pushed the swing for a moment. "And then?"

"And then and I went to lunch. I was on my way out when I decided to stop at the library and I saw Mrs. Eldridge. Sat down with her."

"And she told you that Joey had been poking around in old files before he died."

"That's right."

"Is that when you called me?"

"Yeah, and I called Isabel to tell her I was staying. After that, I went into the Collections Room and had a look at some of those books."

"But you didn't find anything."

"I didn't. When I left, I saw the Sable. I was at the ATM getting some cash and Crystal showed up."

"Crystal again," she said. "And the Sable."

"Right."

"Then we went to dinner…"

"Yeah."

"And saw Elmer."

"After that, we drove to Nock Hill." I let her ponder all this for a few moments "Well, counselor?"

She said, "A couple things. You keep crossing paths with Crystal." She smiled slightly. "I'll take your word that it's not your doing. Second, Elmer and John Miller have popped up twice each. Of course, Elmer's one of those people you can't avoid. He has a lot of time on his hands. So I wouldn't put too much stock in that." Her brow furrowed. "We need to find out what kind of car she drives."

"Who?"

Her eyes slid sideways. "Miss-fucking-America," she said. "Crystal, dummy."

I said, "We're back to her?"

"Well, I could see it," she said. "She's an odd person. I've heard rumors around that her home life was a mess. She came here and got into a little trouble with the law. That's where she met Dewitt."

"What kind of trouble?"

"Minor stuff. Pot. Shoplifting. A DUI. That kind of thing. She definitely has some issues. It's a good thing you didn't bang her." She stopped again and her mouth dipped. "You didn't, did you?"

"No. But I've only been here a day and a half." In the silence that followed, a lurid little movie began and I saw –

"Hey!" Angela snapped her fingers in the air. "Stop that. It's not polite to me and your wife wouldn't like it, either."

Crystal vanished. Angela was frowning in distraction "So maybe it doesn't have anything to do with Joey at all."

"So what happens now?"

She gazed into the darkness. "I guess that depends."

"Depends on what?"

"On your plans. Are you going home tonight?"

"I told Isabel I'd head back tomorrow."

"Tomorrow," she said. Then I guess it's finished. I'll check after you're gone and see what kind of car she drives. If it's a white Sable, then we'll have an answer. I can let you know."

"And if it's not?"

"Then I guess it's a riddle we'll never solve." After a few seconds' silence, she said. "Whatever it is won't bring my brother back, will it?"

She stared into her glass and I watched the night's quiet shadows.

"And what if I wasn't leaving tomorrow?" I said. She didn't answer me. "Angela?"

She stood up. "I think it's time to go in."

I said good night to her and climbed the steps, undressed and crawled into bed. The streetlight was casting a swath of dim white across the floor. A train went clacking through the yards down by the river. Far down the valley, lightning flashed behind gray clouds and thunder echoed.

I heard her pad up the stairs and into the bathroom. Except for the sound of running water, the house was still. Then that stopped, too.

I felt her presence before I saw her. I hadn't heard the door open. Her hair was braided down her back and she was wearing a T-shirt that stopped above her knees. She was backlit from the hallway and I couldn't make out her expression.

She said, "Were you asleep?"

"No." I propped myself on an elbow.

She stepped into the room and placed her hand atop the footboard. Now I could see her face, as the light from the streetlamp cleaved it into halves of light and shadow. She kept her eyes averted from mine and fixed on the framed print on the wall.

Her voice was gentle. "I've been thinking about you a lot since that night you called. I've been remembering what happened between us. And all the time you've been here, I've been..." She took a moment to steady herself. "I just keep thinking, I don't want him to leave. I've been trying to stop it, but it just keeps going through my mind."

For an odd moment, I wondered if she was about to confess to having arranged all the strange occurrences so I would stay. But she wasn't that sort; and if I had any doubt, she put it to rest when she said, "The problem is you're a married man. You have children. I don't want to do anything to harm that."

I said, "Me, neither."

"And I won't. I won't." She let out a sudden laugh, low and sweet. "My God, Richie, I was so crazy about you. You could have snapped your fingers and I would have done anything you asked. And that we had to keep it a secret made it all the more precious." She stopped again. "You broke my heart when you went away, but while you were here, it was so, so wonderful. I loved my husband, but it was never like that. It was never like that with anyone again. That's in thirty years. Amazing, huh?"

I stayed quiet. This was her moment.

"But it's okay," she said, talking more to herself than to me. "The broken heart was worth it. It really was."

She backed away from the bed. "I'm leaving my door open," she said. "In case you want to talk." With that, she slipped into the dark hall.

I lay awake for a long time. I felt a lingering edge from the night's adventure. I thought about what Angela had said, what she and I had been to each other so many years ago, and what we were and were not now. I thought about Joey and his strange death, about Crystal and Leo and Mrs. Eldridge, and John Miller and Elmer Smalley. I thought about whoever had followed us to the top of Nock Hill and the white Sable.

I arrived back at Angela. Somehow I knew that she was lying awake and staring out her own window and feeling the same scramble of guilty shame and excitement as I was. What would happen if one of us got up and traveled the few steps along the dark hallway and whispered a name?

I wondered what it would be like after all this time. Would she again open up as an exotic flower? Would she still quiver like a bow-string beneath me? Would she let out the same sweet moaning music that told me she had lost herself?

I stopped. No, it was Isabel who did all that. I sat up again, as a wave of remorse swept over me for betraying my marriage, though it had only been in my mind.

I knew that neither Angela nor I would take those steps down the hall. Even if we wanted to. Settling back to gaze out the window at the lights of town and the stars that hovered over it, I waited out the last remnants of the faraway storm.

8.

She was gone by the time I woke up. I let out a huge sigh of relief that nothing had happened. Which was followed by a small sigh of regret that nothing had happened.

It took a few minutes for me to rouse myself and carry the clothes I'd been wearing down to the basement, where I found a washer and dryer. After a shower, I stepped into the kitchen for a cup of coffee, wearing only one of Angela's towels. Standing at the window and gazing out at the tidy garden, I punched the key on my cell phone.

Isabel said, "Good morning." She sounded only a little guarded. My wife has great antenna and could sense a threat, even from 160 miles away, and would catch any odd note in my voice. Had Angela and I crossed a line, she'd picked up on it in an instant. But she sensed correctly that nothing had happened and her tone was gentle as she told about the girls' day.

We got the family matters out of the way and I moved on. "There's definitely something going on here," I said.

She said, "Oh?"

I told her the story, including all the suspicious angles, though I left Crystal out of it and jumped over the last moments of the night. I felt I had earned those small deceptions. Plus I was a coward.

She didn't seem convinced and cut to the chase. "Does this mean you're staying longer?" she asked in a tone that told me she already knew the answer.

"I'm not sure."

"Your daughters want to know where their daddy is."

"I've been away before."

"Not with an old girlfriend, you haven't."

I gaped into the phone. "You told them that?"

"Of course not. That was me."

"How did you know?"

"Oh, come on. How dumb do you think I am? Your friend's little sister. I bet she was cute. Still is. Am I right?" When I didn't answer, she said, "What? Is there more to it? Is she holding a candle for you?"

A second passed and I started to laugh. She said, "Well?"

"That's not what I'm doing here."

"I'm very glad to hear that."

"I want to find out what happened to Joey," I said. "Because I'm not so sure it was an accident."

By the way she sucked in a breath, I could tell she was startled. "What then? Someone killed him?"

Hearing it put so plainly gave me a start. "I don't know about that."

She said, "It's still none of your business. You don't live there anymore. And you haven't seen this friend of yours in a long time."

"That's right, I haven't," I said. "And now it's too late. So I can at least do this for him."

"Do what, exactly?"

"See if I can find anything more about how he died."

"Don't they have police for that?"

"They've written it off as accidental. I just want to make sure that it was. That's all."

"So you won't feel guilty?"

"No, I'll feel guilty anyway."

"And if you do find something?"

"I'll tell the state police. Or whoever."

"Wait a minute," she said. "It takes you half a day to find two socks that match. Suddenly you're Sam-fucking-Spade?"

My wife does not often use such language, so I knew to tread carefully. "I need to do this, Isabel."

She kept quiet and so did I. Finally, she said, "I don't understand.

But if it's so important to you..."

"I appreciate that."

"I want to know when you're coming home." Her voice was firm.

I said, "End of the week?"

She said, "I suppose that's acceptable."

"I love you," I said. "And I love my daughters."

"We know that," she said and hung up.

Outside, I found a cloudy mid-morning, with shafts of sunlight washing the street at intervals. The memories of the adventure in the darkness on Nock Hill seemed different in the daylight, and I wondered for a moment if any of it had happened or was it just my imagination wandering loose.

Crystal looked surprised and happy to see me. From the far side of the café, she waved a hand, directing me to the table in the corner by the window. The three other customers were sitting together.

"Well, well, well." A scent of flowers preceded her as she stepped up with a cup of coffee, wearing her best fond look. "I wasn't sure if I'd be seeing you again."

"I said I'd –"

"I know what you *said*," she broke in with a low laugh and a flutter of her eyes. "People say things all the time."

"I guess that's true," I said. We were a profound pair. I gave her my order and she sashayed away.

The street outside was quiet and I remembered how Joey and I used to huddle in the space between two buildings on this street, smoking our first cigarettes. He was also there the time outside the football stadium when my dad caught me with a Marlboro and knocked it out of my mouth. I tried to conjure the stepping-stones of my youth that didn't include him and couldn't think of any.

Crystal brought my coffee with a happy flourish that made her seem even younger. It was true; take away the sweet figure and she could pass for a goofy kid. It made me feel like a pervert. My eldest girl would be a teen herself in another two years. Though she'd never be a Crystal. I'd make sure of that. I wasn't a good Catholic, but my wife was, and they still had convents.

This morning, my favorite waitress left me in peace, bless her, though I could still feel her steady gaze. When she brought my breakfast to the table, she stood for a moment and stared out the window.

"So, what do you think, now that you've been into town awhile?"

"What do I think?"

"About Wyanossing. Pretty dull, huh?"

"Well...

"It's not." Her voice dipped low, almost to a whisper. "There are all kinds of things going on. You just don't see them."

Okay, I thought, *I'll bite*. "What kind of things?"

"Sleazy things," she said, drawing it out. "The kind nobody wants getting around. You know, their dirty little secrets."

"In Wyanossing?" My voice carried just the right hushed tone of disbelief.

She glanced over her shoulder, either checking her other tables or to spot anyone who might be listening in.

"There are some things I could tell you..." Her eyes got wider. "Things you would not believe."

I gave her a look that said I wasn't sure if I should believe her now. She returned it with a stare that held a challenge and an invitation, tilting her chin just so.

"Well, I'd like to hear," I said. "I mean, I this is my hometown." I wondered if I had overdone the con. Then I saw the sharp flicker of satisfaction in her eyes as she gobbled the bait.

"Maybe I can tell you."

"When?" I said.

She liked my show of interest. "I'm going to be busy tonight."

"All right."

"But just until nine o'clock." She paused. "I could meet you after that."

"Where?" I whispered, taking my turn at furtive.

She was ready with a plan. "You know that church on the other side of the park from the library? It's Episcopalian. They have an old cemetery around the back and there's a stone bench at the far end.

Can you be there at, I don't know, 9:30?"

"I can do that," I said.

She treated me to a secret smile, winked, and moved away.

I spent the next moments wondering why I had engaged in a plot to meet a voluptuous twenty-something vixen in the dark of small town night. As I peered out the window, lost in these thoughts, two cars rolled by. One was a police cruiser. It might have been Dewitt at the wheel or another cop. It was followed a half-minute later by a white Sable. I was too distracted, though, and the sedan passed so quickly that I missed catching a glimpse of the driver. I left my table and stuck my head out the door just in time to see the car disappear around the next corner.

From behind me, Crystal said, "Something wrong?"

When I turned around, I found her regarding me narrowly and was caught by surprise. Something about the way the daylight struck her face had added some years, so that she looked like an older sister; the sharp-eyed, devious one. I made an effort to avert my gaze.

"I thought I saw someone I knew," I said, keeping my tone offhand. "From school."

She said nothing and stepped aside for me to make my way back to my table. She didn't come around again, leaving the other waitress to top-up my coffee. When I paid my check, her thank you was distracted. But then she let her fingers linger on my palm as she gave me my change. It was very strange behavior.

I crossed Front Street and headed around the corner to First Avenue, then walked another block to the corner of River Street. Across the intersection was the building housing the police department and borough offices, a one-story red brick with a tidy little lawn arranged around a flagpole. The Stars and Stripes fluttered and snapped in the morning breeze.

A cruiser was parked at the curb and when I reached the other side, made a point of walking very close to the front of the car and letting my right hand dangle near the grill. It was cool.

I stepped into the lobby and wandered down the hall until I

found a set of double doors with a shingle reading "Borough of Wyanossing - Police Department" over it.

Tim Raines was standing beside the front desk, explaining something to a middle-aged woman. He glanced up with a look that was only slightly surprised. I waited until his business with the woman was finished and she made an exit before stepping up and offering my hand.

"Richie Zaleski." He started to smile. "Did you just come by to say hello? Or did you get mugged? Car-jacked? You witness a drive-by? We get a lot of those." He was enjoying ribbing me.

"Nothing like that," I said. "At least, not yet."

He jerked his head. "Come on back."

As I walked around the counter and to the large office that was in the corner, I noticed the way the woman at the desk was staring at me. I whispered, "Maxwell House."

She shook her head, "No..."

"Hyundai? Tegrin?"

"Tegrin." She snapped her fingers. "That's it."

Tim was holding his office door open. He closed it behind me, then drew back to give me the once-over.

"You don't look so different," he said.

"Neither do you."

He waved me to a chair and went around to settle in the taller one behind his desk. He tilted his head in the direction of the wall. "You get tired of that?"

"I just wished they'd remember the movie roles."

"You were in movies?" he said.

We both laughed. He said, "Sorry," and I waved it off. He folded his hands before him. "You've still done well for yourself."

"I've been lucky."

"I lost track of you," he said. "What I want to know is how you got from Wyanossing to having your face on television sets all over the world."

Just as I started my career spiel, his phone buzzed and he held up a hand. While he listened to the call and murmured back, I took a look around his office. The space was simple enough, small and neat, with walnut paneling. There were bookshelves on the right and left walls and a window gave a view of the lot where the borough vehicles were parked. A credenza was adorned with pictures of Tim's wife and three kids – I remembered he had married a pretty blond girl named Cathy Carter – and one of the 1972 Wyanossing High School football team with a banner reading District Champions. Along with rows of official books, the shelves held plaques and trophies and some Nittany Lion paraphernalia.

I took the opportunity to study him for a moment, too. He still had a boyish look about him, one of those guys you can look at and still see the kid. He was right at six feet and still in good shape. He had kept most of his hair, a modest cop brush cut that had gone mostly gray. His eyes were brown and intense. He could have played the sheriff in a western or the tough sergeant in a war movie.

We had been pals where we were little kids, but by the time we were in high school, he was a star athlete and lived in a different universe, breathing the rare air of hometown celebrity. He had led the football team to the Districts two years in a row and had lettered in basketball and baseball.

Though he and I had been in separate camps, he never shared in any of the tribal hostility that most of his friends had displayed. He always seemed more amused than offended by our antics and I figured that guys like him were so busy being local sports idols that they missed a lot of the fun. Of course, it made a difference that I wasn't a total slouch. I was a second-string football player until my junior year when I broke my wrist and I'd a earned a letter in track.

Apparently, he was not the type to let his athletic glory remain the high point of his life and appeared quite settled into his role as chief of police in his hometown.

He finished his call and hung up the phone. "Sorry about that," he said. "You were telling me about your path to fame and fortune."

I went through the tale for him. Then I asked about his family. One of his kids was a freshman at Penn State. The other two had graduated.

"One broken condom and I'm a grandfather." We chuckled over that, too.

In the pause that followed, he eyed me in a speculative way. "Why do I get the feeling that this isn't a social visit?"

"It's not," I said. "Not completely. I wanted to know if there's anything you can tell me about Joey's death. I mean anything other than what people are saying."

He placed his hands palm down on his desk blotter and regarded me with a cool cop expression designed as a signal that I was now officially meddling.

"It was pretty much what was in the paper," he said, barely shrugging his shoulders. "He was goofing off in the park up there in the dead of night and somehow got turned around and went off Council Rock." He shook his head slowly. "It's over six hundred feet to the old track bed. No way to survive a fall like that."

I nodded, considering, then said, "I was just wondering if there might be anything else to it."

He gazed at me, a slight frown tilting his mouth. "What kind of 'anything else' are you talking about?"

My actor's ear caught the harder edge creeping into his voice and I eased up a bit. "Well, for one thing, I spent enough time up there with him to know he'd never go out on that damn rock. He could never handle heights at all."

Tim watched me as if waiting for more. I didn't have anything, except for the business about the white Sable, which I didn't want to go into. I thought it might sound foolish. That, and Joey's research at the library, which I also chose to omit. It didn't seem so ominous in the placid light that was streaming through the window.

Switching channels, Tim said, "When was the last time you saw him?" That question again.

"It was a while ago."

"Maybe he got over it. The fear of heights, I mean."

"Yeah, maybe," I said. "But whether he did or he didn't, he'd been sneaking up there to screw around since junior high school. He knew that hill like the back of his hand. And somehow he loses his way and takes a header over the side? And off Council Rock, of all places?"

Now he picked up a pen and tapped in lightly into his palm, a bit of stage business as his brow stitched in faint annoyance. "What I can tell you is that there was a full investigation. We went over the scene from one end to the other. The State Police were in on it, too. There was no evidence of anything but an accidental fall." He paused. "Unless he jumped, of course."

"I don't think he'd do that."

Tim smiled slightly. "No, I don't think so, either. Between you and me and most of Wyanossing, he still smoked pot all the time. Maybe he sampled some other substances. I can tell you off the record that there was THC in his bloodstream."

"No surprise," I said.

"No. But God knows, we're all getting older. It gets really dark up there. So maybe he got high, and a little disoriented, and stumbled, lost his balance..." He raised his hands, palms turned upward. "Good-bye, Joey Sesto. May he rest in peace."

A low murmur of conversation gurgled from the outer office, followed by a tap on the door. It opened and Tim looked past me. I turned to see Officer Dewitt gazing in at us with the flat expression that never seemed to leave his face.

He held up a file folder and Tim said, "I'll get with you on that."

The officer stared for another moment, then moved off, closing the door again.

"Your deputy seems like a pleasant fellow," I said.

Tim let out a short laugh. "Yeah, Mr. Congenial. He's a good cop, though." He tapped his pen on the blotter. "Anything else?"

"So the investigation is closed?"

Though another small spike of annoyance flashed in his eyes, he kept his voice steady. "Well, yes. Unless something else comes to light. Which I really don't expect. Not at this point."

I said, "All right, then," and pushed myself up from the chair. "Thanks for your time."

He got to his feet. "I'll walk out with you," he said.

We stood on the sidewalk in front of the building. Tim and I had played as kids on these same streets. Now we were into our gray years and far apart. And yet he still struck me as a decent guy. He had found his place and would occupy it for the rest of his life, spending not a moment fretting over what could have been, like a certain actor might do.

"How long will you be here for?" he asked.

"I don't know. Another day, maybe. This is quite a break from New York."

He smiled at that. "So what have been doing with yourself?"

I figured he knew I was staying with Angela, so I didn't bother to mention it. "Just poking around," I said. "Seeing what's changed and what hasn't. It's been years since I was back.

"Well, it's all pretty much the same. Seen anybody?"

"Just Leo. Mrs. Eldridge at the Library. I ran into John Miller and Elmer Smalley. That's all."

He asked if I remembered a certain girl who had been the head cheerleader, homecoming queen, and all-around class beauty. When I told him that she wasn't someone you'd forget, he whispered that she now weighed over two hundred pound and was as ugly as a river rat and as mean as a snake. He swore it was so.

I said, "And what's this I hear about Louie Zag?"

He sighed and grimaced. "That's some sad business. You know he always had problems with drugs. Always. Even back when, he took it too far." An old clash raised its head for a moment. "He never gave it up, never slowed down. And then one night he put something in his system that screwed him up but good. It was bound to happen. Like Russian roulette. The only thing that surprises me is that he dodged it as long as he did." He looked off down the street. "At least he's no trouble anymore."

"Where would I find him?" Tim turned to look at me with a baffled expression. "I just want to say hello," I said. "See if he remembers me."

"Seventh Street School."

I didn't understand. He had named our old elementary school. "I thought they closed it down."

"They did. But the playground is still there. And the basketball court. Louie shows up twice a day, at 10:15 in the morning and at 1:45 in the afternoon."

"Why?"

"You don't remember?" I shook my head. "Recess," he said. He glanced at his watch. "You can catch him, if you hurry."

I studied his expression to see if I'd missed a joke. He was serious.

I said, "Maybe I will."

Tim offered his hand again. "Good to see you, Richie," he said and started back up the walk.

"Hey," I called after him. "Do you know anyone around town who drives a white Mercury Sable?"

He puzzled for a few seconds. "No, not off hand. Why?"

"I saw someone I thought I recognized. I couldn't place the face, though. Driving a white Sable."

"No," he said. "Doesn't ring a bell." He waved and continued up the walk.

As I headed to Front Street, I glanced back after a few seconds to find that Tim had gone back inside. I caught sight of a face in one of the windows. I was not surprised when I saw who had been watching me.

When I was a kid, the Seventh Street Elementary School playground had been a rough gravel expanse with a full bevy of monstrous steel contraptions – merry-go-rounds, monkey bars, and slides – that racked up hundreds of broken bones over the years. In my miniature view, it had stretched for miles, a landscape over which our happy games and fierce battles had taken place.

I pulled to the curb across the street to find that the gravel had been dug up and replaced by rubber carpet made from recycled tires and all the old playground gear had made way for devices of thick and safe plastic with no splinters or metal edges. The school building had been converted into elder care apartments and in its shadow was a little park with benches for the old folks and young mothers with their infants and toddlers. It was another small step toward a condo future for Americans in large towns and small.

For all this renewal, the basketball court was still in place. And I saw standing at center court a lonesome scarecrow.

This particular scarecrow held a ball on his hip as he tracked my approach from the sedan. I made my ambling way across the playground and reached the edge of the court. The scarecrow waited until I put a foot on the sealed concrete to start started bouncing the ball in an even, hypnotic rhythm: pock-pock-pock.

I stopped when I was twenty paces away. In the next long half-minute, I conjured Louie Zag thirty years before, the bony frame, long black hair, hook of a nose, and flashing Italian eyes.

I stayed where I was, waiting to see what he would do. He was staring at some point just to my left, not meeting my gaze. Then he stopped bouncing the ball and came up with a sweet and quizzical smile.

"Hey, Richie," he said softly and looked at me for the first time.

"Hey, Louie."

"You're on TV," he said.

"I have been, yeah."

"But you don't live here no more."

"New York," I said.

"Says here this stuff's made in New York City," he said, putting the country twang on the lines from a popular commercial. I smiled and he smiled back.

Something told me drawing too close would alarm him, so I began a slow back-and-forth arc that became gradually smaller.

"So, how have you been doing?" I asked him.

"I'm doing fair," he said, tracking me absently "Just fair. Better than Joey, though. He's dead. Joey's dead, Richie."

"Yeah, he is."

"*He* knew," Louie said, his eyes shifting.

"Who, Joey?" I said. "Knew what?"

Louie switched channels. "You got anything to smoke?" he said.

"You mean as in..."

His smile went wicked. "Listen to this guy." He jerked a thumb and muttered to an invisible third party. "They used to call him 'Two-Toke.' You know why?" He returned his attention to me. " 'Cause he took two tokes for every one for the rest of us."

I had forgotten that bit of trivia. *Two-Toke*. That had been me for a few drug-addled months.

"Guess the answer's no, huh?" he said.

"Sorry." I nodded toward the moms and their kiddies. "I don't think they'd appreciate it, anyway."

"Well, I was gonna insist that we *share* with them." He cracked into a hoot of happy laughter that stopped just as suddenly, as if he'd tripped a switch. "Ah, what the hell. I've got some. Come on." He started walking and dribbling and did not look back to see if I was following him.

We made some kind of strange parade. Louie walked ahead of me, bouncing the basketball with the perfect, unceasing tympani of a metronome: *pock-pock-pock*. He looked like the caricature of a movie madman, his bony shoulders hunched inside a greasy trench coat, and so intent on the ball that I didn't know if he was aware that I was traipsing along in his wake. This, on a Wednesday morning in late spring on a quiet residential street in the borough of Wyanossing, our hometown.

He led me on a jagged trail down the long incline of streets to the river down from Seventh to Race, then over to Sixth, and then from Sixth to Royal. He never looked up, guided by private radar.

We eventually reached River Street and crossed over, Louie striding through the traffic without looking one way or the other, me trotting after him and dodging the cars in stops and starts. Once we reached the opposite side, he led me across a convenience store parking lot and into the old rail yard.

We traversed a half-dozen sets of unused tracks and were within a quarter mile of wading into the Susquehanna when he veered off, hopping over ties and rails on his way to the far edge of the yard and an old switchman's shack. The narrow, forlorn-looking, shingled building looked like the last thing standing after the visit of a tornado or something out of Dr. Seuss, a collection of crooked corners. The tracks that ran by it were all dull with rust. I guess few trains passed that way any more.

Louie had lost some of the rhythm of his dribble when we entered the yard and now he gave up and tucked the ball under his arm. He stepped over the last set of rusty rails and stopped to regard me quizzically. Now he looked as if he *had* forgotten that I was there. A moment later, he produced a sneaky, lopsided Louie grin, threw an arm wide and said, "Welcome to Rancho Zagarelli."

The gravel edged to the front door with a corrugated steel awning hanging over it at a crazy angle. Louie stepped under it, digging around in the pocket of his trench coat, his brow knit, all business, as he pulled out one large, old-fashioned key with a cloverleaf head. The lock turned and he barged inside, leaving the door open behind him.

"Close it," he cracked over his shoulder. "My neighbors have nose trouble." There wasn't another domicile within a half-mile.

Louie and I went way back. As the only two "Z's" in our class at Seventh Street School, we sat next to each other for seven years. So I watched his talent sprout and grow and had learned little tricks that I had used down the road.

He developed the wild imagination, sharp tongue, and timing to turn mundane moments into routines. It was Louie who discovered Lord Buckley and Brother Dave Gardner and practiced their spiels until he had them cold. He was a natural-born wit who could have built a career as a comic or a writer, but the love affair with herbs and chemicals held him fast. He had abused substances before it was a catchphrase. From what I witnessed that afternoon, they had abused him right back but good.

And yet some of the Louie Zag I remembered was still intact, and leave it to him to end up in such weird digs.

It was just as rough-and-tumble inside. The front room was only ten by twelve feet, with a worn couch, a worn armchair, some crates and a board for a coffee table, and a TV on a stand. The walls looked to be so paper-thin that they wouldn't stop a healthy fly. The ceiling was low and the linoleum on the floors was ripped and broken where it wasn't covered with the patchwork rug. He had figured out a way to cadge an electrical hookup for the old Airline record player that perched on another crate, with a stack of vinyl albums next to it. The only digital device on the premises was the phone in my pocket.

A tiny kitchen was attached to the back, looking like a photo out of a junkie tenement. Off this room was a closet that served as a bathroom. I preferred not to venture there.

The place probably would have reeked with age and other odors, but it was so drafty that any stench would blow away. A gas-fired heater took up a portion of one wall. The place would be an icebox in wintertime and would bake at the height of summer, with windows that didn't open, a tin roof, and no shade in sight.

In the past, the shack had served as a way station on the nights when switchmen had to stay on duty. Now Louie had claimed it for his home. I wondered if this had been arranged or if he was squatting. Living in such a hovel could not be legal; though it was also true that if it was plucked up and placed atop a four-story warehouse in Manhattan, it would fetch an easy half-million.

And Louie would have made a great New Yorker. He had his own wild jive going on. At least he once did, years ago when we were kids. Now I beheld the worn, crazy, loose sack of a middle-aged man stumbling through life in that little burg with his brain checking in and out as if he could never quite get the antenna adjusted.

I watched him for a moment as he stood there fretting over having a visitor on the premises. Maybe I was wrong about him and New York. The city would have chewed him up even faster. Lots and lots and lots of drugs, good and bad, on that island. Lots of "friends" to speed you along on your road to hell. And too many with too little mercy once you fell.

The way his eyes were flicking about reminded me of a frightened bird, and I said, "Hey, are you all right? Maybe I should take off."

He gave me a confused look that lasted five seconds. Then his face relaxed into a kind smile that brought back good memories.

"Naw, stick around," he said. "You're goddamn invited, okay? Siddown." I started for the chair and he barked, "Not there!" so sharply that I jumped.

Moving gently so as not to startle him, I shifted to the couch and sank into what felt like a damp marshmallow. Louie claimed the armchair with a sigh of pleasure.

We sat without talking for a long time. He retreated, deflating as if the pallid flesh was sagging from his bones. I saw hollow cheeks and gray stubble where he had missed the last time he shaved. I caught a whiff of something, unwashed laundry and sour mold. His head was cocked to one side and his eyes were so blank that I wondered if he had fallen asleep with them open.

A rumbling sound rose up and I turned to look through the kitchen doorway and out the stained window. An engine was rolling through the far side of the yard, pulling a string of empty cars. Only when the engineer blew the whistle in one long, low note did Louie rouse himself. His gaze cleared. He straightened, put the ball down, placing it precisely at his feet and watching to make sure it wasn't going to roll away, and then regarded me with frank curiosity in his gray eyes.

"Hey, Richie," he said. "You live here again?"

"No, I'm visiting."

"Why?"

"Because..." I paused. "I came to see Joey."

"Joey's dead, Richie. He fell down."

"I know. I went to visit his grave."

"What for?"

"I don't know. To say good-bye."

"Well, it's a little late for *that*, bro!" He chortled suddenly and rolled his eyes, clowning.

I sighed and nodded. "I guess that's right."

"That is right," he said, jerking forward abruptly. "That is *exactly* right. That is exactly, right on the fucking *money* right!" He was getting excited.

"Louie?"

He blinked and sat back. After a quiet moment, his devilish smile returned. He said, "Hey, man, you wanna get stoned?"

Okay, I did it, and to this day, I don't know why. I hadn't touched anything illegal in at least twenty-five years. After my first derelict year or so, it was clear that I was not a talented herbal imbiber. The experience became a drag. Once the initial five or ten minutes of giddiness passed, I would labor under a muddy cloud that wouldn't go away. The last few times, I ended up drinking myself into a beer stupor just to chase away the buzz.

Even so, I now confess that I smoked marijuana with Louie that day. He went into the kitchen and came back with a sandwich bag and a little pipe. The bag held a small handful of green-gold leaf.

"Where did this come from?" I asked him.

"Growed it myself," he bragged, smiling broadly. "Down by the river. I found a spot where the soil and the sunlight were fucking perfect. This is the last of it."

Yes, I was stupid. It still could have been sprayed with something. What was that stuff back in the 70s? Paraquat? It was a risk, but I had a strong curiosity about how it would affect me after all that time. I told myself I wanted see if it would loose anything in Louie's brain. To be honest, though, I decided to join him because I hadn't done it once in the decades since the time when we were young and foolish. I knew it was dumb, the kind of thing that would make my wife or Angela or anyone else with any sense say, "You did *what*? Are you *crazy*?" I did it anyway.

We smoked from his little glass pipe. After two hits and one cough, I felt it come on and promptly sank down like a turtle into mud. It was as if I had put on one of my old denim jackets and found that it still fit me. My mind shifted for a tense second. What if the cops came busting in? It was too late now; might as well ride it out.

Louie had dropped back into silence. I didn't want to look at him, so I let my thoughts narrow. I could feel the whole history of that little shack, the dirty, sweating men that had parked their butts there during the years when the railroad ruled. I gazed out the front window at a small slice of the panorama of my hometown: Louie's, Joey's, and mine. It had been our world when we were kids, but all that was gone. For my part, I had left it behind with barely a look back. Louie stayed and lost his mind. Joey stayed and died a terrible death.

So Louie was fried and Joey was dead. I, on the other hand, was a visitor who could walk out the door at any time, cross the tracks, go get my car and drive away. And with that thought, I realized that when I left this time, the last thread connecting me to this place would be broken.

I felt a slow wash of homesickness for my little town. Which made me want to run back to New York and dive headfirst into the embrace of my family. Then I spent another moment longing for the empty peace of this quiet little nowhere village.

After riding this rollercoaster up and down and around until it became nonsense, I returned my attention to Louie. His eyes were fixed on something that only he could see hovering in the air before him.

I decided to see if I could make my brain work again. "So, Louie..." I said. He didn't respond. "Louie?" Nothing. I snapped, "Louie!"

His gaze skittered my way. "I fucking heard you. I'm sittin' right here."

"What's been going on around here?"

He shifted in his chair and his eyes narrowed. "Why you asking me?"

"I don't know," I said. "I've been away for awhile. I was just wondering. How's it been going?"

"Oh. Same as it's always been. Can't buy a thrill." He held up the pipe. "This is about as good as it gets. You want some more?"

"No, I'm fine. Save it." I *was* fine and, except for the flashes of guilt about what I had done, mellow as could be.

"I guess I might as well leave, now that Joey's gone," Louie was saying.

I returned to the present. "Why's that?"

"Because there's only about four people in this town worth a shit. And he was one of them. You know why?"

"No, why?"

"No, why, no, why, *know* why? Because he never treated me like I was insane. That's why." He flinched, wounded. "And I'm not. Insane, I mean. I'm just not myself lately. Joey knew that. The rest of them, they wanted to lock me up and throw away the fucking key." Now his expression shifted to appalled. "They put me in Danville, Richie. The cracker factory. The funny farm. They wanted to shut me up for good, so I couldn't tell what I know. But Joey had his little sister Angela get me out!"

He stopped to catch a breath and I said, "What you know about wha –"

"You were banging her."

I stared at him. He was grinning all sly and wagging a finger at me.

I said, "What?"

"Angela," Louie said. "You were banging her. Joey didn't know. But I did."

I said, "Uh..."

"If he would have found out, he would have cut your nuts off. That was his little sister, Richie."

I stared at him in wonder. "You knew?"

"'Course, I knew. I could smell it on you. The both of you. I could feel the heat whenever you guys were around. And the way you two looked at each other?" He shook his head in a musing way. "My, my."

"I can't believe you remember that. It was thirty years ago."

"I remember everything, man." He eyed me wisely. "At least everything that matters."

"Okay, hold it," I said. "What did you mean when –"

"So, anyway..." He cut me off, this time with a stern fussiness and began counting down his fingers. "There's Angela. And Leo. A couple other people here and there. The rest of them are *frog shit*!"

That one almost put me on the floor.

We hung out day and night at Jimmy's. The namesake was a creep who had inherited the place when his father dropped dead from working sixteen-hour days. Jimmy, Jr. was fat and greasy and reeked of sweat, even in the dead of winter. Having gained a career by default, he exhibited no ambition, letting the store slip year by year deeper into dusty disrepair. The good news was that we got to spend our hoodlum days there, reading the magazines, eyeing the girls who came to buy chips and sodas, and stealing whatever we could sneak out the door.

This one lazy afternoon, a little girl came along on an errand, one of those blond, pigtailed snits who go through childhood sticking out their tongues. As I recall, Louie was there and Doug Harman, and Joey, too. The little girl marched inside, casting bratty glances our way. She bought her candy or whatever, reappeared, and proceeded to start preaching to all of us, and Louie in particular, about the error of our ways. She was about eight, and she was running us down like we were schoolboys.

"You don't live here," she snipped. "Don't you have homes? Why don't you leave Mr. Johns alone? My dad says you're nothing but hoodlums. And troublemakers. He says..."

She railed on until Louie finally got tired of it, gave her his best psycho look and said, "Hey, shut up, ya little pissant! Jesus! I can't hear myself think."

She gave a start, then bolted, running up the street, and around the corner. Louie settled back, quite pleased with himself.

Five minutes later, a Chrysler sedan swung around the same corner with tires squealing and slid to the curb in the front of the store. The driver lurched out, forty or so, in a shirt and tie, and stumbling drunk from too many afternoon martinis. He stared at our faces, jabbed a finger, and shouted, "All right, which one of you punks called my daughter 'frog shit?'"

We got a laugh out of that one. Then Louie sobered. "Joey was on my side," he said. "And that's why they killed him." He tumbled into another brooding silence.

I found myself jerked out of another memory. "What did you say?"

"That's why they killed him."

"Who killed him?"

"Those fucks, that's who."

"Who?"

"It's a wonder they didn't get me, too," he muttered. "Cause I know all about them."

I took my time. It was like walking on a shaky branch. "Who are you talking about, Louie?"

His gaze steadied and he gave me prim frown. "Oh, you know *who*," he said. "They're here.

They're everywhere. You know Zeloco?" I nodded. "It's owned by some German corporation. Or maybe it's Dutch. Whatever. Anyway, they cannot tolerate people like Joey and me. We know what they do. They had their agents zap my brain so they could put me in a mental institution and they throw Joey off the side of Nock Hill."

His tone was severe, but he was also lucid, except for the fact that what he was describing was loony.

I said, "Joey had an accident, Louie. He fell."

He gave me a long look. "Oh, really? Is that what happened?"

I sat back. In my affected state of mind, I wasn't in the mood for dark fantasies. Which worked out fine, because in a little spasm of alarm, Louie snatched up his ball, shot to his feet and said, "Time to go."

We walked out of the train yard, and by the time we got to River Street, Louie had ducked behind his wall. He wouldn't look at me, and when I tried to catch his eye he glanced away. From the tight lines of his face, I could see what an effort this was, so I let him go, backing away, my hands up. The more distance I put between us, the more he calmed. At the next corner, he stopped and I crossed over.

He waved shortly and lunged up the sidewalk, the ball picking up that steady heartbeat of a rhythm. I was a dozen paces along when I heard him shout my name. When I turned around, he was wearing his sweetest, most wicked smile.

"Don't forget to blow the dog!" he yelled. Then he laughed and hurried away, bouncing the ball before him.

All through high school, we spent our Saturday afternoons at Jay Derlack's house. Jay's dad had passed away and his mom worked, so there was no one in the house but his little sister, who tried to impress us by strutting around, trying to act cool, and pushing her miniscule breasts into our faces. We ignored her.

Jay's mom kept a note board just inside the back door. So that when he or his sister walked in the house, they would read through their chores and errands. One afternoon, as we were leaving, I happened to glance at the board and see the following: Jay - Call Grandma about market Saturday. Get a gallon of milk. Shovel Mrs. Manetti's walk. Underneath was scrawled: "Jay: Don't forget to blow the dog."

That was Louie Zag.

The afternoon's diversion was too weird and too weighted with strange memories and was not something I'm likely to repeat. I felt as if I had been locked in a room where a movie was looping through odd vignettes from my past.

As I walked to my car, I encountered more of the houses and alleyways and vacant lots that had been settings for my youth. Had I been in a more stable frame of mind, the experience might have been bittersweet, but at that moment it was just creepy. In one of those pot-induced revelations that almost always turn out dumb, I surmised that the past is called that for a reason. It's over and done, passed by. Oh, yeah, that was brilliant.

I walked faster, getting a good pace going as a way to burn off the effects of the herb. My thoughts jumped back to Louie and I recalled his strange strings of words and snide asides. He had displayed his usual humor right along with the dark weight of his broken sanity. I dissected his crazy ramblings and couldn't find a pattern that made any sense.

The cloud began to disperse when I got to Angela's house. I let myself in, went into the bathroom, and took another quick shower to wash off the sweat and somehow, I hoped, the effects of the cannabis. After I finished, I called her office.

She picked up the phone. "Richie?" she said. "Hello?"

"I'm here," I said.

"Yes, and?"

"And?"

"And why did you call?"

"Because..." I couldn't remember.

"Because why?" When I didn't answer she said, "Are you all right?"

"I'm fine."

"What are you doing?"

"I'm just, uh..." I came around. "I saw Louie."

"Oh? How was that?"

"I went to his house."

"His house? What house?"

"That shack down in the railroad yard."

"What are you talking about?"

"The place where he lives. The old switchman's shack in the railroad yard."

"Really?" She didn't sound pleased. "That's very interesting. Because he's under a court order to stay at a halfway house out on Route 11."

"Uh-oh."

"I wish you hadn't told me that."

"Let's say I didn't."

"It doesn't work like that. I'm his attorney."

"You are?" I had to push my mind to grab onto this.

"Joey asked me to take care of him," she said. "I mean with his legal matters. It's pro bono. I'm the one who got him released from Danville. If he doesn't toe the line, he could get sent back."

I endured a guilty silence.

"So, how is he?"

I gurgled out a laugh. "He's crazy."

"That's not news. I meant how is he feeling?"

"Okay, I guess. He seemed fine. Just..."

I let the next pause go on too long.

"Okay, then..." She was prodding me along. "What did you guys talk about?"

I took another second for me to refocus. "It was very interesting. You know what he told me? He said that agents of a multi-national corporation got him sent away. And that they also murdered Joey."

She sighed. "I've heard his theories on that subject. Now Joey's death is part of it, too?"

"That's what he said. He's just rambling, then?"

"Well, what do you think? Do you believe there's been a high-level corporate conspiracy against two residents of Wyanossing, PA?"

"It's just what – "

"That's pretty amazing, all right."

"I guess he's –"

"For what reason?"

"I don't know, but –"

"But what?"

"Nothing, I guess."

She stopped to take a breath and I remembered how she would get irked whenever Joey, Louie, and I would go off on a goof. It always drove her crazy.

She jumped in on that memory. "What are you going to do now?"

After considering for a moment, I said, "I think I'll go back to the library. See what else I can find."

"You don't know what you're looking for."

"No, I don't." I thought of something. "Hey, where did he live?"

"Joey? He had a mobile home on a little piece of land he bought years ago out in the Heights." She meant Merion Heights, the west edge of town, where the borough limits edged into rolling acres of farmland.

"What happened to it?"

"I put it for sale, but I haven't found a buyer yet," she said. "It's only a single-wide. I'm going to keep the land for now."

"Where's all his stuff?"

"In storage," she said. "Why are you asking about this?"

"Have you been through everything?"

"No. I'm not quite ready for that."

"I'd like to see it," I said. "The trailer. And his stuff."

She stayed quiet for a few seconds and I could almost hear the little gears in her lawyer's mind beginning to turn.

"Why would you want to do that?"

"Maybe I can find something there."

"Something, as in what? Evidence that Louie's right? That there's an evil cabal working away in the shadows?"

I didn't care for her attitude. "I'm just making sure that your brother's death was what everyone says it was, that's all."

That stopped her, though only for a moment. "You really think it wasn't?"

"I don't know. Do you? All I know is pieces keep turning up that don't fit. So can I see the place or not? You can just give me the key if you don't want to go."

I sensed a *no* coming down the track, but she surprised me. "See it when?"

"Whenever," I said. "Soon, though. Today sometime."

"I've got things on until late this afternoon."

"We can go then. And get something to eat after."

"Okay."

"Burgers and stuff."

She laughed a little and some of the chill went away. "All right. So you'll be at the library?"

"I'm going to grab a sandwich now. I'm really hungry."

"Go to Frankie's on Third Street. Unless you want to see Crystal again."

"I'll go to Frankie's."

"I'll pick you up out front of the library at five," she said. Another pause. "You sure you're okay?"

"Yes!" I said it too sharply, and she laughed again as she clicked off.

The stroll through the streets took away all but the faintest reminder of my herbal adventure.

But I was hungrier than I'd been in a good while.

Frankie's was busy. I didn't see anyone I knew. There were the usual stares, but now they seemed unsure and the notion that my looks might be changing as I lingered in Wyanossing crossed my mind. From my reflection in the storefront glass, I thought I did look different; less like the New York actor and more like a small town nobody. Or maybe it was the cannabis having its way with my perceptions.

I ordered tuna salad on sourdough and a ginger ale and carried the sack to the park, where I picked out a secluded bench that still afforded a view of the two blocks of downtown.

As I ate, I considered that I was making a fool of myself with all the backward behavior. So far, I had flirted with a sweet young piece, flirted with an old girlfriend, gotten high with an old doper buddy, and hung out at the town library. What was next? Riding around town on a bike with a balloon in the spokes?

So why I was still hanging around? I had done what I had come to do, paying my respects to Joey. I missed my wife and my daughters. I was not going to bed Angela; or, God forbid, Crystal. Leo's happy life would go on and Louie Zag wouldn't miss me. It was a waste of time trying to figure out what had happened to Joey. Small towns were good at keeping secrets. There were a dozen reasons for me to go and next to none to stay. So why was I still there?

Another moment and the answer came to me.

The thought that my old running partner had not died in peace, that something awful had happened to him, came upon me with a sudden surety. I sensed a shadow on the edge of my vision and a shudder crept up my backbone. Somewhere in that dark shade lurked an evil that had been visited upon my friend.

Something unkind was hiding in this quiet town. Odd hints were being tossed my way and odder things were happening. Now my gut was telling me to heed the whispers and shadows, for Joey's sake. I owed him for all the good years so long ago. For sharing the trail with me. If I walked away, I'd be doing damage that I'd never be able to repair. Angela was right about that part.

I stood up, picked apart what was left of my sandwich for the birds, and left their gobbling multitude in peace.

When I reached the library doors, I stopped to turn my cell phone to vibrate and used the moment to make a scan of the block, using my acting skills for something other than hawking garbage. This brought me a quiet, private moment of humor.

The streets were quiet. I didn't see the white Sable. Which didn't mean it hadn't been around. I had been distracted.

Inside, I found an assistant on duty and as far as I could see, there was only one patron, a silver-haired old man in baggy trousers and a golf shirt. I announced myself and a half-minute later, Mrs. Eldridge appeared to whisper an invitation for me to join her in her office for a cup of tea. So I wandered up and down the familiar aisles until I heard the faint whistle of a kettle.

She waved me to the chair next to her desk. She had cleared a place and had put out cups, milk, honey, and a plate of little cookies, the whole bit. Once we had settled in, she said, "How has your day been?"

"Interesting."

"How so?"

"I've been seeing some people I haven't seen in a long time." She waited. "I paid a visit to Tim Stark at the police department." She nodded. "And I ran into Louie Zag. Zagarelli."

"Ah, yes. That poor man. Nothing to be done for him, is there?"

It was not a question. I stirred my tea, getting past the moment. "I'd like to spend some more time in your Collections Room, if that's all right," I said.

She tilted her head back. "You think there's something back there?"

"I don't understand why someone like Joey would be digging around in old plats," I said. "It doesn't sense." I didn't mention any of the other weird little things that had been happening. The less I shared, the better.

The librarian sipped her tea. "People look at those when they're buying some old place and want to know its history. I don't think he was doing that." It was her polite way of telling me that he was too broke to be in the market for property. Which I already knew.

The tea was doing wonders for my head. I could once again progress directly from one thought to the next.

"Oh? So they're not just historical records?"

"No, some of those structures are still standing. Most of them were constructed of stone or brick. They used to build things to last." She waved a hand at the walls around us. "This building will soon be two hundred years old. 1816. And it will stand for another two hundred. If it's left alone."

I nodded my admiration for the materials and workmanship as my brain worked on the puzzle of Joey digging around in antique building plans. I could see him poring over papers about issues that concerned him. Which, from what Angela said, would be zoning, what Zeloco was doing to the river, the police nosing into private behavior. Instead, he was gathering information about old farms, none of which he could afford to buy.

"I think he also spent some time in the records room at the Borough Office, too." Mrs. Eldridge continued.

I came back around. "What? Why?"

She lifted a vague palm. "He asked me where the current versions of the plats would be. I mean the ones he was looking at in back. I told him they keep them at the Borough Office. And he went to see."

I spent a moment sipping and then switched tack. "Was he working on anything else?" I asked.

She glanced at the doorway, then lowered her voice. "Not back there, he wasn't. But he was using my computer to do some research about drugs."

I managed to hold a sober expression. "Drugs."

"That's correct."

"Why your computer?"

"The ones out front have filters on them."

"What drugs exactly?"

"I don't have any idea. I just happened to notice that he was looking at a web page that had information about illegal substances."

This didn't seem quite so strange, given his past habits. At the same time, with so much first-hand knowledge, he wouldn't need to do much in the way of research. That drugs fuck you up was about all the information he required.

"He must have found some of what he was looking for," Mrs. Eldridge said.

"Why do you say that?"

"Because he would get all absorbed and I'd hear him talking to himself, and every now and then, he'd make some noise."

"What kind of noise?"

"Talking to himself. It sounded like he found something that surprised him. A couple times, I had to ask him to be quiet." She produced a sad smile. "Just like when you two were kids. Too noisy."

"About your computer... I can go through the history and see what pages he was searching. It's not very hard."

"I'm afraid that's not possible," she said. "We delete our histories once a week."

"Why?"

She sat back. "Because we're in a period in which libraries are targets for certain government officials who have problems with privacy. It just seems a prudent thing to do. I'm sorry."

"I understand," I said and stood up. "Thank you for the tea."

Mrs. Eldridge rose in kind and fixed her gaze on me. "Do you think what he was doing here had something to do with his death?'

"I don't see how that could be, but..." I waved a hand. "The whole thing has me a little spooked."

"But you do think there's something wrong about it?"

"I don't know what to think," I said. "That's why I'm here."

"Well," she said, "We have our mystery section on the second floor." She gave me a wry smile. "I'm not much of a fan, though. They all seem so, what's the word... *implausible*."

"Yeah, I know what you mean." I hesitated and then said, "You know, I wonder if I don't want to let it go. Because I don't want to let him go."

She watched me, waiting to see if I would resolve this on the spot. When I didn't, she ushered me gently to the door.

The woman at the desk behind the counter glanced up, dropped her eyes, looked up again, and started to smile.

"Richie?" I didn't recognize her. "It's Sharon Anders."

I stared. I wouldn't have known her. Cute and curvy had given way to sweet and round.

"I heard you were in town," she said. "Everybody's talking about it."

We went through the exchange of information. She had married and divorced. Two kids were grown and gone. In return, I gave her the shorthand version of my career and home life. After we'd covered all that ground, I switched channels to ask her if she remembered Joey Sesto coming in there to examine records.

Her reaction was a slightly startled look. Some color rose to her cheeks. "Joey," she said. "The poor guy. That was so terrible what happened." She pushed a piece of paper from one hand to the other. "He was in a few times. I don't really remember what he was looking at. I guess I could, uh..." She blinked too many times.

I got her off the hook. "What all do you keep here?"

She waved an absent hand. "Birth and death records. Real estate. Plat books. Business transactions. That kind of thing."

As she fidgeted, I thought about what Joey would have wanted from these shelves. The only connection I could discern would be the plat books. He had been looking at old house drawings at the library.

"You don't remember what he was looking for?"

Sharon's eyes skittered to the door of the office behind her and then back to me. "I don't," she said. "We get so many people in here."

I understood and took my leave. She looked abashed and faintly unhappy as she wished me good-bye.

9.

I returned to the Collections Room and began working my way through the old plat books. The bindings creaked when I opened the half-dozen oldest among them and the paper inside felt like parchment. I could tell that these volumes hadn't been handled in a long time and decided to leave them alone, fearing that they would crumble to dust under my fingers.

Three others had seen some recent use and it gave me a moment's pause to consider that Joey's hands could have been the last to touch them. These contained hand-drafted designs of houses and barns on the acreage far outside of the borough limits, beyond Line Road, the two-lane that ran along the ridge over which was the next valley. I couldn't imagine a reason why Joey would care about the buildings on those plots of land. And yet Mrs. Eldridge claimed these were the books he had been studying.

Page by page, I perused the drawings, some of them so faint they had faded almost to white. There was something about the crafting of these homes and barns and the careful way the had been depicted with pen and ink that gave me pause. The drawings and their subjects struck me as beautiful and for a few moments, I dreamed of living in just such a home. My girls, Isabel, and me, ensconced in a castle that had been built stone by stone.

It was an idle diversion. I still might have a rustic bone or two left in my body, but my wife and daughters would not thrive in rural America. They were hothouse flowers who loved living in the city.

Still, there was no harm in me pretending just a bit more and I studied another drawing, this one of a farmhouse with a broad front porch that had no doubt looked out over the sea of green corn or whatever. Just the place to while away a summer evening with a glass of something while the cows lowed in the lower forty and someone plucked a banjo.

Okay, I told myself, enough of that, and turned to the next drawing, a barn, tall and staunch. It was the last page and I went about closing the book.

Then I opened it again. Something caught my eye: a smudge of some sort in the lower right corner, odd only because the other pages were so pristine. I lifted the page and inclined my head until it was almost resting on the table. From that angle, the corner of the page was set against the lamp in the corner.

It wasn't a smudge; it was a fingerprint. One placed so precisely and so visible in that manner that it seemed that someone had pressed a digit very hard and quite clearly with bare skin.

Someone.

After a moment's pause, I rose from the table and poked around until I found a pencil and a scrap of paper. Resuming the chair, I removed the cotton glove and spent a minute rubbing the end of my right index finger with the soft graphite until it was coated with a patina of light gray. Then I pressed down hard on the scrap of paper, leaving a fingerprint of my own. With the glove back on, I pinched the piece of paper next to the corner of the page and again tilted my head and held it to the light.

The two prints were the same size. Joey and I were the same height and weight. Our hands would match and so would our fingertips.

I sat there for a good while longer, studying the page and then staring at nothing at all.

I went back through the entire book, peering down at every page to see if I could detect any other prints or marks or smudges. I kept turning the pages without finding anything else of interest until Angela showed up a little after five. I heard her exchanging pleasantries with Mrs. Eldridge before she stepped into the doorway.

"What's all this?" she said, leaning against the jamb.

I showed her the collection of plat books, pointing out the three that I believed Joey had been working through. She looked tired or bothered about something and I decided not to go into the business about the fingerprint, but keep that detail myself until I could make something of it.

She couldn't offer an explanation for her brother's curious research and seemed a mood to write it off as another of his weird tangents. I didn't push it. Her expression was distant and it occurred to me that she was distracted over the trip we were about to make to the trailer.

After I put the last book back on the shelf and stashed the gloves we made our way to the front so I could thank Mrs. Eldridge. Angela stood by in silence. Whatever the librarian was thinking about the two of us having a rendezvous she kept to herself. Her eyes were curious but kind as she wished us farewell.

As we drove through town, I told Angela about seeing Louie. She glanced my way, sensing something, and under that gimlet gaze, I blurted that I had shared his pipe. She gave a start, then let out a startled laugh. It was a nice break from her brooding little cloud.

"That's one I'll definitely pretend I didn't hear," she said. "I'm an officer of the court."

"So does that mean you can arrest me and hold me for questioning? Because you'll have to frisk me first."

She rolled her eyes once more and said, "Dream on."

The section we called "the Heights" was once a poor section of town where grimy kids played in the dirt front yards of rickety frame houses that huddled along the dirt roads. Now it was Wyanossing's own little patch of sunny suburbia, the streets paved, the houses replaced by cookie-cutter bungalows that boasted manicured plots bordered by flower gardens. A few blocks further on and we were into the fringe again, with the rundown homes still standing or leaning throwbacks to the old days.

When we reached 17th Street, Angela pulled up to a singlewide sitting on a lot that was bare except for a lonely poplar tree. A "For Sale" sign listing her phone number had been planted near the road.

She shut off the engine and peered through the windshield. "Uh-oh." She pointed a finger. "The door's open."

I looked. The door was standing wide. She started to get out of the car.

"Wait a minute," I said. "Maybe you should let me go in first."

She said, "Oh, please," climbed out, and marched up the metal steps. I hurried along behind her.

Someone had done a crude job of jimmying the lock. The cheap metal frame had been chewed by a crowbar or the claws of a hammer. I followed Angela over the threshold.

The living room was standard thrift-store Americana, with mismatched couch and chairs. All the cushions had been tossed in what had been a small frenzy. The kitchenette had suffered the same treatment, with the cabinets flung open. In the city, such a scenario would be a loud signal to hightail it right back out the door. Angela went stalking across the worn, dull-red carpet and down the hall. She poked her head into each of the two bedrooms and then the bathroom, and reported that the whole place had been tossed, one end to the other. I made the tour; she was right. Nothing had been left out of the rampage.

She stood in the middle of the living room, arms akimbo. "The neighbors should have called me," she said. "Look at this place."

"You think it was kids?"

"Who else? Little bastards. Somebody should have called me."

"Maybe it just happened."

"Yeah, maybe."

We were both quiet for a moment. I let it soak in that this humble space had been Joey's home.

I said, "When was the last time you were out here?"

"Saturday. I stopped by for a minute and everything was locked up tight."

We must have both been thinking the same thing, because I saw her brow furrow.

I said, "What?"

She paused, then shook her head. "Naw, it was kids. Had to be."

I jerked a thumb in the direction of the tiny bathroom. "What would kids want in a toilet tank?"

"People hide things in those," she said. "Guns and drugs. Other valuables. Believe me, I know. I've done criminal defense work."

She stepped into the kitchenette to close the cabinets. I began placing the cushions back on the couch. She saw me through the doorway and said, "No. Leave it."

She used her cell phone to call the police department. I overheard her explaining to Tim Raines or Deputy Dewitt about the break-in. Then she said, "Yeah, he's here." She listened for a moment, her studied gaze coming to rest on me. "All right, she said. "We'll come back in." She clicked off. "That was Raines. He says there's a problem with your rental car."

"What kind of problem?"

"He wouldn't say. He said we need to get back to my house right now."

I could see from a distance that the sedan was pitched forward at a weird angle, resembling a hound sticking its snout in the dirt. When we pulled to the curb behind the borough police cruiser, I saw why that was: both front tires were flat.

Tim was standing in the street, watching with a blank stare as we got out. He held a metal clipboard in one hand. Three old geezers had assembled on the opposite sidewalk to talk and point.

I stepped around the front of the sedan to find that along with the tires, the passenger side window had been smashed. A rock the size of a tennis ball had landed in the passenger seat amidst hundreds of bits of glass.

"Jesus," I said.

"You have any enemies?" Tim asked directly. I stared at him. "It was a joke, Richie."

"This doesn't seem very funny to me," I said.

Angela said, "What the hell happened?"

"Someone vandalized the vehicle," he said, stating the obvious. I glanced his way, figuring this was another quip, but he was now frowning with distaste. "Two slashed tires and the rock through the window. That's what we can see."

"You have a lot of problems like this around here?" I asked.

"Not really," Tim said.

In the silence that followed, he looked at Angela in what I thought was a curious way, stole a glance at me, and then started writing on his pad. I could guess that he was trying to put together a likely scenario. Such as the jealous wife finds out about her hubby and the former hometown flame and drives out to pay a visit. He didn't know Isabel, of course. She wouldn't dream of –

"And what's this about your brother's place?" he said.

"Somebody broke into it," Angela said. "It's all torn up."

"Vandalized?"

"More like tossed. Like they were looking for something."

"You mean something to steal?"

"There was nothing there but old furniture," she said. "I was going to let Goodwill take it, if they wanted to bother. But nothing worth stealing."

Tim said, "I'll send Officer Dewitt to investigate."

Angela nodded, though she didn't look pleased.

"What about the car?" I asked.

Tim continued writing. "You need to call Leo and have him come get it," he said. "He can replace the tires for you. And the glass. You'll also want to call Avis so they can send someone out to inspect the damage. And get you a replacement vehicle."

He closed the cover of the clipboard. "You can come by tomorrow and pick up a copy of the report." He took a last glance at the car. "Keep your hands off the vehicle. And tell Leo to touch it as little as possible."

"Why?"

"We might want to dust it," he said. He sounded like a cop on a TV show and I tempered an urge to snicker. "I doubt we'll find anything. Unless we find a witness. And we can't count on that."

"You mean because it only happened in the middle of the goddamn day?"

Tim turned his cop stare on me. "Richie..." His expression that told me he didn't appreciate the attitude. The moment passed and he switched back to cop mode. "You were the victim of a property crime, that's all. It happens. I'm going to guess you have incidents in New York now and then. It happens here, too."

On that note, he walked to his cruiser, climbed in, and drove off.

Angela watched him leave, then went digging for her cell phone. She said, "I'm going to call Leo."

"Sure is a *friendly* little town," I said.

Leo paced from one side of the Lumina to the other, shaking his head and muttering, "Sonofabitch." and "Holy shit."

He went to work winching the car onto his wrecker. Once it was secure on the bed, he treated it to another inspection. He told me that replacing the tires were no problem, but that it would be late on Thursday before he could get the window installed.

"And I'll have to check and see if there's any more damage," he said.

"Like what?"

"They could have torn it up underneath. Or popped the cap and dumped something in the tank."

I hadn't thought of that. "Who's 'they'?"

"What?"

"Who's 'they'? Who does things like this? Teenagers?"

"Nobody, that's who," Leo said. "Not around here. Ain't ever happened that I remember." He scratched his chin, leaving a smear of grease. "I'd say somebody wanted to mess with you, Richie."

Angela was sitting at her kitchen table drinking a beer. She looked up when I walked in. "What'd he say?"

"Won't be done before tomorrow," I said. "You know, if you wanted me to stay, you could have just asked."

She wasn't amused. She tipped her bottle toward the fridge. "Help yourself," she said.

"Not right now," I told her. "I better call Isabel."

"She's going to think this is like *Deliverance* up here."

"Yeah, but she's a city girl. She thinks any place beyond the Hudson is like that."

Angela didn't find that funny, either. She was in a serious funk over the two incidents, so I left her alone and went out onto the back porch to call New York.

"*What* happened?" I explained it a second time. Isabel listened in baffled silence and then said, "So what's this mean?"

"It means I need to get the car fixed. And wait for a replacement."

"Are you coming home?"

"What? Of course, I am." I realized Angela could hear me through the open windows and lowered my voice. "You think *I* did this? You think I –"

"I don't know what to think," my wife shot back. "But what I know is that you left for one day, and then it was three, and now it's going to be a week, because somebody vandalized your car so you couldn't leave even if you wanted to." She took a breath. "Do you?"

"Do I what?"

"Want to leave."

"Yes," I said, trying to calm the waters. "I want to leave. I want to come home." I waited; Isabel didn't speak up. "I can't explain to you what's going on. But I found out that Joey was digging into something just before he died. I don't think this other stuff is just bad luck."

"And so?"

"And so I don't want to just walk away now."

She was quiet for a few tense seconds. "And what if this has nothing to do with your friend? Have you thought about that? What if somebody out there has a grudge against you going way back? And figures that now's the time to settle the score? What if this is just getting started? Forget about the car, what if someone comes at *you* next? What then?"

I was gazing absently at Angela's little yard. Patches of shade mingled with lingering sunlight. Long-stemmed irises waved prettily in the evening breeze. A bird flitted in and out of the shadows.

"No one's got a grudge against me," I said, keeping my voice steady. "I barely know these people anymore." At least the last part was true.

"All right, then," Isabel said. "You stay, if that's what you need to do."

"I can still get back by the end of the week."

She didn't acknowledge this and I guessed that meant she wasn't buying it.

"There's one more thing," she said. "With all that drama out there, I want you to watch yourself."

"What do you me –"

"I *mean* that if you lay one finger on that woman, you're dead meat." She waited to let it sink in. Then she said, "I love you. And your daughters miss their daddy." She clicked off.

When I stepped through the back door, I found Angela reaching into the refrigerator. She eyed me as she twisted the top off another Urquell. "Everything all right?"

"Yeah," I said, "She's just concerned."

"She should be. This is getting strange." She lifted the bottle. "Okay, I'm going to drink this and then brush my teeth and then we'll go eat. If you're still in the mood, that is."

"I am," I said. "But do you mind if we take your car?"

I called the Avis office while Angela was working on her second beer. The customer service guy was puzzled. I guess they didn't get a lot of major vandalism reports from little towns like Wyanossing. He sounded suspicious when I described the damage, as if I was at fault. His tone said it likely had something to do with a female or a money deal gone bad.

Once he had the information he needed, he told me the company would have "an associate" drive out in the next twenty-four hours to, as he put it, "Address your problem with the vehicle."

The Landing Drive-In sat on the bank of the river a few miles north of town and still hired high school girls as carhops. There were only a half-dozen cars spread out along the lot and we got quick service. Our server brought us baskets of sandwiches, fries, onion rings, and sour pickle slices. We passed on the thick milkshakes for reasons of health.

"I can't be eating this stuff," I said with a full mouth.

Angela bit into her double cheeseburger. "Yeah, me, neither."

It had been a regular stop when we were teenagers. I recalled the food tasting better in those days, but it was still pretty good. That's what I thought before it hit my stomach with a leaden thump. Letting out a quiet groan, I placed my basket back on the tray. Angela kept nibbling.

Between sips of water, I filled her in on what Leo had said about the damage to the rental car. "He doesn't think it was random."

"Well, guess what?" she said. "I tend to agree."

I selected a French fry, dipped it in ketchup, and took a bite. "I think it could be about Joey," I said.

"Oh? How so?"

"Like you said. It was all laid to rest, right? His death was an accident. I show up and start asking questions. Poking around at the library. And this stuff started happening." I counted down the list. "The Sable. Nock Hill last night. Joey's trailer. Now the rental car. That doesn't include all the rude attitude from John Miller and Elmer Smalley. "

"That, you're going to get, one way or another."

"And there's that cop. Dewitt."

"Don't forget Crystal," she said. "She's another card in the deck."

At the mention of the name, I suddenly remembered that she and I had a date for later that evening.

"Maybe." I moved on. "Joey didn't get along with some of these people, did he?"

Angela said, "Like who? John and Elmer?"

"Leo said there were others, too."

"That's true," she said. "I think 'didn't get along' is putting it mildly."

"So what was he doing that was pissing them off?"

"Plenty." She took a sip of her drink. "Something I learned early in my career is that once you take away brute force, power comes from two sources: money and information. Joey didn't have any money. So that leaves information." She shrugged. "He dug things up and outed these people for their misdeeds."

"Such as?"

"Oh, he kept a running tally of violations. He knew the municipal codes better than I did. He kept his ears open. He nailed those assholes on various infractions, and more than a few times."

She saw that I wasn't quite following and sat up, waving her cup for emphasis. "Some of the people you guys went to school with have spent the last decades building little fortunes here. They feel like they've earned the money and all the privileges that go with it. Whether they did or didn't is beside the point. But they came to believe that they own this town and can do whatever they want here." She smiled crookedly. "My brother was out to get them. He busted them left and right and made it hard for them to add to their piles of gold. They had to pay fines, answer lawsuits, all that. His legal nitpicking drove them crazy."

"Did they smack him back?"

"Oh, yeah. They were always siccing the borough on him. They got citations issued all the time. Sanitation, parking, loitering, whatever they could find. They tried countersuing him for mounting frivolous lawsuits, but he didn't have anything to take, so there was no point. And that made them even madder at him. He had them."

I thought about what she was telling me. "Okay, so what if

whatever he was after at the end there would have caused one of these characters a lot of trouble?"

"That wouldn't be a surprise."

"Then how does this sound: I come here. I talk to you and Leo and Mrs. Eldridge. I have something like a conversation with Jimmy Zag. Someone hears about all this and starts to worry that I might stumble on something. Maybe the same something that Joey was after. Something that would cause this person a serious problem. Or persons."

I felt a cold prickle on the back of my neck. Angela was peering out the windshield, her brow knit.

I went ahead with it. "What if he didn't fall?"

She turned to face me. "That's crazy. You know how crazy? It would mean that Louie Zag is right. That's how crazy."

I nodded. "I guess that's right."

"But who would do something like that?"

"Someone who wanted to shut him up about whatever he found at the library or at the borough office or wherever." I rattled the ice in the bottom of my cup. It seemed odd that no one else had caught this. "He never said anything to you?"

"No."

"Or did he, and you just didn't pay attention?"

Her eyes cooled and slid my way. "I listened to every stupid word he said. Most of the time, I was the only one who did. Me, not you. Okay?"

"Don't bark at me," I said."

She banged her fist on the steering wheel as if she hadn't heard me. "But then you show up after he's dead and try to take over where he left off. Now. After all this time."

"Well, then, how about if I just go home?" I said. "We'll leave whatever happened to him alone and you can all live happily ever after?"

"*Fuck* you, Richie!" Her eyes were completely black and her olive skin had flushed red. She was close to throwing her drink in my face. "Go ahead. Go back to New York. Nobody wants you here, anyway."

I stared at her. "What was that?"

Her hands were shaking. She picked up her cup and put it down again. Her mouth formed a hard line, but her eyes had turned soft and sad.

I said, "Don't you want to find out what happened to him?"

"Yes." The word came out on a shaky fall. "Of course, I do."

"Then what's the problem?"

She didn't speak for a moment. Then she said, "You. You're the problem."

"Why me?"

"You're selfish. You always were."

"Excuse me?"

"You take what you want and then you go away."

"This is –" I stopped, now feeling my cheeks getting hot. "What's that got to do with Joey?"

She looked at me for a brief second with hurt and anger drawing her fine features, then turned her face away. "Nothing," she said. "It has to do with you and me."

"Oh." I was being careful. "What about you and me?"

She stared out into the darkness. "You're married to someone who's probably a fantastic woman and you have two beautiful daughters," she said. "You live in New York and when you leave, you'll never come back here again. I might live the rest of my life here, and I might meet someone to spend my days with, but that's not very likely. It's slim pickings. But, whatever, after you go, chances are I won't see you any time soon. Maybe never."

"And?"

"And I still have feelings for you. No, that's not right. I have feelings for you *again*. After all this time."

"By feelings, you –"

"I want to finish what we started, okay?" she said. "I want to pick up where we left off. Or I want to start all over. I don't know." She let out a sigh that seemed to fill that closed space with regret. "What I do know is that we can't."

"So?"

"So nothing. We can't." She grabbed the handle, gave a rough tug, opened the door with her shoulder, and slid out. The car rocked when she slammed it behind her. She walked off along the narrow deck and into the darkness.

She stayed away until I started to worry. I got out and walked to the fence. She had descended the plank steps and was sitting on a tree trunk that had fallen a few feet back from the water's edge. The moon was up and the surface of the river was dappled with glittering points of light. Her dark shape was hunched over and I wondered if I should just leave her alone with whatever thoughts she was entertaining.

It was getting late, though, and so I followed her down the steps to the soft, mossy earth of the riverbank. I gave her plenty of space, moving around to brush off a place at the opposite end of the log. A bass broke the surface of the water with a slap and a splash. Angela wouldn't look at me. I sat and waited.

Presently she said, "Joey had a boat."

"A boat."

"Some piece of shit motorboat someone gave him. One of those old wooden ones. I'm going to have to get rid of that, too." She paused. "Or I guess I could get in it and sail away from this fucking place."

I didn't have a comment on that. She sat forward and I felt a change in the air. Something had been carried away on the night breeze.

"I thought about what you said." She sounded reasonable. "And I agree that there's a possibility that Joey didn't just fall. That he was pushed." She paused. "Murdered, in other words. Or maybe whoever it was didn't mean for it to happen that way. But it did."

I said, "What are you going to do about it?"

"I was going to ask you that. Since you're the one who opened the door in the first place."

"The problem is there's no evidence," I said. "I'm not a cop and neither are you. I'm definitely not a detective. I don't know what to do next."

She looked at me, her face cool in the moonlight. "So, what, you started and now you want to drop it? That seems to be a habit of yours."

Though she was wearing a small, tight smile, her tone was not kind, and I decided to let it be. I was in no mood to resume the battle.

"We could talk to Tim Raines," I said.

She shook her head. "He won't do anything. None of them will. Nobody believes it was anything but an accident." She tossed a stone into the water. "We'd have to find something to change their minds."

"Maybe what he was working on at the library?" I offered.

"Maybe. I don't know..." From her quiet tone, I got the impression that she was regretting her outburst in the car.

"Also, there's, uh..."

She glanced at me. "What?"

"Crystal. She's been kind of hinting that she knows something."

She returned her gaze to the glittering water and tossed another stone. Hard. "Why don't you just do her and get it over with?"

"Because I'm married. And she's too young for me."

"Then let her give you a blow job. I won't tell." She threw a third stone, this one even harder. It chopped the water in an angry little spurt.

"Why are you mad at me?" I said. "I came here to help."

"No, you didn't," she said. "You came here to make yourself feel better."

That caught me. It was true, or at least partly so. That wasn't all of it, though, and I felt the heat rising again.

"Maybe," I said. "But if it turns out that Joey was murdered, and we find out who did it, it will be because of me." I threw a stone of my own. "So fuck you."

I stood up and walked over the slippery moss and climbed the steps to the deck. I had half a mind to drive off in a huff and leave her there. Then I remembered we had brought her car. I wasn't going anywhere.

So I leaned against the fender and waited. It was another ten minutes before I heard the slap of footsteps on the wet earth and then the creak of the wooden steps. She walked slowly to the Volvo, then opened the door on her side.

"I'm sorry about what I said back there." She wouldn't look at me. "It was really unfair. I want you to know that I'm glad that you came here. I know you did it for Joey. And it matters that you're the only one who cares what happened to him." She paused again before raising her eyes. "Listen, I need to tell you that I am definitely not in love with you."

I said, "I didn't think you were."

"It was kind of touch-and-go there for a little while," she said. "But I ain't gonna let that happen. No way."

"Okay."

"Though I've been wondering if your wife might be up for a threesome."

I snickered, relieved that we had pulled back from the edge. "I can ask her." I said. "Except that right now, she's kind of upset with me. But I could introduce the two of you."

Now she laughed. It was nice music.

I said, "Can we go?"

"Yeah," she said. "Let's go."

We got out of the car. She started up the steps. I stayed where I was. She peered at me. "What's wrong?"

"I promised I'd meet her tonight."

"Her who?" She watched my face. "Oh... my... God," she said. "I don't believe this."

"It's not what you think," I said, sounding lame.

"What I think is that you're a fifty-year-old man and you're running off to meet a cupcake."

"Oh, okay, then it *is* what you think," I said. "But I'm not fifty. Not yet. I've got eight months to go."

She was waiting, her mouth twisting into a smile, enjoying my discomfort.

I said, "She made a point of telling me that she knew things about people around here. Things that I wouldn't believe. *Secrets*. That's the way she put it."

"That's probably true," Angela said with a short laugh. "I'm sure she knows quite a few secrets. Especially about the men."

"Maybe Joey was one of them," I said. Her eyebrows arched. I backed up a little. "I think it's possible."

Now she regarded me with a wise expression. "You've just got to know, don't you?"

"Know what?"

"If you still have anything going on." Her smile returned, though now thinner.

I knew I wasn't going to win this one. "I need to go," I said, and started backing up.

"You can take my car, if you want." She let out another laugh. "Just don't get anything on the seats."

"I'll walk."

She wagged a finger. "Be careful."

Careful, indeed.

Wyanossing lay silent under the purple veil of the spring night. I was again amazed to be able to look up and see stars by the thousands. When I was a kid, I had imagined God walking across the heavens and spreading them out of a sack, like Johnny Appleseed. It was a nice memory.

Especially on this night, with innocence nowhere in sight. The shadows were murky rather than kind and the quiet was eerie. Where were the cars? The shouts and laughter? Where was the music? I heard nothing save for the occasional sound of a door slamming somewhere far off. Even the air was still. Moving along the sidewalk, I could imagine someone dogging me on soundless steps.

So it was too perfect to find the little church cloaked in an even deeper darkness. Narrow and austere, the building was shingled in dark green and huddled among four pine trees that stood sentry on the small lawn in front. Rose bushes showed dots of pale white on either side of the stone steps.

St. Michael's bells tolled nine times. The stillness and silence that followed the last dying echo brought on some creeps. It was too quiet. I told myself I was going to give this experiment about five minutes, and then be gone. After what I had seen at Joey's trailer and the vandalism to my rental car, I was in no mood for foolishness. My visit had been intended as a melancholy homecoming, sad but simple. The plan was to pay my respects to a departed friend and then return home to my life. Instead, I found myself standing in a lightless churchyard, waiting for a girl who came off as too young for me to be even looking at without adult supervision.

I whispered into the night. "Joey, man, you see what I'm doing for you?"

"What was that?"

I almost jumped out of my skin. Once my heart came down off the spike, I stood gazing at a vision that had appeared from the shadows between the trees.

She was wearing a wraparound skirt of lily white and a blouse just a few shades darker that was tied under her breasts to reveal her stomach. Her hair was tied back and she wore hoops from her ears. She was, in fact, as lovely an image of femininity that I had ever beheld, and yet there was something off about the picture. She had been blessed with a fine face and body, and she knew how to dress. And yet as she stepped out from beneath the limbs of that evergreen, she reminded me more of a clumsy child making an entrance in a school play.

"You're here," she said.

She sounded pleased. At the same time, I thought I caught a hint of a vague disappointment as she discovered that the New York actor was just another man who would hasten at her call. She was probably also thinking that I would try to get my almost-fifty-year-old bones fastened on her. Indeed, with that look, she had to know she'd draw vampires of all ages. And so she struck a pose, standing quite still and allowing me to feast my eyes. Which I did for a few seconds more before averting my gaze. This wasn't why I had shown up.

"So." That was my opening line. "What are we doing?"

"Around the back," she said and beckoned me with her fingers.

I followed her, watching the sweet sway of her hips and thinking that if Roy Dewitt or some other mug was waiting to knock me cold, watching Crystal walk ahead of me was not such a bad way to face it.

I am a fool.

I'm thankful to say that no such thing happened. She led me along the path of flagstones that circled to the rear of the church to the tiny graveyard, a patch of ground with no more than two dozen stones, all of them weathered by a hundred years of wear. The plot was enclosed by a low wrought-iron fence and, yes, the hinges of the gate creaked when she opened it.

In the far corner was a bench with a seat and back of hardwood slats. Crystal made a show of swooping down to perch there, waving a hand like a gypsy dancer for me to join her.

Once I was settled, she regarded me with the sort of ardent stare that children produce when they want to be taken seriously. She had dropped the carnal act and was instead regarding me with grave eyes. This was a relief: I do not know how I would have handled her pussycat act, alone and in the inky darkness.

The first words out of her mouth were, "I meant what I said about getting out of this place."

That was her starting point. She next launched into a rambling litany of complaints. The people in that town were stupid. They treated her like *she* was stupid. The men were all jerks. She went on with it for a couple minutes, earnestly, trying to convince me of how dim her prospects were in that little burg. I knew all this, of course; it was much of the reason I had made my own escape.

That was me. I doubted she had the tools to perform the same leap. She assumed that getting out was the hardest part. That was only the beginning. She was having enough trouble in Wyanossing. The city was a far tougher game. Too tough for the many who went running home, defeated.

None of this occurred to her as she rambled on and I found my mind drifting to thoughts of my kids and my wife, Angela, Joey, my little town. It was some drama, all right…

It dawned on me that she had stopped talking and by her

expression, had just asked me something.

"Well, I'll help you if I can," I said.

She cocked her head, her eyes narrowed, and again the empty-headed, hometown tart stepped out of the way for another character, one who was measuring me with a sharp and knowing stare.

I sensed that whatever the question, I had given the wrong answer.

"But you can't, isn't that true?" she said.

"I'm sorry," I said, "I'm –"

"It was terrible what happened to him."

I stumbled on the sudden change of subject. She was studying one of the gravestones. "I'm so sorry for your loss." It wasn't an act; the troubled look in her eyes was for real. Her voice had changed as well, dropping a notch deeper and slowing. I was seeing and hearing another side of her I'd never imagined. So much for stereotypes. And for blonde jokes.

I was moved by her kindness and said, simply, "We were best friends when we were kids."

"I thought so. That makes it hard. I know. I've lost friends, too."

She clasped her hands together and bowed her head slightly, folding inward with an odd sort of gravity. I got a sense that she was waiting for me to say something about Joey. As in something that might give her an opening to tell me what she knew.

"That's why I'm still here." I said.

"Because you think there's something wrong about the way he died."

I nodded, feeling my way. "That's right." I paused for a few seconds, then said. "What do you think?"

"I don't know," she said. "The police say it was an accident."

"Police meaning Officer Dewitt?"

"It's what was in the paper," she responded smoothly. "They said the investigation is closed."

"They said."

She was quiet, gazing at the white stones. "He made trouble for some of the people in this town," she said. "I would overhear them talking about him at Charlotte's. They didn't think I was paying attention. But I was."

"Who's them?"

"Oh, you know. John Miller and Elmer Smalley and that crowd. The businessmen and political people. I always knew when Joey had done something that got them upset. They would call him names. You know, *freak*, and *dopehead*. And worse." Her voice dropped another notch. "Sometimes they'd talk about what they wanted to do to him. To shut him up. This one time I heard John say, 'One of these days, we're going to fix his ass,' or something like that." She came up with a wan smile. "He used to call them names, too. Some really nasty things. And not behind their backs, either. He didn't care if they heard what he said. He liked making them mad."

"Yeah," I said. "He always did."

We were both quiet, conjuring our own visions of crazy Joey. I let the moment pass and then said, "Were you and he good friends?"

She said, "Well, he was around a lot, you know. I thought he was funny. We hung out a little bit." Her tone sharpened. "But that was all."

"Did you ever go to Nock Hill?"

"Sure. Everybody's been to Nock Hill."

"I meant with Joey."

She lingered over her answer. "A couple times, yeah."

"What were you doing?"

She turned her head to give me a hard look. "Why don't you just ask me if I did it with him and get it over with?" Her face appeared pale and baleful in the blue light. "Didn't you hear what I just said? The answer is no. I'm sure that surprises you. I bet you think I've laid down for every guy in town."

"I didn't –"

"You really shouldn't make so much of first impressions." In the next moment, she let out a small laugh and shook her head in a wistful way. "He was cute and really funny. For an older guy, I mean. I liked him right away. He was nice to me. Now and then we would hang out. But he never tried anything. Never. The truth was he thought I was too young for him."

Joey? I marveled. What I was hearing defied the laws of the universe.

"The first time we went up there, we just walked around," she continued. "I could tell he loved it. I think he knew every tree. The second time we went because I wanted a private place to talk to him. I had something personal…" She stopped, took a breath. "So we talked. That was all. Just the two of us."

I didn't ask what they had discussed, figuring she'd share it if and when she was ready. Though I was nothing to her, certainly not a friend like Joey had been. Not someone she could trust with private matters.

"So he knew some of my secrets." She pondered for a few seconds. "He died with them." I saw a tear well in the corner of her eye and her shoulders hunched as if she was cold. She sighed and dabbed the rivulet on her cheek with the side of her hand.

I realized that I was getting caught up in her little drama and needed to get on firmer ground. "Did he tell you any of his secrets?" I said.

Cooler eyes shifted my way. "Like what?"

"For one thing, I've been wondering why he was spending so much time in the library in the weeks before he died."

"The library?" She frowned. "I don't know. He didn't say anything to me."

"He was looking at drawings of old farms outside of town," I said.

She started to shake her head and then stopped and said, "Okay, wait a minute. There was this one thing. It was a Sunday morning, and he called to ask me if I wanted to go for a hike."

"When was this?"

"Maybe a month ago. It was just a walk, really. We drove out there and parked and walked across the fields. He brought along a camera. And he took some pictures of the old farms."

"This was where?"

"Between Line Road and the ridge. You know where I'm talking about?"

I remembered how the road ran along a secondary rise in the topography. Farms had been laid out in the shallow valley between there and Mahoning Ridge. It was the same section of land catalogued in the plat books at the library. The ones Joey had been studying.

"So you were, what, walking around people's houses?"

"There aren't many houses anymore," she said. "A couple of the old barns are left. But someone still farms the land."

"So he was taking pictures."

"Yeah, he kept snapping away until the memory was full," she went on. "And he did take a couple shots of me. Just goofing, you know."

I did know. Goofing was what Joey had always done. And yet in his last weeks, he had been conducting research of the plats of old farms outside of town. Including, as Crystal claimed, a trek to those same parts to take pictures. Something on that rolling farmland had snagged his interest. And then he had died.

These musings were interrupted by the sound of an engine and a flash of headlights. I stood up and took a few steps toward the gate, but the car had already cut around the front of the church.

I turned back intending to ask Crystal about the Sable to find that she had slipped into the darkness as if blown by a breeze. I surveyed the shadows, searching for a shred of her white skirt and saw nothing. It seemed the young lady knew the dark corners of her little town very well.

I walked out of the churchyard and followed the flagstones around front in time to peer down the block and see a car pull away from the curb and cut into the narrow alley that connected First and Second streets.

I was standing at the sink, sipping a glass of water, when Angela appeared in the kitchen doorway. She was wearing the t-shirt that hung to her knees. Her hair was pulled into two braids. Isabel did that sometimes and I always thought it was adorable.

"So," she said. "Did you have a nice time?"

"It was interesting."

"I can imagine. You can tell me all about it tomorrow."

I smiled at her. "You waited up for me?"

She said, "Good night, Richie."

I heard her climb the steps, pad along the hallway, and close her bedroom door.

I said, "Good night, Angela."

10.

I woke up a little before nine. After a few moments spent sifting through a dreamy photo album of my wife and daughters, my thoughts turned to what had transpired in the past twenty-four hours, from Tim Raines to Louie Zag to the library to Joey's single-wide, and then back to Angela's house and my trashed rental car. After the drama on the banks of the river, I had topped off the night with an encounter with Crystal that had answered nothing.

I rolled out and made my way downstairs to find that Angela had left a note for me to call her at work. I decided to put that off and took a shower, after which I carried my two sets of clothes to the basement. Once again, I would spend an hour wrapped in towels while I waited.

My first call was to Isabel at her office. She surprised me by sounding cheerful, though in an absent workday way. I gave her a report of what was going on and for the first time she didn't get all bent out of shape, instead listening thoughtfully. I heard a hint of resignation in her voice, as if she had given up on talking me out of this silliness. Maybe she thought it was a midlife crisis. If that was the case, she had to be thinking this jaunt to my hometown was better than a Harley and a bimbo.

I told her about Crystal, too.

"She sounds like some piece of work."

"I can't get a fix on her. I think she knows something, but she's playing it cool. She's got this game going on."

"Is she pretty?"

I was ready. "If you like that sort," I said. "She'd be prettier if she didn't push so hard."

She had heard enough about Wyanossing. She told me her sister, who was having husband problems of a far more serious nature, had come up from Philly to hang out with her and the girls. They had turned the visit into a big pajama party and were making a game out of daddy wandering off and the womenfolk holding down the homestead. Hearing this, I felt a little sad and quite useless. It wasn't the first time; I lived with three females.

Isabel ended the exchange on a placid and trusting note, which made me feel safe and boring. *Welcome to middle age*, I reflected. We traded some sweet talk and then said good-bye.

I made the call to another of the women in my life while I sat at her kitchen table with a second cup of coffee before me.

"Well, how was your date?" When I didn't respond, she must have sensed that the joke had gone thin, because she dropped it for a more even tone. "You going to tell me what happened?"

I knew she was dying to ask if anything wicked had occurred or what carnal goodies Crystal had dangled. I told her what had transpired in the churchyard, including the story about Joey and Crystal and Nock Hill.

"She said he never tried anything with her."

"That's good to know."

"You know, I think she's gotten a bad rap. I mean the idea that she's some kind of hussy or whatever."

Angela said, "From what I've seen, she doesn't do much to discourage it."

"I know, but I had her wrong, too. She puts on a show. She really cared about Joey and he cared about her. They were friends."

Angela didn't know what to say to that. I told her about Crystal evaporating when the Sable drove near, thus ending our evening.

We left it there. I said I was going to see Leo about the rental car and asked her if there was anywhere in town I could buy some clothes.

"We don't have Louis Vuitton, if that's what you're asking," she said, her voice lightening.

"No? Then, forget it."

"But we do have a Dollar Store right down on First Street," she said. They sell khakis and sport shirts." She started to laugh. "I think they have a tailor on the premises, if you need something fitted."

I was telling her how glad I was that she was enjoying herself when I heard her doorbell ring.

Angela heard it, too. "Who's that?"

I carried the phone into the dining room and peeked through the front door glass. Beyond the thin curtain, I saw a profile I recognized and the unmistakable cut of a uniform.

I said, "Shit."

"Who is it?"

I lowered my voice. "It's Tim Raines."

I considered ducking him. But he of course knew I was there, so I had to face him, no matter how ridiculous I appeared. I returned the phone to the kitchen, crossed the living room, and opened the door.

"Good morning," I said.

Whatever he thought about me presenting myself that way, he didn't show any reaction. In fact, he didn't look surprised at all. Of course, he'd had a lot of practice putting on stone faces. For all I knew, he could have been chortling behind those tight lips.

"I catch you at a bad time?" he asked

"I only brought one change of clothes," I said. "Everything's in the, you know, the dryer." I made a vague gesture in the direction of the basement.

"Is Angela here?"

"At her office."

"Do you have a few minutes you can spare?" He was being extra polite this morning.

I said, "Sure," and held the door wide.

He stepped into the living room, looked around, and said, "I always thought this was a great old house."

I offered him a seat in the armchair as if I owned the place, then went through some gymnastics getting myself and my two towels arranged on the couch. It remembered hearing that cops liked to get suspects stripped down to make them feel vulnerable. I understood the feeling. But I wasn't guilty of anything; I was the victim.

That was what he had come to talk about. "We went over the vehicle and didn't find anything," he said. "I mean nothing that would point us to any suspects." He opened his metal clipboard, produced a sheet of paper and handed it over: my incident report.

I glanced at the entries on the form. "So it was random?" I knew the chances of me being that unlucky were small and perked an ear for his reaction.

"It's possible that you were targeted," he said. "The question would be why." He shifted his position. "A couple things. And I know this might sound crazy. But is it possible that someone was holding something against you from way back? Someone who might have been nursing it all these years? So then when word gets around that you're back in town..." He cocked an eyebrow. "Does that bring anything to mind?"

It was the same idea Isabel had put forth. I said, "I didn't have that many enemies," at the same time, thinking, *Joey, now, he had enemies*, but kept it to myself. "Anyway, who would care, after all this time?"

"Well, with some people, you never know."

I noticed that he looked uncomfortable, more so than me.

He said, "There's something else that came up."

I waited.

"Crystal Nash."

I went on alert, wondering how I would explain our rendezvous the night before. "What about her?"

"She's been going around bragging on you a little bit," he said. "Telling people that you're going to help her become an actress or something like that."

I put on my best laconic smile. "She's been talking to me about that, yeah. She has this idea in her head. I think she's just dreaming out loud. What's that got to do with anything?"

"Well, Crystal is…" He hesitated again. "How can I put this? She's popular."

"You're saying she's got admirers?"

Tim laughed. "That's it, exactly. *Admirers*. She's very attractive and she's a flirt. She gets guys buzzing around her like bees sometimes."

"Like Officer Dewitt?"

"Yes," he said in a more measured tone. "Like him. He's kind of a hard-ass, but he's a very good cop. That's not who I mean. What I'm telling you is that she doesn't mind one bit making guys jealous. So I'm thinking, if one of them hears her talking about this acting business, and thinks you're helping her run off, who knows what he might do?"

I thought that over while keeping an eye on my visitor. He seemed just a bit too composed. and his spiel came off as rehearsed. But to what end? In any case, the short view, it didn't make any sense that someone like Tim described would trash my car. That would only keep me from leaving.

I decided to throw out a fastball. "So you don't believe this has anything to do with Joey?"

He stopped to treat me to a thoughtful gaze. "What would make you think that?"

"Well, I came here because of him. To visit his grave and pay my respects. I know that got around town. And I told you that what happened to him doesn't add up. Because of the height and all that. I talked to Angela and Leo about it. And Mrs. Eldridge at the library."

He watched me, looking pensive. I went on.

"Anyway, I'm in town a few days and his trailer gets ransacked. Then someone slashes the tires and busts out the windows on my rental car. All that might point to something."

I could tell by the set of this eyes that he didn't much care for the amateur sleuth routine. He said, "Such as?"

"Such as that somebody in this town doesn't like what I'm doing."

Tim considered for a moment, then shook his head. "Joey fell off that rock, Richie," he said. "I know that might be hard to take because you two had been friends and all, but that's what happened. We conducted an exhaustive investigation and his death was determined to be accidental. But even if it wasn't, I don't see how it connects to you at all. It's not like you know anything."

He paused and I noticed the tiny question mark that he ended on; almost inaudible, but it was there. I wasn't about to give anything else away and sat back with a shrug. Nothing I said was going to change his mind.

In the next moment, I was saved by the bell. Literally; the little alarm on the dryer went off.

"My clothes," I said.

"That's okay, we're done here," Tim said, and stood up. "We can talk again when the Avis people show up. They're going to bring you another car, right?"

"That's what they said."

"You'll be able to head back home, then."

I have a good ear. If I didn't, I wouldn't have caught the little note that told me that it wasn't a question. I saw him out and watched him get in his cruiser and drive away.

The Dollar Store was down the block and around the corner from Leo's garage. I bought two pairs of khakis that fit when I rolled the cuffs, two thin polyester sport shirts in pastel colors, a three-pack of boxer shorts, and a six-pack of white socks. Everything was cheap, dull, and pedestrian. Maybe I would create a whole new style when I got back to New York. Though I assumed someone had already beaten me to it. *Nerd chic* or whatever.

Neither the manager of the store in her little cubicle, nor the kid stocking shelves, nor the dull-eyed girl who rang my purchases recognized me and I wondered if I had begun a slow fade into the wallpaper, devolving by the day into a fellow who could live out his days as a happy hometown fool.

Leo and I stood in the open bay, looking over the Lumina.

"I can't see where anyone's been under the hood," he was telling me. "I haven't cranked the engine yet. I'll pull a plug and open the fuel line. But I'm pretty sure the engine's okay." He tugged a shop rag from his back pocket and wiped his hands. "The other shit, the tires and the windshield, that's a mess, man. I think this was your basic hit-and-split."

I said, "I can't believe they had the time to get away with it. Anybody could have looked out a window and seen."

Leo eyed me. "You don't remember Halloween? Get in, do the damage, and duck down an alley. Ten, fifteen seconds, maybe. I can see it."

"That was in the dark of night, Leo. And we were little guys."

"Yeah, well..."

"What I want to know is why."

Leo shrugged as he wiped his hands on the rag. "Maybe somebody saw those tags and thought they'd teach the New Yawker a lesson. We got some punks around here." He stopped for a moment. "And maybe they had some help."

"Meaning?"

He shrugged. I could tell that the matter bothered him mightily. This was no way to treat guests, especially a homeboy who was a true friend.

After a few more moments studying the damage, I said, "You know I've been talking to other people about what happened to Joey."

He looked at me. "Yeah?"

"I'm just saying."

He mulled that, frowning.

I said, "I keep meaning to ask if you know anybody in town who drives a white Mercury Sable."

His forehead creased. "Seems like I do. Why?"

"I was just curious. I thought I saw someone."

"I can't remember right now, but it'll come to me." He went back to fiddling under the hood.

I was gazing out at the street, pondering all the strange business, when a new Chrysler approached the corner, stopped, and sat idling.

After a few seconds, the sedan rolled onto Leo's lot and up to the bay.

Elmer Smalley was behind the wheel. He pushed the door open with some effort and hauled his tonnage out of the seat. Freed of the extra weight, the Chrysler bobbed like a buoy.

He strolled up and spent a few moments staring at the Lumina. "I heard what happened," he said. "Looks like somebody did a hell of a job there." He edged into the bay. He and Leo had not exchanged greetings and I noticed Leo was watching him with a rude stare.

Elmer waddled around the car. "Damn miscreants," he said. He looked at me, his eyes cold blue orbs in the folds of his face. "Sorry as hell to see this happen here."

"I'm sure it's bad for the tourist trade," I said.

He gave me puzzled look. "The what, now?"

Leo said, "He said it's bad for the fucking tourist trade." It was impossible to miss the raw edge on his tone. He didn't like Elmer, a fact that the man either didn't comprehend or decided to ignore as he went about asking questions about the car, to which Leo gave snide answers. He asked me what Tim Raines had said about the incident.

"Just one of those things," I told him. "It's what happens when we don't patrol our borders."

Leo snickered. Elmer blinked, then smiled slightly, getting it this time.

"Well, I'm damned sorry about it." He couldn't have meant it less. He turned around and ambled out of the bay. Leo didn't look up from the engine again until the Chrysler had pulled away at a lordly pace and swung into the street.

"I should have known that fat prick'd be around," he said. "He has his nose in everybody's beeswax."

I said, "I wonder how he found out about it."

"His buddy Roy Dewitt probably told him. Plus he keeps one of those police scanners in that damn boat. So he can stick his nose into the cops' business, too. Fucking Nazi."

I laughed, but Leo was serious. "No, really, you see the bumper stickers? Him and Dewitt, John Miller and that crowd, they're all wingnuts. They think Oklahoma City was the chickens coming home to roost. September 11th really has them cranked up. They want people like you and me locked up in concentration camps, man. For real."

It was an echo of one of his rants from twenty-five years ago. If Louie was the comedian, and I was the artist, Joey and Leo were the bomb-throwers, the guys who seethed to mount a working-class revolt.

Joey had turned his words into action. Leo was mostly talk, berating us mercilessly about the coming Revolution until someone would say, "Hey, Leo, why don't you shut the fuck up?" Which would send him stomping off into the darkness with a string of furious curses. A few minutes later, he would return as if nothing had happened, goofing, his stoned eyes aglitter.

He'd say, "Okay, what were we talking about?" and everyone would crack up.

Now he was back to Elmer Smalley. "Those guys like to call up these goddamn radio shows and blow their stacks about how the country's going to hell. He's on the Borough Council and he's always trying to run that. He shows up at school board meetings to see if he can get books banned. He's like our local Joe-fucking-McCarthy, that guy. Meanwhile, he's getting jerked off by every developer in the valley because he lets them off on zoning or whatever."

He stopped and looked around, his eyes flitting about for spies. I smiled, falling into yet another momentary time warp.

"Oh, yeah, I forgot to tell you," Leo said with a hard laugh. "They march around in the woods."

I didn't understand. "Who does?"

"Who do you think? Dewitt and Miller and a bunch of their dipshit friends. They put on fatigues and pretend they're in the Army."

"Are you talking about a militia?"

"More like Cub Scouts with loaded weapons. I don't think Elmer does much marching, though." He got an odd look on his face and looked behind him before he spoke again. "But you know, Richie, those guys..."

"What?"

"They all hated Joey, man." He glanced around again, then leaned closer. Keeping his voice furtive, he said, "And I've been thinking maybe it was one of them who did him."

I watched his expression, trying to guess if this was a goof I wasn't catching. I didn't tell him that Angela and I had discussed the same notion. But that had been in the dark of night, when imaginings ran wild. This was in the clear light of day and I couldn't see it. And in such a small town, somebody would have talked by now.

I kept it light. "Say what, now?"

"I said, what if one of those guys killed Joey?" He crossed his arms, and started to pace, two steps in one direction, two in the other. He was dead serious. "They wanted him out of the way. You know that, right? Couldn't stand his ass. Because he fucked with them all the time." His eyes were shifting back and forth, like a hack actor in a B-grade mystery film. "You hear what I'm saying?"

"Do you have proof of anything?"

"I know what I know," he muttered.

He was watching me closely to see if I was buying any of this. I could have kissed Angela for choosing that moment to call. As I flipped my phone open, Leo gave me another long look, then went back to the Lumina.

"Where are you?" she said.

I told her what Leo had explained about the car. I also mentioned that Elmer Smalley had just happened to drop by.

She said, "What a surprise."

"What's this I hear about these guys tramping around in the woods with guns?" I asked her. "Leo said that John Miller and Dewitt and some other people have been playing 'GI Joe' around here."

"Oh, that." She laughed shortly. "All I know is what was in the paper. They say they're *training*."

"Training for what?"

"For the day when Wyanossing is attacked by terrorists, I guess. I don't know. Why?"

I hesitated. "Because Leo says they might have been after Joey."

She sighed and said, "And yesterday it was Louie Zag and his evil conspiracy. Leo doesn't know what he's talking about. Those guys are clowns."

"Clowns with guns."

"Nobody was shot here," she said tersely.

"Well, no, but..."

"But what? You two just can't give it up, can you?"

I didn't want to answer that one.

"So now what?" she said.

I thought about it and said, "You up for some sightseeing?"

She picked me up in her Volvo a half hour later and twenty minutes after that we were turning off a two-lane onto the gravel road that sliced over the top of the ridge and into the next valley and the town of North Cumberland. I recalled that for years, various secluded clearings on this high ground had been the scenes of wild parties, chosen at the last minute and then drawn on maps that were passed from hand to furtive hand as if they contained atomic secrets.

The road was narrow and steep and crowded with a tangle of brush. Angela took her time steering up the slope. When it flattened at the crest of the ridge, she pulled off into a cleared spot at the base of a fire tower that stretched a hundred feet into the afternoon sky. When we were teenagers, anyone could climb the twelve flights of steel steps to the landing that was just beneath the ranger's observation platform and from there see for miles into the distance. Those days where over; the base of the tower was now enclosed by an eight-foot cyclone fence topped with coils of barbed wire and festooned with signs warning of the dire official fates awaiting those caught within its confines.

Angela turned off the engine and we got out to look around. The lock on the gate was beginning to rust and weeds were running riot around the bottom of the fence. When I circled to the back side, I found a section where the barbed wire had broken loose and was hanging down in a limp curl. I called Angela to join me.

We didn't discuss it. She studied the fence for a few seconds, then treated me to a sidelong glance. "You're not too fat to get over, are you?"

I laced my fingers into a step-up. "I'd say 'ladies first,' but since there ain't any present, you can –"

"Yeah, yeah, let's go," she said and placed her shoe into my webbed hands.

She made the climb with medium effort and minor cursing. I was grateful that she didn't stand on the other side to watch me take my turn, instead poking around the bottom of the tower while I inflicted torture on my bones and muscles getting up and over. She did turn around when I hit the ground like a sack of potatoes.

"You all right?" she said.

I gave her the gift of a withering glance as I brushed the dirt from my knees and hands. She didn't wait for me to start up the stairs.

I wasn't terrified of heights, as Joey had been. At the same time, climbing steep metal steps with nothing between me and a growing drop except a thin steel railing was not my first choice for a fun afternoon. The spring breeze became a whipping wind the higher we progressed and the tower swayed with creaks and groans. I distracted myself by following the motion of Angela's butt as she climbed ahead of me. I was sure Isabel would understand, though at that point in the jittery ascent, I didn't care.

Halfway up, I started to slow, and Angela looked over her shoulder, all cool-eyed. "You want to stop and take a breather?" she said

Another few minutes on the treadmill and we reached the top landing. The trapdoor was padlocked, preventing access into the observation booth and the maximum. Still, we were forty feet above the highest treetops.

I sat on the steps to relax my burning thighs and catch my breath while Angela leaned on the railing to gaze at the panorama. The haze had burned off and the view was clear for a good ten miles up the valley. She looked very pretty with her face bathed in the light. Happy, too, as she surveyed the rolling hills and forests of new green all the way to the river.

I hated to dispel the mood, but we weren't up there to admire the scenery. I rose to stand at her side, my knuckles white on the rail.

She said, "Okay, what are we looking for?"

"Joey was looking at the plats of properties out here."

"Which ones?" There were only a half-dozen structures spread across the sloping acres of farmland.

I peered for a few moments, then noticed something familiar and pointed. "You see that stone barn?"

She stared narrow-eyed, shielding her eyes. "I see it. Looks like it's all covered in vines and stuff."

"I think he was interested in that one."

"How do you know that?"

It was time to tell her. "Because when I was in the library, I saw a – " I heard her catch a breath and stopped in mid-sentence. "What's wrong?"

"A car. Coming up the road."

I stared down the slope. It took a few seconds for me to catch the motion through the foliage. "Is it the rangers?"

"Don't think so."

"Tell me it's a white Sable."

"It's a white something," she said. "I can't see what. It keeps going under the trees."

"You sure it's not a cop?"

"No." She kept her gaze fixed. "Wait, it stopped."

We had two choices. One was to stay where we were and see what developed. The other was to rush down to the ground and confront whoever was stalking us. Angela, being the smart one, came up with a third plan.

"I'll go down. You stay up here."

"What will that accomplish?"

"You can watch and tell me where it is. I'll see if I can spot whoever's driving."

"Why don't we try –"

"We don't have time, that's why."

I got it. We couldn't afford the minutes it would take for me to creep down the swaying steps and then haul my carcass over the fence. She was fit and it was something she could do more quickly. My pride was bruised, but I saw the logic. Not that it mattered at that point; she was already three flights down and scampering like a squirrel.

I grabbed the swaying railing and scanned the forest until I picked out a patch of white roof creeping upward. The overhang of the trees and the steep angle of the road made it hard to get a clear view. All I could tell was that the vehicle was moving very slowly, as if the driver was trying to approach undetected.

Angela let out a sharp whistle. I looked over the railing, then closed my eyes at the dizzying sight. When I opened them again, I saw her peering upward, her arms wide, waiting for me to share what I could see. I looked down the slope of the ridge and caught sight of the car a quarter-mile off and still moving at that turtle pace.

I spun my left hand in three quick circles, signaling her to get over the fence. Without the help of a leg-up, it was twenty seconds before she could drop to the ground on the other side.

Now the white car was fifty yards closer. Angela's Volvo was in clear view and if the driver hadn't seen it already, it would only be a matter of moments. I couldn't call down instructions because the sedan was closing in near silence and it was quiet enough for any shouts to be heard.

So I motioned by pushing my hands downward. She ducked back from the fence and into the brush and trees until I couldn't see her anymore. As the car topped up the last rise I saw that it was indeed a Sable – *the* Sable. From my high perspective, I could see only the two white hands gripping the steering wheel.

The road flattened out for a hundred paces, passing the tower before it declined again. The sound of tires crunching on gravel stopped and I looked down between the gaps in the steps. The car had come to a complete stop. I froze. A tense ten seconds passed before the driver's side window came down with a soft electric whirr.

It happened before I could react. The muzzle of a pistol appeared, pointing into the woods and in Angela's general direction. A second later, it flashed and shot echoed through the trees.

I yelled, "*Sonofabitch*!" and bolted down the stairs.

A second shot cracked. I had no idea what I was doing. At the next landing, I looked down and came to a halt, my feet sliding and butt smacking a steel step. The pistol was now angled upward. It snapped again and I heard a sharp metallic bang off one of the struts over my head. I flattened myself on the landing.

At that moment, the Sable's engine revved and the tires spun on the gravel. I waited a second before peeking over the edge. The car was rolling down the road in reverse, lurching side to side. After fifty feet, it whipped to one side, then swung around ninety degrees, raising dust and spraying pebbles into the trees. A few seconds later, the last white swatch had disappeared into the web of green.

I shouted "Angela!" and rushed down the rest of the steps, half-stumbling and in danger of pitching over the thin railing.

I was on the fourth landing from the bottom when I heard her called out, "Richie?" I stopped and looked. She was looking up at me from outside the fence.

"You all right?" I called.

"Yeah. You okay?"

"Yeah..." I wheezed. "You believe that?"

Her terror gave way to anger. "That sonofabitch *shot* at me!"

I made it down two more landings and stopped again, now only twenty feet off the ground.

"Did you see who it was?"

She shook her head. "I looked out from behind the tree just in time to see the pistol. The first shot went by about four feet away."

"Okay, wait," I said and made my slow descent of the remaining steps. When I reached the bottom, I met her on the opposite side of the fence.

"What the hell?" she said.

I shook my head, dumbfounded

"I was." She was shaking at little. "I was scared."

"Me, too," I said. "I never had anybody shoot at me before. And you were down here alone."

"Whoever it was saw me. I'm pretty sure he could have hit me if he wanted to."

"Or put one in my ass," I said. "It was a he?"

"I don't know. I think so." She gave a nervous start and said, "Can we get out of here before he comes back?"

I said, "Yeah, yeah, let's go." Having escaped, I was feeling a little giddy.

Angela repeated the courtesy of walking off while I huffed and grunted my way over the fence. I had just reached the top when I heard her say, "Goddamnit."

"What's wrong?"

I found out when I joined her in front of the Volvo, looking down with a grim expression.

"The crazy bastard shot out my tire," she said, sounding stunned. "You believe this?"

"Must have been to keep us from following."

She stared at the flat. Then glanced at me, looked at her tire, looked at me again. "Well?" she said. She was waiting.

I went to the trunk for the jack and the spare.

It was after four o'clock when we limped onto Leo's lot. He was observing a high school kid do an oil change in one of his bays. He turned to peer at us as we drove up.

He saw the skinny spare right away and said, "Holy Christ, now what?"

We got out of the car. I steered him aside and dropped my voice to a whisper to relate our adventure.

"Jesus and Mary!" he said. "The guy took a shot at you?"

"At both of us," I said. "And he put one in the tire."

The young kid had wandered out of the bay to eavesdrop. Leo shooed him back inside and opened the trunk to examine the flat.

"The slug's likely still in there," he muttered. "Unless it was something huge, like .357 magnum. But a cannon like that would have blown it to shreds."

"The pistol wasn't very big." Angela's voice was muted.

Leo stared at her and then at me and said, "What the hell is it with you two?"

He didn't want his helper to know what was going on and sent him on an errand. He drove the Volvo into the bay and went about pulling the ruined tire off the rim. Once he got the wheel on the changing machine, he found the slug right away.

"Twenty-two," he said, and dropped it into my hand. I stashed it in my pocket rather than show it to Angela. She was sitting in the passenger seat and did not look well. The rush had faded, leaving her shaken. I felt the same way when I let myself think about that ball of lead flying so close by.

Leo took me into his office to explain that he'd have to get a new tire from Goodyear. It would probably take a few hours, but he'd stay however long it took to do the replacement.

I left him and Angela and walked across the street to the convenience store, where I bought a six-pack of Yuengling Black and Tan. When I appeared at the window with a cold bottle, Angela roused herself and climbed out of the car. Leo wiped his hands on a rag, twisted a top, and took a long swig.

"Somebody's screwing with you guys," he said. "Yesterday it was a brick and a knife, today it's a pistol. I mean, what the fuck's going on?"

"I wish I knew," I said.

"Well, what are you going to do about it?" His face was pinched with worry. "This is no joke."

"I guess I need to report it to the police." I went digging for my cell phone.

Angela exchanged a glance with Leo and then put a hand on my wrist. "Wait a minute," she said.

"What's wrong?"

"That could be one of the problems."

"She means the police department," Leo said. "Or at least one member of it."

"You mean Dewitt?"

"You have been chatting up Crystal," Angela said.

"He's a cretin," Leo said. "And he's trained on firearms. I guarantee a guy like that could hit a tire at fifty yards, no problem."

I shifted my gaze to Angela to see if she was buying any of this. She shrugged and said, "It's something to think about. What if he is involved?"

I nodded. "All right, then. How about if I see if Tim will talk to me about it?"

"What, for old time's sake?" Leo was sneering. "You remember high school? He was one of *them*."

"Give it a break, Leo," I said. "You sound like Louie."

"Yeah, well, maybe Louie's smarter than you think." He treated me to a wise look. "Maybe he's the Fool on the Hill. Know what I mean?"

Angela let out a little hiss of annoyance at these dramatics. She looked at me and said, "Tim's a pretty straight arrow, so I don't know if he'll talk off the record or not. If not, he'll give you the speech about *if you know of a crime, blah, blah, blah*... In that case, you can refer him to me."

She gave me a mocking smile. "Your *attorney*."

Leo laughed without much humor and drained what was left in his bottle. He snatched a fresh one and went back to work on the tire. After watching him for an absent moment, Angela said she was hungry.

"Really?"

She nodded. "If I don't eat, I'm going to get sick."

"Where do you want to go?"

"Not Charlotte's." She eyed me. "Unless you want to see into your little girlfriend."

"She's not –"

"Don't worry, Richie." She patted my shoulder. "I had someplace else in mind."

I had forgotten the Lunchbox, a tiny hole in the wall crammed between two storefronts a few blocks down River Street, one side vacant and the other occupied by an auto parts store. The restaurant had seen much better times when the railroads were busy. Somehow it had survived, though just barely.

The bell over the door tinkled in a dull way when we walked in. The narrow room with its counter and half-dozen tables was empty. It had the look of a tired old snapshot.

"I don't believe this," I said.

"Yeah, how about it?" Angela said.

A stout, gray-haired woman in a dingy white waitress dress and apron appeared from the kitchen in back. She didn't greet us exactly; instead, she said, "Help you?" with a wheeze of weary breath.

I let Angela order sandwiches, chips, and soft drinks while I looked around. Time seemed to have stopped. From what I could see, the place hadn't changed a bit since the days when I perched with legs dangling on a counter stool, devouring hot dogs.

We sat down at one of the tables. The novelty of returning to another little landmark was dissolving in a hurry. Maybe I was growing tired of too many memories. Or maybe it was the returning shock of having live ammunition whistle within reach of our bodies not two hours before.

We were seated in the back corner. I didn't want to think about what had happened at the fire tower and was glad for the distraction of the rumble of a lonely train moving through the yard behind the building.

I said, "Oh, yeah. I keep forgetting to ask about your plans for Louie."

"Right. Him." She began turning her glass between her fingers. "If I was doing my job, I would have reported what you told me. But he's not hurting himself or anyone else. The halfway house gets paid one way or another. Him not being there means they have another bed they can collect on, so they're not going to say a word. They'll be doing the explaining if anything happens." She took a sip of her ginger ale and put the glass down precisely. "So I'm just going to let it alone for now."

I took a chance on another subject. "Are you all right with me, Angela? I mean with everything that's going on."

She raised her eyes. "With you?" She considered for a moment. "I think I settled some things at the river last night. I know where we are, you and I. I don't have any illusions and I don't have a secret agenda. I'm not saying I've got it all worked out. There are still a lot of moments when I..." She let the thought hang for a few seconds. "But those things pass. And here we are. With more pressing problems, if you know what I mean."

I said, "If having me around your house is making things harder, I can go someplace else."

Her eyebrows hiked. "Don't exaggerate your effect on me, pal," she said.

"I didn't. I just meant it's getting a little dangerous."

"I know what you meant. It's cool. And I'm not going to let whoever's pulling these stunts jerk me around."

"I think it's more serious than that, don't you?"

"I don't know," she said, then leaned my way. "But listen. The truth is, I like being around you. I always did. I know that back when what you wanted from me was some tail, and that's okay, because you were that age. I still liked you. I thought you were a good guy. I still do. So you can stay."

The waitress made her slow way to the table with our plates in hand. Angela picked up a sandwich half, took a bite, and said, "You've certainly kept me entertained these last few days."

"I just came to say good-bye to Joey," I said.

She laughed quietly and said, "Yeah, well, you should have known he'd stir up trouble, dead or alive."

She decided to go back to Leo's to check the progress on her tire. After she left, I put in a call to the police department and asked for Tim. The dispatcher took my number and said she'd get a message to him.

Slouching at the table, I gazed out at River Street. It was as serene as it had been when I was a kid. Lost in a childhood daze, it never occurred to me what sorts of rancid roots might be creeping beneath the surface of my little town. I had been busy growing up and the bad seeds were being sown out of sight and mind.

Now I had come back and for reasons I still could not fathom, someone was intent on wrecking every day I spent there. Mine and Angela's. Isabel and Tim Raines had both posed some ancient grudge as the motive. I wracked my brain and couldn't come up with anything that would inspire such violence. Had I stolen someone's girlfriend or committed some other malfeasance? I had no such recollection, but decades had passed. Who could remember?

But even it was a matter of mean pranks committed by some vindictive moron with a long memory, it had gone way too far. My rental car had been badly trashed. Gunshots had been fired, narrowly missing Angela and me. This was serious; and though I didn't buy the mad conspiracy theories spouted by Leo and Louie, I believed it had something to do with Joey's death. Whatever it was had been buried with him, until I came along with my nostalgia and guilt and started scratching in the dirt.

I fell into such a deep muse over this story line that I gave a start when my cell phone jingled.

"Richie? Tim Raines."

"Tim." I returned to the present. "Thanks for calling back. I need a couple minutes of your time."

"Can you come by the office in the morning?"

"I'd rather not do that," I said. "And I'd rather talk today."

He paused. "I see." He had to be wondering if I was turning into some kind of pain in the ass. "Tell you what," he said. "I'm driving over to Middlebury to pick up some equipment. You can ride along if you want. We can talk then."

"Will you turn on the siren?" I said.

He laughed and told me to be waiting at the corner of River and First streets in fifteen minutes.

On the drive out of town, Tim explained that he was collecting some new chemical and biological warfare materials that had come from Homeland Security and were being doled out to police forces up and down the valley.

"I don't know what they're thinking," he said. "Something tells me this part of the world is not going to be a prime target for terrorists. But when they're giving it away, you take it." He smiled. "We still have Cold War stuff from the Fifties lying around somewhere."

We were crossing the river bridge. His glanced at me and said, "So what's on your mind?"

"Is this in confidence? Between you and me?"

He frowned slightly, then nodded. "I guess I can agree to that," he said. "As long as you're not going to tell me that you've committed a crime. Or know that someone else has." He took his eyes off the road again. "What's this about?"

I decided to lay it out. "I have concerns about Officer Dewitt."

"Why? Did he do something?"

"I don't know. That's kind of the point."

Tim kept silent for a few seconds. "Okay," he said. "You tell me what's going on and for the next couple minutes, I won't be a police officer. How about that?"

I took him through it. At least most of it. I left Joey out of the conversation as much as possible, once again avoiding the subject of his library research. I finished with the incident on the ridge.

He slowed the car and shot me a glance. "This individual fired a weapon at you?"

"And Angela. And it was close, too. He shot out her tire."

I told him about the white Sable and the gunplay and Leo finding the slug in the tire.

Tim mulled this, then said. "What were you two doing up there? Or would you rather not say?"

My face got warm. "I wasn't doing anything a married man would need to hide, if that's what you're asking," I said. "We used to climb that tower when we were kids. You remember."

"I do," Tim said. "Everybody did that. Lucky no one ever fell off. The state put up the cyclone fence to prevent that."

"Well, we found a place we could get over and we climbed to the top."

"Hell of a view from up there." He looked at me again and said,

"But aren't you a little old for that sort of thing?"

"Yeah, well, it's what happens when you come home, I guess." Let him think it had just been some foolish stunt.

Running through the other details of the adventure took us into Middlebury. He parked in the county courthouse lot and shut off the engine.

He said, "So I understand this, you think that Roy Dewitt might be the person who followed you up there and fired those shots. And that he's the one who vandalized your car?"

"There was Joey's trailer, too."

"Uh-huh. So Officer Dewitt is committing these acts why? Because of Crystal Nash? Is that what you're thinking?"

"I don't know, Tim. I don't know anything about the guy. Maybe it's Crystal and maybe it's something else. Maybe he doesn't like Polacks. What I do know is that it's not some silly shit anymore. This person shot at us."

Tim nodded gravely. "That is serious. As in felony serious." He pondered it for another moment. "Okay. I'm going to look into it. You understand that I can't tell you anything more than that. But I'll see if I can find out who's behind this. It just might take a while."

"I'm not going anywhere," I said, mostly because I wanted to see his reaction.

He did hesitate, though only for a second. "I'll keep you posted as much as I can, then." He opened the door. "Help me carry some government issue?

I had him drop me off at the garage when we got back to Wyanossing. From Leo's expression, I had just strolled out the side door of Gestapo headquarters. He watched the cruiser drive away before turning a baleful eye on me.

"What?" I said.

"What? What are you doing riding around in a cop car, that's what."

"I needed to talk to him in confidence."

"Oh, yeah? And who says he won't go tell Dewitt whatever it was you said to him?"

"Come on, Leo."

"He's a cop."

"He's Tim Raines," I said.

Leo wasn't having any of it. "No, he *was* Tim Raines," he said. "What do you want to bet that he's going to drive right back to his office and tell Dewitt that you're on to him. Then you're really going to have trouble."

"Like I don't already?"

Leo shook his head. "The bastard is screwing with Angela, too."

"I know that."

"So, there you go."

We were both getting angry and I stopped to let things cool off. "Anyway," I said. "It's too late, because I already told him what happened."

"And you're going to be sorry you did, man."

I gave up and asked him where Angela had gone.

"She drove over to her office," he said. "Oh. And a lady called from Avis about the car. She said someone would be here in an hour or so." He came up with a sudden grin that washed away his pique. "She asked me for the details. Of the *incident*. I said you got caught banging some man's wife." He saw the look on my face. "I'm kidding, Richie. Jesus, lighten up."

The moment passed and I found him treating me to a frank look.

I said, "Okay, now what?"

"Angela. Any chance this is about her?"

"I don't think so."

"Uh-huh. And what's going on with you guys?"

"Nothing, Leo. Nothing at all. I swear." He laughed at my rueful expression. "By the way," I said. "Who's in your bed these days?"

A sly grin cracked his face. "Do you remember Chuck Dawley?"

"What, you're gay now?"

"No, ya dickhead. His little sister, Brenda."

"Brenda Dawley." It took a few seconds for me to remember her. "Well, good for you."

"Yeah." He nodded complacently. "We get along."

"Well, what more can you ask?" I said.

With nothing else to do, I decided to take a stroll up First Street. I had just reached the next corner when I caught a flash of white out of the corner of my eye and turned just in time to see the back half of a white car creeping into the alley that cut through to Second Street, moving an a taunting pace.

I yelled out a curse and started running. I must have been some ridiculous sight sprinting like some maniac in my street clothes. As I reached the mouth of the alley, I saw a white fender just disappearing onto Second Street. Another miss. I stood there, catching my breath and wondering if I had really spied our tormentor or was now hallucinating white cars everywhere I went.

As I turned around, I heard the sound of a basketball snapping off concrete. After a few seconds, I saw Louie walking up the middle of the park, his trusty ball pounding out that steady rhythm. *Pock-pock-pock*. I walked to the corner and called to him. He looked around and saw me. I crossed the street and stepped onto the manicured grass.

Louie stopped bouncing the ball. "Hey, Richie," he said. "I thought you went to New York."

"Louie, did you see a white car?"

"Did I see what?"

"A white car."

"When?"

"Just now. A mean, a few seconds ago."

"A white car." He spent a few seconds puzzling. "No, I can't say that I did."

"Do you know anyone who drives a white car? It's a Mercury Sable."

He didn't answer the question. He was gazing at me with his brow stitching. "Richie, I'm worried about you."

"Why's that?"

"You know what they did to Joey?" he said. "You see what they did to me?" He held up a solemn finger. "You better watch your ass or you'll be next."

"Do you know something, Louie?"

"Oh, yes." He nodded solemnly. "I've known all along what they've –"

"I mean do you know anything about what's been going on since I got here?" I was curt with him and he flinched. "Like my car getting busted up. Joey's trailer getting torn apart. People taking potshots. And a goddamn white Mercury Sable that has been stalking me everywhere I go in this fucking town."

My voice had shot up and Louie cocked a disapproving eyebrow. "Well, you're certainly not going to get any cooperation with that tone," he sniffed.

I coughed out a laugh, coming down from the ledge. The whole thing was insane.

What'd you do today, Richie?

Oh, well, I got grilled by a cop. Then I bought me some duds. After that, I went to check on my car that was vandalized. Then I went up on the mountain with a woman I used to lay and got shot at. After which I rode around in a cop cruiser. Then I chased a car up an alley like some stray mutt. And now I'm standing in the park talking to a lunatic. You know, the usual.

Louie was watching me with a dim smile. "You were always too serious, Richie. And you were always going somewhere. You never stayed put."

"Well, I'm not going anywhere right now." I gestured to the nearest bench. "You want to sit for a minute?"

Louie peered fretfully at the bench as if it was something unfamiliar to him. I sat down and after a few seconds' hesitation, he stepped over and lowered himself onto the seat.

"There," he said. After a moment, he perked up. "Hey, I just thought of something. You remember Janet Laster? That young lady played a tune on an upright organ on this very bench." His eyes shifted slyly. "Mine, to be exact."

I was shocked that he recalled the incident and all the more so that Janet Laster was the one who committed the lewd act he had described, because in school she had been known as our own little church lady, as neat as a pin and prim as a saint, disapproving of everything guys like Joey and Louie and I did. Just picturing her sitting all stiff and proper as she serviced Louie's stiff prick had me snickering.

He laid a pensive finger to his chin. "Yeah, that was what, two weeks ago?"

I cracked up. He hadn't totally lost his touch. I glanced at him with affection and felt an urge to put my arm around his shoulders. I didn't know how he'd react, so I settled for a gentle pat.

"Louie," I said, "I always said you should have been a comedian."

"I am a comedian," he said. "Just not the kind on TV. I'm one of God's clowns." He eyed me, again in earnest. "You know what that means? It means that everything I say is a joke. Nobody's laughing, though. You know why?" I shook my head again. "Because they just don't get it. You don't get it. I think you will, though. I hope you do. Before it's too late."

With that, he got to his feet, patted my shoulder in return, and dribbled away without looking back, out of the park and down Second Street, going home to his shack by the railroad tracks. As I watched his scarecrow figure grow smaller, I thought about little Janet Laster going through her pious days wondering if crazy Louie was one day going to blurt to the world how she had treated him to just about the best gift a fellow could receive.

This riff darkened into thoughts of little secrets, and of petty sins, and of cruel, dishonest, and discourteous acts. We were all guilty. Small tortures could never be forgiven because the victims were gone. I had forgotten so many of the ones that I had committed; now an assortment of them came back in a slow march and I felt the onset of an unslaked shame. I had done so many people wrong at one time or another, and at that moment, I wished dearly that I could have every one of them line up in front of me, so I could fall on bended knee and ask forgiveness. But that was just more selfishness. My failings were a curse that would follow me forever.

I had betrayed Joey, betrayed our friendship, just as Angela had said. I left him behind and turned him into a box of memories that included the afternoon when we first shared "She Loves You" as it burst from the little speaker of an old radio. Now it was too late to do much of anything about it.

I caught myself before I descended further into this pit of regret and stood to walk away from the bench as if had transformed into a bed of nails. My remorse was deep and I wasn't sure what good it would do to tumble in all the way.

In need of some normalcy, I crossed the street to the library. Though it was past closing time, I saw Mrs. Eldridge framed in the window as she worked at the front desk. I tapped on a pane and she looked up to peer at me through the thick lenses of her glasses. Her kind face broke into a sweet, ageless smile. She left the desk and appeared to unlock the door.

She frowned. "You don't look good," she said, and stood back.

She allowed me to hide there while she finished her work. It was solid and peaceful within those centuries-old walls. I located the drama shelves and took down one book after another. I was sure that some were the same volumes I had read as a kid. I recalled memorizing the opening scenes from *Macbeth* and *Hamlet* because I loved how the lines dripped with such dark mystery. I kept my family amused by disappearing into this character or that. But being the center of attention was never as enticing as the experience of becoming someone else.

I closed a book, wishing I could somehow transport myself through time and into Joey's skin in his last moments and so solve the puzzle that had now entangled me. That was not going to happen. Gazing past the window at the falling night beyond, I brooded on reaching nothing but dead ends.

So it was a perfect time for my cell phone to start singing. The sound roused Mrs. Eldridge. She appeared at the end of the shelves, glaring in displeasure, just as she had done thirty years ago, only this time she caught me with a noisy electronic device instead of a giggling girl.

Her old eyes fixed on it as if it was a dead rat as Leo's voice squawked, "Hey! Richie! What the fuck? You there?"

With a severe look, Mrs. Eldridge said, "Not in the library."

I whispered "Hang on," and hurried out the front door and away from that unflinching stare. I hit the sidewalk. "Leo?"

"What the hell?"

"What's going on?"

"The Avis guys are here."

"All right, on my way," I said, and clicked off.

I went back inside to apologize to Mrs. Eldridge. She was not mollified. Open or closed, the library was sacred space.

"I swear, those *things* are the first sign of the end of civilization," she said. "People never stop talking! Yak, yak, yak. Walking down the street, in their cars, from morning until night. When do they have time to think anymore?"

"I mostly use it for emergencies," I offered weakly. "For my kids..."

"But not in a library."

Yes, ma'am." I made gesture toward the door. "They're here about my car." I gave her a small wave. "My apologies about the phone, Mrs. Eldridge."

"But not in a library," she repeated. "Not here."

The two Avis guys were waiting, one black, one white, young sports wearing Avis shirts and jackets.

Leo was showing them around the car when I walked up. The pair turned to me with quizzical stares, curious to see the character responsible for their trashed vehicle. The black kid was grinning and I wondered if Leo had decided that the banging-someone's-wife joke was too good to lose. His partner was glancing between me and the car, all officious, a rookie.

The black kid had finished the paperwork on the car and was talking to Leo as they fell into some kind of instant bonding mode. I could hear them laughing in the bay while Whitey fussed over the forms for the replacement vehicle, a Pontiac Grand Am. Presently, he held out the clipboard for my initials and signature and then handed me a new set of keys. I got the impression from the pinched look on his face that he wanted to scold me with something like "and don't destroy this one," but he had the sense to keep his yap shut.

He called out, "We're done here, Alvin."

Alvin and Leo emerged from the office, still chuckling. We shook hands all around and then they took off. Leo watched their car roll north along River Street.

"Nice guy," Leo said. "I wish they were all like that."

"Who, black people?"

"No, dumbass," he said with a grimace. "Corporate drones." He blinked. "And speaking of worthless dicks, look right there." He nodded his head and I turned to see Elmer Smalley's Chrysler rolling past.

"So?" I said.

"So he's spying again," Leo said and went back into the bay.

I followed him. "What do you have on for this evening?" I asked.

"Same as usual. Not much."

"You want to come out for some drinks with me? And Angela, if she's up for it. I could use it. You can bring your lady."

He wiped his hands on a shop rag, considering. "To where?"

"Definitely someplace you won't have to wear a tie," I said.

Leo nodded. "Well, in that case, I accept."

Looking back, my mistake was letting him choose the place. He claimed that I wasn't getting the old homestead experience by hanging around peaceful cafes like Charlotte's or munching arugula at the Riverside Hotel.

"Where then?" I asked him.

He gave me a big Leo grin.

At first, Angela laughed as if it was a joke. Then she said, "Don't go there."

"Why not?"

"Because it's a dive. Was. Is."

"That's kind of the point. Anyway, Leo says that's really it when it comes to the joint department around here. And that just about everybody in town still hangs out there."

"I don't. Pick another place."

"I already said I'd go."

She laughed again. "Well, have a good time." I stayed quiet and she said, "What?"

"I said you'd go, too."

11.

If there was anything akin to an infamous door in Wyanossing, it would be the one that welcomed the patrons of Sonny's Lounge, on the east end of town.

My dad and my uncles had quaffed beers there when it was decent roadhouse. Later, it went on the skids and became a hangout for hoodlums. The brawls often produced more Saturday morning talk than the high school football games generated. Times changed and the place toned down some, though fights were still breaking out with regularity when I had last been in, right after I got out of the Army. Visiting Sonny's that one night helped to convince me to leave town for good.

The original Sonny had died in the 1950s and the place had passed from hand to hand, with each owner managing to honor the tradition of cheap food and drinks, loud music, and a threshold testosterone level. I was curious about its most recent incarnation.

It took some more convincing to get Angela to join us. Then she got into the spirit – sort of. She wore painter's pants and a t-shirt under her leather jacket and put something on her hair that gave it a hard sheen. I told her she looked a little dykey.

"Good," she said. "Maybe I'll get laid." She was in one of those moods.

A fair part of the reason she had agreed to go was Leo's lady Brenda. Or so she said. They had been classmates, sophomores to our seniors, and they hadn't seen each other in months.

Leo came by to collect us in a monster of a 1974 Chevy station wagon that had been in his family since it was new. He had cleaned up and in his jeans, hiking books, khaki work shirt and photographer's vest, looked dashing in a funky way.

His date came along behind him. Leo said, "You remember Brenda, don't you, Richie?"

As crude as it sounds I did remember her, because she had been the proud bearer of the largest bust in high school. Those fixtures had held up well and she had kept her cute, too. She blushed and made a minor fuss about meeting the "famous actor."

Angela broke out a couple bottles of wine and we polished them off as we sat around talking on her front porch. Then Leo said it was time to go.

"You guys sure about this?" Angela said.

I said, "Yeah, sure. Why not?"

She turned to Leo and, wagged her finger, said, "He's your responsibility."

"He'll be fine," Leo said, rolling his eyes at me, as if to say *womenfolk*.

We piled into the wagon. As we rolled through town and out onto the two-lane, I felt excitement mixed with an odd dread. Like I sensed that something was going to happen.

Angela had caught the same vibe. Or maybe she was just wary in general. All the way there, she slipped glances my way that let me know she was having her doubts. At the same time, she chatted away with Brenda about the fates of various classmates, as if it was just another outing.

We pulled into the parking lot after a twenty-minute ride and I saw that Sonny's hadn't changed much, almost homey looking with the same log cabin construction with the timbers blackened with pitch and the chinking in between painted white.

It was clearly the place to be on a Friday night in Cumberland County. The parking lot was crowded with pickup trucks, SUVs and Jeeps, and fewer Saabs, Volvos, BMWs and Mercedes. A hornet's nest of motorcycles were arrayed near the front door, the black-clad bikers with their half-shell helmets lounging with studied cool.

Inside, we found the house on its way to filling up. The front door was at one end of the horseshoe bar and the tables were arranged to make room for a small dance floor. Electric lamps attached every few feet along the walls threw a yellowish cast over the room and Christmas lights were hanging haphazardly from thick old ceiling beams. Four windows on the far wall gave a view of a full moon over the dark river.

We were greeted by the usual turning of heads whenever a new party comes through a door. Then a ripple passed from table to table along our side of the bar and more heads turned. People were staring. In a series of fast glances as we moved to an empty table, I caught some smiles along with a few brittle stares.

Leo stopped at the bar to order a round of drinks while I followed the women. Four people got up to greet me. I remembered all of them, though vaguely. No one stepped forward to embarrass me, but the night was young.

The stage for trouble was set before we even took our seats. Angela gave me a sharp look and the slightest tilt of her head. Fifteen feet away, three four-tops had been pushed together for a large party that included John Miller and Elmer Smalley. They were watching us with stares that were not kind, though they managed fake smiles. Around the table were men and women I didn't recognize and like pack dogs picking up a scent, each one turned to gaze at the new arrivals.

I was just about to whisper something to Angela when I heard a throaty, "Hey!"

I smelled her sweet perfume before she was on me with a gentle hand sweeping over my shoulder. Angela muttered something under her breath and I saw her and Brenda exchange a look.

Crystal said, "Richard! What are you doing here?" She gave no hint of our rendezvous the night before, careful not to come on too familiar. Still, the people at the tables around us, including the ones occupied by John and Elmer and their crew, were watching.

Mostly because she was such a sight in her short black skirt, black tights that ended in beatnik boots, and sleeveless top of black and red vertical stripes. She had spent some time with her makeup and she looked wicked, like an Apache dancer. The lady was some sight.

I was trying to decide whether to invite her to join us when Leo stepped up and said, "Hey, Crystal."

She eyed him. "Hello, Leo."

Jerking a thumb, he said, "Damn, you got a whole table full of hussies over there."

I glanced around to see two other young, pretty, decked-out ladies sitting over cocktails a few tables away.

"That's a club sandwich if I ever saw one, eh?" Leo yelled and smacked my back.

Crystal wasn't amused. She offered a quick good-bye and moved away, touching my hand as made her escape.

We had just settled in when the evening's entertainment began. Someone at the Miller and Smalley table muttered a comment that brought a round of raw laughter.

Leo cocked an ear. "What was that?" he said and glanced my way. "You hear something, man?"

"Couldn't quite catch it," I said. "But it sure sounded stupid."

Angela was glaring between us. "Both of you shut up."

"He started it," I said.

A waitress arrived with our drinks and the waters calmed. The peace lasted as the couple at the next table paid their tab and left, leaving no bodies between the four of us and John and Elmer and their crew.

Still, Leo and I behaved, ignoring them. We shared a toast and worked our way through the first round without incident. Brenda wanted to hear stories from Sin City and she was dismayed to learn that as a married man with a wife and kids, I couldn't relate any tales of cocaine parties or weird sex. She asked if I knew the model in the SlimQuik commercials or the darling little girl who lisped her way through the Provident Insurance spot. I explained that the actress in the SlimQuik spot was a lesbian meth whore and that the little girl was actually a 28-year-old male midget named Tiny Tony. Then Leo guffawed and she realized that I was putting her on.

We were having such a fine time that it took me a few minutes to pick up on the static from the table across the way. I didn't catch the muttering until I noticed a change coming over Leo, his mouth smiling but his eyes going hard as they flashed a message. I saw Angela staring over my shoulder and the lines of her face draw tight. Her black, bleak gaze was tracking something that she didn't like at all.

It was Elmer Smalley, floating to our table like a balloon in the Macy's parade. I shifted in my chair in time to avoid his hand on my shoulder. He turned the motion into a clumsy wave and stood waiting for a word of greeting. Angela just stared at him

He had to raise his voice over the music. "It's really good to see you out and about."

She gave him a puzzled look, as if she didn't understand. "After your recent loss, I mean."

It seemed not to occur to him that he had appeared at our table at Lightfoot's. Or how gauche it was to bring up such sad news when we were trying to have a good time. Whatever his point, the response was four blank gazes.

His fat cheeks flushed to pink, a few beads of sweat popped on his brow, and his eyes turned from wide with sincerity to small and piggish. He said, "Well, then..." and ambled back to his table.

I heard whispers and grumbles as he took his seat. After a moment's bemused silence, we picked up our drinks and the conversation. I was trying to dream up another spicy scandal to entertain Brenda when I heard Angela say, "Now what the hell are *you* staring at?"

I turned around to see John Miller slowly rising from his chair like a man who's *had enough, damn it.*

"What's wrong with you?" he snarled back. "The man came over there to offer his sympathies."

"Sit down, John." Leo said. "Have another drink."

John shifted to his steely gaze. "I wasn't talking to you, Leo," he said. "So stay out of it."

"No," Angela said. "You were talking to me and *I'm* telling you to sit down. And shut up."

Instead of sitting, John took a fuming step forward, bumping his left thigh into the empty table so that it shifted a few inches in our direction. I felt something percolating in my gut and swung around to fix my eyes on him.

He caught this and said, "Yeah, what, Richie?You don't live here, so you can stay out of it, too."

The drinks on our table rattled as Angela rose to her feet in an abrupt motion.

"Okay, Johnny boy, that's enough," she said. "Here's how it is. You guys don't get to talk about my brother. You don't get to say his name. You didn't like him, he didn't like you, and we both know you're not grieving his passing. So drop it, you fucking asshole."

Leo and I traded a stunned glance and the customers at the closest tables fell silent. She was on. John, his eyes bugging, lifted a righteous arm with a righteous finger extended and opened his mouth to say something.

Leo cut him off before he got whatever it was out. "Christ Almighty, did you not hear the lady?"

Now Elmer ascended from his chair to put his two cents in. "All right, all right. Angela, I apologize if I insulted your brother's memory. Sit down. Catch your breath. I *apologize*, okay?" It came out pure huffing sneer. He resumed his seat and I swear the chair creaked in protest.

Angela's eyes glinted as if she was shooting razor blades. "I don't want to sit down, motherfucker."

Now about half the room had noticed the commotion and customers were craning their necks and rising from their seats to see what it was all about.

Angela stared directly at John and said, "Okay, what?"

There was no way he could let her beat him in front of that crowd. It happened in a few sudden seconds. In his anger, he took another step forward and bumped the table again. This time, the edge jammed my forearm against the back of my chair. That did it. I jerked my arm free and shoved the table, catching him above the knee with its edge.

He let out a grunting curse. He couldn't go after Angela, but he was happy to have me in her place. I saw what was coming, pushed my chair back, and shot up. He took it as signal enough to charge around the table, his fists clenched.

I don't know what he expected. Maybe that I would throw up my hands, scream like a queen, and run away from his badass country self. He didn't figure on the time I had spent in the boxing gym in Queens and that I'd remember my basics enough to handle him.

I choked down the first thrill of fear that comes with a brawl, planted my feet, and ducked under the arms that were swinging wildly for me. The room tilted, the lights swirled, and I heard shouts and screams and the sounds of shattering glass as the table cleared.

I jammed my forehead into John's chest, brought my left hand up for cover, and used my right to start hammering his rib cage. He huffed in pain and tried to wrap me in a headlock, but every time I hit him, he shuddered and his grasp went weak again. He was not a small man, though, and his weight was pressing down on my neck and shoulders. So I wriggled free with one fast jerk, stepped back, and caught him looking, throwing an uppercut that clipped him under the jaw. His head snapped and a searing bolt shot through my knuckles and up my arm to my shoulder.

John staggered sideways and crashed against another table, sending more glassware flying. He was coming in for more when two of the bartenders broke from the crowd and placed their thick bodies between us. I backed away, my legs shaking and my fist throbbing. It was over, after all of fifteen seconds.

I looked around and saw Leo posed to my left with his dukes up. One of the guys from John's table was holding a napkin to his bloody nostrils. Leo had kept him at bay with a shot to the nose while I did battle with John. Angela and Brenda were standing behind the table with eyes wide and their mouths agape, as if they couldn't believe what they had just witnessed.

The room had gone mostly quiet. The bartenders looked between us and shook their heads over men our age behaving in such a way. They told us to cool it and went to putting the tables and chairs back where they belonged and cleaning up the spilled drinks and broken glass.

Leo and I sat down. The adrenaline was making my arms tremble and bringing a bitter taste on the back of my tongue. I felt a little sick and my throat was so tight that I didn't even try to talk. Angela kept quiet, her stare now fixed on the table, mortified that it was her mouth that had started the fracas.

Second by second, the surreal swirls before my eyes settled into hard shapes and angles. The other customers returned to their drinks and chatter, but was too late to make nice with the enemy and we were still glaring back and forth when blades of blue lights shot across the windows and then through the open door.

A few moments later, Officer Dewitt walked inside with another cop on his heels. This one was a she, and looked to be about sixteen. The crowd parted as they stepped around the bar and walked directly to ground zero.

Dewitt took a moment to examine the combatants.

"Anyone need medical attention?" he said. No one spoke up. He looked at the guy holding the bloody napkin. "What about you, sir?"

The guy honked something that no one understood. Dewitt turned to speak to the female officer. She took the injured guy by the elbow and led him outside, stopping for a half-second to stare at Leo. He ducked his head. The blue lights on Dewitt's cruiser flashing on the windows mixed with reds as an ambulance from the hose company pulled up.

"I want everyone involved in this incident in the parking lot," Dewitt said.

We filed out as if we were once again on our way to the principal's office. Dewitt lined us up against the building and pulled out a leather-bound notebook. Starting with John and Elmer, he moved from one to the next, asking questions about what had happened. The bikers watched and snickered, sharing the bartenders' amusement at the middle-aged melee. With the last bit of the rush fading, I was starting to feel ashamed of myself, and I kept my eyes on the ground.

Dewitt was questioning Leo and me when an SUV pulled into

the lot and Tim Raines climbed out, wearing street clothes, though with his badge displayed in a small wallet on his belt. He took his junior officer aside for a report, keeping his arms crossed as he cast his cop stare at each of us in turn.

"When's the last time?" Leo asked me, his voice down low.

"What, a fight?" I had to think about it. "In a bar in Brooklyn," I said. "And I lost." That wasn't quite true; the guy had sucker-punched me and I didn't have a chance to get a lick in before someone else jumped him and broke it up. From some corner of my memory, I recalled that my last real fight had been behind the YMCA after a dance, with Joey, and over a girl.

"What about you?" I said.

Leo tried not to grin. "You ain't gonna believe this. It was ten years ago, and I kicked Miller's ass in the parking lot at the Hook and Ladder."

Angela stepped outside, carrying a bar towel and some ice for my ear, which had begun to swell where John had clamped his arm on it. She looked unhappy as she handed it to me and then took a step back. She wouldn't meet my eyes.

Tim Raines regarded her absently as he listened to the rest of Dewitt's report. He murmured something to his deputy, then stepped up to address Leo and me.

"You're both being placed under arrest for causing a public disturbance," he said. "Mr. Miller will be charged as well. And anyone else who might have been directly involved. Officer Dewitt will take you to the station. We'll dispense with the handcuffs."

"I'll be representing them," Angela said in a subdued voice.

Tim nodded. "All right, then. Both of you please accompany the officer."

Dewitt was waiting and we did our perp walk ahead of him. A few of the bikers clapped. It occurred to me that it was the first live applause I had received in a long time.

The officer opened the door and ushered us into the back seat of the police cruiser. He left us there and went over to speak to the female cop, who was standing with the EMTs at the ambulance. Leo and I tried to be sober, but our eyes met and we traded guilty smiles.

"We shouldn't have done that," I said.

"Yeah, well, Miller started it." He shook his head. "I can't believe they still have a hard-on for us. After all these years."

I said, "Aren't you the one who keeps calling them Nazis?"

"That's more like a, whaddyacallit, figure of speech." After a moment, he said, "Oh, my God, I wish Joey could have been here."

"Yeah, he would have –" I stopped, gazing past him and out the window. "There it is again."

He looked around. "There's what?"

"The white Sable." The car sat idling at the edge of the lot.

The door on my side opened and Officer Dewitt bent down to speak to us. "We'll take you in for booking now," he said. "Then you'll be released."

"What about that cocksucker Miller?" Leo said.

I was surprised to see a flicker of a smile cross Dewitt's lips. His chin tightened. "Mr. Miller will be booked and released also. Same charges." He closed the door.

Through the windshield we saw the female cop escorting Miller to Tim Raines's SUV.

"Look at that shit," Leo groused. "He gets to sit in front." His gaze shifted. "Hey, man, there's your girlfriend."

Crystal and her two friends had stepped outside. I had forgotten she was there and had witnessed the whole shebang. She leaned over slightly to give me an odd smile and a wave of her hand.

"Hope Dewitt didn't see that," Leo said. "You could be shot while escaping."

A few minutes later, the driver's side door opened and the female cop slid in behind the wheel. She started the car, then turned around, her face stern but oddly affectionate, and somehow familiar-looking.

"Uncle Leo," she said. "What the hell?"

Leo sighed and said, "Just don't tell your mom, okay?"

Leo's niece Kelly and Officer Dewitt escorted us downstairs into the basement of the borough building where there were two holding cells and a small office. We did fingerprints and then signed something about having heard the charges. Dewitt explained that in the morning the magistrate would set a hearing date and we would proceed from there. Then he let us go.

On the way out, Kelly – Officer Malick – explained that most likely the charges would be dropped, but we still had to go through the rigamarole.

Brenda and Angela were waiting on the sidewalk. Tim's SUV pulled up as we were leaving. We avoided staring at each other as he and John made their way inside.

Brenda drove and Angela sat in front. Leo and I were consigned to the back seat like the miscreants we were. No one spoke a word all the way to Angela's house. Leo and I bumped forearms when we got there. He climbed in front and they drove off.

I followed Angela inside. She locked the door, tossed her keys, and crooked a finger. She led me into the kitchen and pointed to a chair. I sat. She turned on the lamp on the table, tilted and shade, and said, "Let's see the ear."

She gave it a good tug, making sure I felt it, then opened the freezer and packed some ice cubes into a hand towel. I let out a little yelp when she slapped the cold compress against the side of my head.

She said, "Shut up, you baby."

Ducking my head, I took over the ice pack. She sat down, her face composed in a way that reminded me of when we were young. I remembered that she had often treated me to that same baffled look, unable to figure out what I was thinking that made me act so crazy. I made sure she never did, and then I left.

There was something else flittering in her black eyes: a profound shame over having lost control. Her show at the bar had been a sight and a blessing in disguise. There was no way she could go ballistic on my sorry self now.

Though she could still sting me. "I don't need you to stick up for me, okay?"

"Okay."

"What happened tonight wasn't your fault. I understand that."

"It wasn't yours, either," I said.

"But I could have stopped it." She tapped a sharp finger on the tablecloth. "I could have handled it. I'm a lawyer. That's what I do. Handle things." She paused for a thoughtful moment, before coming up a faint smile. "I'm pleased to report to you that I've never seen John Miller's cock. I have seen yours, though it's been a while. I'm going to go ahead and hazard an opinion that yours is bigger. Do you think that if I had told you that before, we could have avoided the fisticuffs?"

I wanted to laugh; instead, I bit my tongue and shook my head, all solemn. "No."

She sat back. "No, I don't think so, either. It was bound to happen, one way or another. But it wasn't about me or Joey, was it? It was you and Leo and John and Elmer trying to get your licks in one more time. Trying to settle something. And I helped you."

I had the sense to keep my mouth shut. She mulled something for a moment and then went on.

"Speaking as your attorney, I'm reasonably sure that if you leave town, I can get the charges dropped. I can make that happen. You can be on the George Washington Bridge by lunchtime tomorrow, if that's what you want."

I hiked an eyebrow. "I'm not going anywhere. Not now."

She nodded. "I didn't think so, but I'm obligated to explain the option."

My ear felt sufficiently frozen and I got up to dump the cubes and the soaking towel in the sink. Leaning against the counter, I said, "I don't believe Joey fell off Council Rock, Angela. I think he was pushed. And I think that what he was doing at the library, and what he was doing on the other side of Line Road, is the reason."

She gazed at me with intent. "I agree."

"I don't want to go until we deal with that. So I'm staying."

She nodded. "Then call your wife."

"I do that every day."

"This time you ask her to come out here."

"Why?"

"So that she can see that there's nothing going on."

"I told her there wasn't. And she believes me."

"Good. So invite her. I know you miss your kids. I'd like to meet them. And her, too. If they want to come tomorrow, everyone can stay over here."

"I don't know if she'll go for it."

"Why not?"

"It's a lot of trouble, for one thing."

Angela frowned. "How much trouble? She rents a car and drives out. What, three hours? Isn't that what you did?"

"Yeah."

"So you'll make the call?"

"In the morning."

She nodded, satisfied. "Okay, then."

"Now what?"

"Now we go to bed." She caught herself. "I mean go to sleep. And in the morning you call and invite her. I'll get on the phone with her it if will help."

I didn't want to think about it. My muscles ached, my ear throbbed, and I had a headache. Angela said goodnight and left the kitchen. I heard her climbing the stairs.

In that quiet room, I let myself think about her suggestion and saw some sense to it. I missed my family. I wanted Isabel to know that Angela was not after her husband. The thought stirred in the back of my mind that maybe the two of them together could save me from my folly and failure. *That* was foolishness, and I let it go.

Climbing the steps was no easy task. I was exhausted and aching and felt a childish need to be mothered. When I reached the second floor, I found myself staring down the hallway at Angela's room, hoping she might be thinking the same thing and waiting for a chance to take care of me.

I knew she was far too wise. Her door was closed and if I came knocking, she'd know better than to let me in.

12.

Most days, the first images that come into my waking head are clips from a little filmstrip of my wife and my daughters. And so it was on that Saturday. It my drowsy state, I remembered that Angela had insisted that they drive out to bring me back home, and pictured a sweet little reunion.

Then I heard thunder rumble and the crackling of lightning far off, and the movie made a jump cut to the chaos at Sonny's. I felt my gut sink to the floor. Had I really been in a bar fight, after all these years? It couldn't be true. And yet the stinging throb on the side of my head told me it was. If I needed harder evidence, I had been charged with a crime, a matter of police record.

To provide a backdrop for this humiliation, the storm that had been rumbling when I went to sleep had come rolling in all gray and sodden, bringing a thick spring rain that dampened and silenced the streets of Wyanossing. It would have been lovely to lie there and daydream childhood scenes of splashing through puddles, a little Norman Rockwell painting of my very own. Except that Rockwell never painted the aftermaths of bar fights, which turned those memories into so many broken balloons.

I rolled off the bed with a groan. It felt as if every muscle in my body had been pummeled and I winced with each step toward the door. I hadn't had that many aches since my first day in the Brooklyn gym. When I finally made the eight feet to the hallway, I peeked down to see Angela's bedroom door standing open. Craning my head in the other direction was no simple task, either. I was pleased that the bathroom was free, so I wouldn't have to wait. There was no question of going downstairs to use the half-bath. I'd pee out the window before I'd make that painful descent.

I had just reached the end of the hall when I heard her voice behind me. "I wish I could think of a song for what you're doing there." I managed to turn around. "You look like hell," she said.

The shower was torture. I was being lanced with hot needles. I yelped so many times that Angela rapped on the door.

"You all right in there?"

"I am way too old for this shit."

She laughed and went away.

I dressed gingerly in the duds I had bought at the Dollar Store and made it downstairs with tender steps, wincing a bit less. The twinges of pain in my right wrist to my shoulder were starting to ebb, too.

Angela had laid out breakfast, a nice touch. A nicer touch was the bloody mary sitting next to my plate.

"I figured you'd need some medication," she said.

I sat down, grateful for the kindness. She served an egg scramble with Italian sausage, diced potato, asiago, mushrooms, and red bell pepper. Through the open windows, I could hear the hush of gentle rain. I started feeling human again, which in this case meant mortified, as the night before jumped right back into focus.

"I can't believe I did that," I said.

"You did," she said. "And by noon, it'll be all over town." She sat down with her own plate. "I gave you a chance to get away and you said no."

"I know, I know."

"Your hearing is scheduled for Monday. But it could be postponed."

I put down my drink. "Postponed why?"

"Because they might decide to screw with you. I'll raise holy hell if they try anything. But just so you know, you might have to come back."

"All right." I didn't like the sound of this at all.

"You going to call your wife?"

"As soon as I'm finished here."

"I'd like to talk to her, if she's willing."

"About coming out?"

"I want to explain your legal situation." She stopped to peer into my eyes. "I also want to make sure she understands that I'm not the other woman."

"I told her that."

"You told her, but that doesn't mean she's not thinking it. I've been in the shadows here. Like we're hiding something. And we're not. So I'd like to talk to her. Please."

I pondered this, trying to think of a reason why I couldn't do what she asked. First in line was my not wanting to tell Isabel that I had been arrested after getting into a fistfight in a barroom. And that was just this morning's headline.

Angela had mixed a nice drink and served up a nice breakfast and I decided to enjoy the libation and the meal before I had to face the music.

The girls took turns babbling happily, then fell to fighting over the phone. It was at that point that Isabel got on the line. I hemmed and hawed until she got suspicious and said, "Now what?"

"There was an *altercation*," I said. "Last night."

"An altercation? Do you mean a fight?"

"Yes."

"Where?"

"In a bar."

"Were you in the bar?"

"Yes."

"Were you in the altercation?" She was getting perturbed.

"Yes."

"And what happened?"

"That's all." She waited. "Oh, well, I was arrested."

"Are you in jail?"

"No."

"Because if you were, I was going to say, good. You can stay there."

"Isabel, I'm –"

"I want you home right now!" She was furious.

"I can't do that." I worked to keep my voice steady. "I have to appear in court."

"Oh, that's just great."

"And Angela wants to, uh, talk to you about that."

There was a silence from the other end. Then: "She wants to talk to me when?"

"Right now."

"What is this?" The way her voice rattled, she sounded as if she was on the verge of losing it. My wife doesn't melt down very often, but when she does, it's a good idea to take shelter.

"She's acting as my lawyer," I said. "That's all. She wants to talk to you and explain what's going on."

A terse pause ensued before she said, "All right."

Another bullet whizzed by my head. I said, "Hold on just a minute," and then scurried like the chicken I was to the bottom of the steps to call Angela. As soon as I heard her on the line, I hung up.

They talked for almost ten minutes. I hid out downstairs until Angela came to the landing and said, "Richie? She wants you." She went into her bedroom and closed the door.

Isabel's voice was calm again. "She sounds like she knows what she's doing."

"I don't think it's very complicated," I said. "They'll probably drop the charges."

"And then what? You'll come home?"

I said, "Angela asked me to invite you out here. You and the girls. You can rent a car and drive out tomorrow. And we'll all ride back together on Monday. They can miss a day of school."

She didn't say no, but she wasn't convinced, either. "And what about your friend? Angela's brother. All that mystery? I thought that was the point of you hanging around."

As I thought about what she said, I recognized a certain sad reality. "I don't know what happened to him," I said. "But I can't just stay here hoping that someday I'll find out."

"No, you can't."

"So, I'll get through this thing on Monday and we can drive back," I said. "Please?"

"All right," she said. "Okay."

"Yeah?" I felt my heart lift.

"Because the girls will love it."

"They really will."

"All right, then. I'll call you when we get on the road." I told her that would be fine. She said, "Tell Angela that I said thank you."

"I will."

"She sounds like a nice person."

"She is. I got her caught up in a mess here."

"You've got everyone caught up in it." She said, "We'll see you tomorrow," and clicked off.

Angela explained that my problems had disrupted her schedule and she was going to spend part of her Saturday at her office getting caught up on work. She warned me to stay out of trouble. As she went out the door, she said, "I like your wife, Richie."

I said, "Yeah, I think she likes you, too."

She left me in an empty house.

Though it didn't stay that way for long.

I decided I'd had enough of the buzz brought on by the early morning cocktail and started a short pot of coffee to chase it away. As I waited for it to brew, I thought about how happy I would be to see my wife and daughters. In the next moment, my heart sank as I realized that I'd be going back to New York with them and would likely never find out how and why Joey had died.

I had learned a lot about disappointment over my career; a fact of the actor's life. This was something else, a far deeper loss, and I didn't know how come to terms with leaving before the story ended. I would, though. Because my family needed me home. That Angela –

and Joey – would understand didn't make it any easier.

The coffee was ready and I drew a cup. Angela had left a blank legal pad and a pen lying on the table and I began drawing little boxes and circles at random. I sketched a picture of a house, like my youngest would create, a construction of craggy angles. It was a mindless exercise, and as I doodled I thought about Joey studying the drawings at the library and his foray to the shallow valley and rolling farmland beyond the ridge. In search of what? I still didn't have any idea.

Next I sketched the outlines of the old barn, half-entangled in brush and vines, as it was slowly being absorbed back into the earth, stone, and wood from which it had been built.

I had been about to tell Angela about the page in the plat book with the faint fingerprint when we were interrupted by the Sable-driving, pistol-packing nut case. She was in such a state the rest of the afternoon that I didn't get around to telling her about it. And then we were at Sonny's and the fun really began. I still had no idea if Joey had planted his print on that page and if he had, what was the point? Was it meant as a hint? *A clue*?

I laughed and shook my head. The dark and stormy morning was getting to me. Most likely, he or someone had simply fingered the page, leaving a trace on the thin old paper. It had just been one of those things.

I lifted my drawing, turned it this way and that, put it down, and laid the pen aside. I glanced up and almost fell out of my chair. A figure was huddled at Angela's porch door, staring in at me from beneath a baseball cap pulled down low. Rising with only a slight wince of pain, I stepped closer.

It was Crystal, tapping the fingernails of one hand on the glass and waving at me with the other. I unlocked the door and stood back to let her in.

She gasped out a "Thanks!"

She was a little out of breath and her chest heaved. I looked, okay? But I took in the rest, too: her khaki jacket, t-shirt, blue jeans, and sneakers, all dappled with raindrops. When she took off the

Phillies hat, I saw that she had tied her blond hair in one blond braid down her back. Her face was flushed and her eyes were bright.

I said, "What are you doing out there?"

"I came up the alley," she said. "I didn't want anybody seeing me." She glanced past my shoulder. "Is Angela here?"

"She went to her office," I said. "You want to sit down?"

"Okay."

"There's coffee."

"I don't need any." She slid into a chair, then took a moment to compose herself. Folding her hands before her, she settled in the grave way people do when they're about to announce bad news. But before she said a word, her eye fell on my drawing of the barn and she cocked her head. "What's that?"

"It's nothing." I pushed it aside.

She let her gaze rest on it for a second. Then she said, "I'm sorry I ran away the other night," she said. "I heard that car and got scared."

"Don't worry about it," I said.

Her gaze darkened. "You've got to get out of here."

"Oh? Why's that?"

"Because I think it's getting too dangerous."

"Is this about Sonny's?"

She said, "That wasn't good. But I'm talking about something else."

She was all drama and it was hard for me to take her seriously. At the same time, I knew she meant well and believed what she was saying. I said, "Something else, as in?"

She turned her head slightly, as if divulging a secret in a shadowy alley. "As in what happened to Joey."

Now it was me trying to read her face. "Where are you getting this?"

"I can't tell you," she said. "Not yet."

She was playing at evasive and I thought about saying something to rattle her, but I didn't want her to jump up and run away again. So I hiked a cool eyebrow and said, "I'm not afraid of those guys."

She shot me a sharp, troubled glance.

I said, "What?"

"That's what Joey used to say."

She let the pause linger. It was a very strange interlude, with rain falling outside the window of the unlit kitchen and the two of us trading whispers about the death of my old friend, the tragedy that had placed me there. In the next moment, I realized what was going on.

It was a scene, one of a string that began with the day I had arrived in Wyanossing. She had been posing this way or that and I had yet to get a fix on the real person lurking beneath her pretty skin.

I was a little tired of it, tired of being a fool for games and the lost time that went with them. Enough. Before she could launch into the next little number I said, "Do you think Joey fell off Council Rock? Or do you think he got some help?"

She flinched – good. In a hushed voice, she said, "I think he got help."

"Why?"

Again, she blinked. "Because he knew something."

"Something that was worth his life?"

She gave a vague nod.

I pushed her. "What could that be? It's not like Wyanossing is one of your major crime areas. If that's what happened, who did he cross?"

"I don't know." Her brow creased. "But you've been looking in the right places."

Now she had switched parts to the role of the messenger. I sat back, watching her.

Maybe it wasn't a role at all. What if someone had sent her? Perhaps some old friend lurking behind the scenes who had heard about me nosing around and wanted to help. Or Tim Raines? No; he wouldn't have dealings with a rank amateur like her. I doubted Mrs. Eldridge had the wiles. Of the homeowners who might be on my side, that left only Leo and Louie Zag. Leo was too straight up for that kind of secrecy and Louie was stone crazy.

The other possibility was my imagination running away with me on a rainy morning.

I felt her green eyes on me as I took another sip of coffee. My thoughts rounded another turn. What if it was a set-up? What if some other someone had sent her to either scare me off or draw me further into the web? John Miller, Elmer Smalley, or Officer Roy Dewitt would be my candidates for that ploy. What if Dewitt had put his sometime-girlfriend up to this as a trap? So I'd be the next one to end up –

"Okay, I've got to get out of here." In a nervous move, she rose to her feet, zipped her jacket, and pulled on her Phillies hat. "I've told you everything I can," she said. "What are you going to do?"

I shrugged and said, "I don't know what I can do, Crystal. My plan is to stay for my hearing Monday and then go home."

She placed a hand flat on the table and looked down at me. "And are you going to take me with you?" She was back to that.

I made sure she saw the roll of my eyes. I said "I can't take you with me." Her eyes flashed. "But if you get to New York, I'll help you. I'll point you in the right direction, tell you where to go and who to see. But then you'll be on your own. You think you can make it in the city? I wish you luck. Just don't come crying to me if it doesn't work out. Understood?"

She looked stung, and I felt like a monster. She was either a better actress than I had given her credit for or I had truly hurt her feelings. She stared at me for a few seconds more, looking too much like one of my girls when they grapple with heartbreak.

"I can take care of myself," she said, then turned around, opened the door and stepped onto the little porch. Within a few seconds, she had dissolved into the gray mist.

I sat at the table for long minutes. The light from outside was muted and there were no breaks in the clouds. It looked like rain well into the afternoon, a day for a book, a comfortable chair by a window, a large cup of coffee or a larger glass of wine. I could pass the hours and tomorrow would be Sunday and my family would be coming in. We'd have our hearing and then I'd be going back to my world.

Sitting there in the silence, I considered for a few more musing minutes that some things are not better left alone.

Years before, I had been on a commercial shoot and we were put up outside of San Antonio. It so happened that my first real friend in the Army was a native of that same city, a Chicano named Jaime Matos. He was a great pal and we were constant companions. Except that he had a drinking problem. He'd get really drunk really fast and stay that way. He was too mellow a soul to get nasty, so he'd just lapse into his languid half-stone that was just shy of comatose.

Another comedian, he would come staggering into the barracks, stand over my rack, and start yelling. "Zaleski! Get down and gimme twenty, man, or I'll *cheat* in your *chews*."

When he was discharged, I saw him to the bus station. We promised we'd hook up. We didn't. Ten years later, there I am in his hometown and I find an address in the phone book and drive out to find this broken-down mobile home with a car on blocks out front. The windows were filthy and the dirt yard was littered with junk. It looked like what a set designer would create to announce a derelict homestead. The kind of place where a dead-end sot would drink himself into oblivion.

I sat in the car for a half-hour, trying to decide what to do. In the end, I drove off. Maybe I didn't want to humiliate him and maybe I just didn't want to face his wreck of a life. So I left and I've regretted it ever since.

Monday was still two days away.

The weather was too nasty for my poor clothes, so I went searching for something to wear. The more I moved about, the less my muscles and joints ached, and I scoured the house, upstairs and down, without poking anywhere I didn't belong.

When I got to the basement, I opened an old steel wardrobe to find a man's rain jacket in forest green hanging inside. I figured it belonged to Angela's ex or her son. It fit well enough, though the sleeves were short. On the shelf above, I found a fishing hat with webbing above a soft brim and a little patch with a trout fly sewn on in front. My Rockports were all weather. I was ready to go.

The rain was falling in heavy sheets. I ducked into the rental car and drove off through the downpour, my wipers slapping time. I turned one corner and then the next, watching in the mirror. But no one else was dumb enough to be out in the deluge and I didn't see a vehicle moving for blocks. Still, I took my time and followed a crooked route to work my way north out of town.

Beyond the borough limits, I located the web of farm roads where we used to ride our bikes. Once hard-packed dirt, they were now narrow blacktops, still barely wide enough for two vehicles. All were lonely on this rainy morning. Driving from one to the next, I saw lights in the windows of far-off farmhouses, glowing through the drizzle like eerie candles.

When I circled back to Line Road, I passed a flatbed Ford crawling by in the opposite direction. A half-mile along, I happened on a utility road and pulled the car over and then out of sight behind a stack of railroad ties that were waiting for a construction project. I gave myself another five minutes to bail on the adventure, then I got out and started hiking.

Joey and I and our little gang of snot-noses had explored most of this same deep green territory, so I wasn't totally lost. A short walk brought me to the creek that wound from the ridge down through the dense woods. In my memory, it was a gurgling brook, clear and cold enough to drink from on a hot summer day. What I encountered that morning was a small river engorged with muddy runoff. I moved up and down the bank for fifty feet before finding a collage of rocks and a fallen tree trunk that formed a rough bridge.

The descent was more like surfing and the crossing was shaky. The incline on the other side rose a nearly-vertical twenty feet and required a hard minute of climbing and sliding back and then more climbing to reach the crest.

I stopped to clean the mud and leaves from my hands and to get my bearings. Through the trees, I could see a fallow farm field a hundred yards directly ahead. The old barn we had spied from the tower stood at some point along the edge of the clearing. Though the rain had settled into a drizzling cloud, I wasn't about to go plunging into the open and instead took the time and the cover of the foliage to circle around.

It occurred to me that the last time I had done anything like this was a basic training exercise that had my platoon creeping through a South Carolina swamp while our drill instructors tried to plunk us with BB guns. It was their way of proving that unless we got with it, the only place such hopeless morons would end up was in a body bag.

The rain was putting down a steady background hiss that was punctuated by the sound of the occasional fat drop slapping a broad leaf. I heard no bird songs, though I did catch the random, lonely caw of a crow. No little feet scrabbled through the underbrush. All God's other creatures had the good sense to stay home.

The empty and silent forest had me on edge. I began to imagine the cracking of branches, but saw nothing when I stopped to look around. Several times, I turned my head and then jumped at what I thought was a moving shadow. Though neither man nor beast appeared, my keyed-up brain kept playing tricks.

I was as isolated as I had been in a long time. In New York, I was never truly alone, never far beyond spitting distance of another human being. Even on our vacations, I was happily surrounded by Isabel and the girls. Only once in a while, when I was on a commercial shoot and found myself in a faraway hotel room did I become invisible enough to wallow in anonymity for a few sweet hours.

Out there, though, I really was on my own. No one knew where I had gone. Though it was true that I hadn't severed all my ties. My cell phone was nestled in the inside pocket of the jacket. I told myself I had done this so that Isabel could reach me in an emergency.

Gradually, I felt more at ease amidst the primeval and made the most of the minutes of solitude, watching the woods and listening to the rainfall that had me lost to the rest of the world. This lasted until I reminded myself that I had made the trek for a reason.

Though it was still unclear. I didn't know what Joey had been searching for out there and so I was wandering blind, hoping to stumble on a hint of what was so important that it had him poring over useless old records. So important that it might have cost him his life.

Through a break in the foliage, I could see the stone barn that we had viewed from the tower. It appeared from the mist as an antique painting in shades of brown. Branches from the taller trees were touching the back and side wall and hanging over the tin roof and vines had crept from the underbrush to begin to claim the lower part. And yet it appeared stone staunch, as if it might stand forever. An old farrow with rusted blades, and the empty sodden land stretching for acres all around added to the bleak panorama. A few hundred feet away, a foundation and some of the fireplace brickwork remained as a lonely and forlorn reminder of a farmhouse.

From the seclusion of the trees, I scanned the landscape to the horizon. Nothing was moving. The closest standing house was almost a half-mile away. With the veil of rainfall, anyone who happened to look in my direction would be hard-pressed to see me. Still, I'd be taking a chance wandering about. Rural folk notice when things are out of place and people don't belong. A quick phone call could bring Tim Raines or one of his officers.

What's your business in this location, Mr. Zaleski?

I stopped to consider that someone might have this patch of land under surveillance. Yes, and then what? Trespassing would be the extent of my malfeasance. At least I wasn't involved in a bar fight. Maybe I was simply reliving the joys of my youth with a nature hike. In any case, the weather was giving me my chance. The choice was to go forward to the barn or to retrace my steps through the woods and forget about the whole matter.

With a glance over my shoulder, I crossed the wet earth to the back wall of the structure. As I drew close, I could make out the expert masonry work, with the heavy stones fitting as snugly as if they had come out of a kit, and only a few having shifted at all.

I took another moment to scan the landscape before circling to the front. Now I was exposed from two directions. The tall doors had rotted and fallen from their rusted hinges years ago and I walked up the gentle incline to stand just out of the rain and inside the cavernous interior. The old floorboards sagged and creaked beneath my shoes.

I recalled that the Pennsylvania Dutch built some of their barns round because they believed that devils hid in corners. Out there, in that gloomy weather, it didn't seem so silly a belief. But the interior, though filled with nooks and crannies, was empty. I backed out. There was nothing to see.

Not there; but as I continued around to the north side and back into the partial cover of the trees, I passed along a foundation that rose two courses above the sloped earth and noticed an odd break, six inches tall and a foot long and just above ground level. The building stone had been replaced with a flat rectangle the same russet color as the stones. I moved in for a closer look and discovered that it was a pane of gray glass mounted in a frame of wood. I straightened and continued on my way.

I reached the corner of the barn, stopped, and retraced my steps to crouch down for a closer inspection. Rapping the glass with a knuckle, I found it solid in its mount, dusty but uncracked. The wood frame appeared fairly fresh and without rot or blemish. It seemed an odd addition to such an antique structure. But what did I know of barns?

Now treading more slowly, I noticed that other stones had been replaced with the same frames at regular intervals, three on the side and two in the rear.

I was gazing at one of the curious additions when I heard a squeaking sound from the direction of the ridge. I perked an ear and heard it again. Lifting my feet like a cartoon character, I crept to the front corner of the barn in time to see a vehicle rolling my way from Line Road, the wipers flapping as it rocked through the potholes.

I froze, staring in stupid shock until my gut told me to move. I scurried back to the tree line, hoping that the combination of drizzle and the driver's attention on the bumpy road would give me cover. I ducked behind a thick oak and stopped to catch my breath. I could now slip off without being spotted or stay and see what had brought some other individual to this same lonely spot on this stormy Saturday morning.

At that point, I figured I was just as likely to be noticed crashing through the woods and so I stayed put, peeking out to track the vehicle's slow approach. When it drew within a couple hundred feet, I recognized an older model Jeep Ranchero. It appeared innocent enough and I considered that the driver might just cruise on by, a local heading for wherever the road led.

No such luck. The Jeep rolled to a stop in front of the barn and the door opened. I cursed under my breath when Roy Dewitt stepped out.

He was wearing jeans and a hooded sweatshirt, the first I'd seen him out of uniform. He stepped to the front of the vehicle and stopped to take a quick glance around before pulling up his hood against the rain.

Joey often repeated the worn old line that I would fuck up a wet dream and I would not have disappointed him on that morning. Dewitt had just taken his first steps around the north side of the barn when my cell phone went off. I had forgotten to put it on vibrate.

If it was possible to freeze any harder, I managed it. Though the phone was tucked in the inside pocket and the rain was rustling through the leaves, it sounded to me like a fire alarm and after the third ring, I dropped chest-down into last autumn's wet leaves in an attempt to muffle the sound. Raising my head to peek through the underbrush, I thought I saw Dewitt cocking his head, but I couldn't be sure.

The shrill noise stopped. I lay there for a fifteen seconds before rising to my knees. Then I stood up again, my heart thumping as if it was about to leap out of my chest. I retrieved the phone and switched it off, making a mental note to find a brick when I got back to town and smash it into pieces, after which I would bash myself in the head.

Dewitt had moved out of sight. I waited for him to reappear around the back, ready to bolt or bluff it out if he turned my way.

Ten seconds went by, then fifteen. When it crept up on a minute, I started getting nervous. I took a few steps to the left and one to the right, trying to get a fix on him.

Another minute passed without a sound or movement. Stepping as carefully as a New York klutz could manage, I wound through the trees until I found myself facing the north side of the barn. From there, I could see the Jeep and the road winding back to the two-lane. It appeared that Dewitt had gone inside. To do what? There was nothing in there; at least nothing that I had noticed.

I felt a jolt up my spine and my heart went back to pounding triplets. What if he had heard my phone and my noisy thrashing and was now circling behind me? That I couldn't see or hear him didn't mean he wasn't closing in. I whispered to myself that I was getting crazy again and that I needed to calm down. While my wandering in the woods might be hard to explain, it wasn't a crime.

A few more tense seconds passed. I couldn't just stay there. For all I knew, the cop was prepared to lurk for hours, enjoying the cat-and-mouse game. So I backed away one soft step at a time, watching through the brush for any sign of motion.

Nothing happened during the time it took me to cover fifty feet and I turned and broke into a fast walk then a slow trot that brought me to the creek. I slid and slipped down the tall bank and one foot went into the rushing water up to the ankle. I climbed up the other side in a soaked sock and shoe, and slogged the remaining quarter mile at a squishy hobble.

I was relieved to find the rental car as I had left it. I jumped in, cranked the engine, turned on the heater, and pulled off the wet shoe and sock. I high-tailed it out of there and drove to a point on the road where I could see over the fields to the barn. Dewitt's Jeep was no longer in sight. I stole a fast glance in the mirror before pulling out again.

When I got to Angela's, I pulled into the alley behind her yard and parked there. Inside, I changed clothes, then turned on the oven and placed my still-damp shoe and sock on the open door. I was fixing my second bloody mary of the day when the lock rattled. She stepped into the kitchen, saw the cocktail, and asked me if I was still going from breakfast. Her gaze settled first on the open oven door and then on the raincoat that was hanging on the back of the chair.

She said, "Where'd you find that?"

Rather than answer, I said, "Do you want one of these?"

"I came home to eat lunch," she said

"I'm using V-8."

"Well, then, by all means." She removed her own coat and sat down.

I finished making the drinks and brought them to the table. We both sipped.

"I found it in the basement," I said. "I'm sorry if I –"

"It's all right," she said. "I forgot I still had it." She didn't elaborate and I decided it would be best not to ask.

I said, "I didn't have anything to wear outside."

She held her celery stalk in mid-air. "I thought I told you to stay here."

"You told me to stay out of trouble."

"You're right," she said. "Did you?"

"Not exactly."

Her black eyes went blacker. "God*dam*nit, Richie."

"You have to hear this," I said.

She glared at me for another second, then crunched down hard on the celery. "Okay, what?"

I told her about my trek through the rainy woods to the barn, Officer Dewitt appearing and then disappearing; and my retreat, which I chose to slow to a stately pace.

Though she was still irked, her curiosity had the best of her. She said, "You didn't see where he went?"

"Inside the barn, I guess. Or maybe he slipped into the woods. Anyway, I think he knew I was there. He could have known where I was the whole time. Just playing with me." I quaffed my drink. "What do you know about him? Is he from around here?"

"No, I think he's from Virginia or West Virginia, I don't remember which."

"That's great," I said. "I had a fucking mountain man stalking me."

It wasn't funny and we both knew it. Because Dewitt was likely one of the fools who were running around those same fields playing army with live ammunition.

"You're missing something," Angela said. "I mean, we are. Joey had pulled out the plats of that piece of land and the barn, right? We were looking at it from the ridge when someone came to chase us off. Now the same place gets a visit from Roy Dewitt."

"You think he followed me there?"

"I don't know. Coincidences happen, Richie. Really. Maybe he goes out there three times a day. Maybe *you* being there was the coincidence."

"I don't think so." It was time to share the piece I had left out. It told her about the page in the plat book.

She didn't see it. "A fingerprint? That's it? Anyone could have left it there."

"But on that page? You don't think that's kind of peculiar?"

"It's just an empty old barn," she said.

"There's something else. I was checking it out when Dewitt showed up."

She sipped her drink and waited.

"It's all stone, right? With the foundation walls sticking up maybe two feet above the ground."

"So?"

"So some of the stones had been removed and replaced with these window-panel kind of things."

She didn't get it, and I explained the frames and the dark glass, all newer than the rest of the structure. I said, "Why would you need windows in the foundation of a barn?"

"I guess to, I don't know, ventilate underneath?"

"These weren't vents."

She puzzled for a few seconds. "So, what, there's something under there?"

In the silence that followed, I felt prickles rise on my arms. Angela was watching me as my expression changed. I finished my drink in one fast swig. "I'm going to the library."

My sock was dry and my shoe close enough to dry to wear. I pulled them on, stood up, and reached for the raincoat.

Angela drained her glass. "Wait," she said. "I'm going with you."

We drove through the pelting rain and when we got there, found that Mrs. Eldridge had stepped out, leaving the sacred stacks in the hands of her assistant and a high school volunteer. The assistant hesitated, not sure if she could let us into the Collections Room, but the combination of what was left of my celebrity and Angela's standing as a local and a lawyer overcame her reluctance. It didn't matter; I was already down the hall and waiting when she arrived with the key.

While Angela made room on the long table I pulled the plat book that I had opened the day before down from the shelf. I flipped through until I found the drafting of stone barn, then lifted the corner of the page so that she could discern the fingerprint in the old paper.

She studied it, then shifted her gaze. "Okay, so this is it."

We had before us a skeletal view from ground-level perspective, drawn in faint blue lines. We both peered closely and I pointed to the places in the foundation where I had seen the window frames.

Angela said, "Then it's got some kind of a cellar."

I said, "I didn't see any door." She waited while I turned some pages forward and backward. "And it's the only one that's built that way. The others are just on slabs."

"So that could be where Dewitt went," she said.

"Maybe." I ran an absent finger over the faint old lines. "I wonder what it is."

"Maybe it's where their little army meets."

"Yeah, but why hide it like that?"

She didn't have an answer for that, either.

The front door creaked as Mrs. Eldridge came in out of the rain. We could hear her talking to the assistant. Then her voice rose, followed by staccato steps in the hall. Angela and I exchanged a guilty glance.

Just as the door opened, I remembered my ungloved hands, and tried to hide them. The librarian stood glaring.

"I'm sorry," I said. "It couldn't wait."

"It's a library. *Everything* can wait." Her mouth was pinched in anger as she turned on my partner in crime. "Angela Sesto..."

"I'm sorry," Angela said. "But we think we found something important."

Mrs. Eldridge's gaze shifted by degrees from ire to grudging interest. After a tense few seconds, she cleared her throat and said, "Found what?"

I jumped to hold a chair for her and she sat with a cool nod. Angela did the talking, tying Joey's visits and drawing in the plat book of the barn beyond Line Road.

Mrs. Eldridge stared down at the page. "Do you think this had something to do with your brother's death?"

Angela said, "We don't know that."

I said, "It does," and she looked at me, then looked away.

The librarian was quiet, trying to grasp the notion that some old papers in her archives could be a piece of the puzzle that led to a murder. She said, "So you think this involves those men and their – what do they call it – 'defense group'?"

"Maybe," I said. "Or some of the members. Who knows what they'd do if someone got in their business? It happens all the time with these nuts."

Angela said, "If you asked me, I'd say no."

"And why is that?" Mrs. Eldridge said.

"Those guys are not like those crazies out in Idaho or wherever. They just like to run around with their guns. I don't think any of them were even in the military. They're playing. I guess it makes them feel like tough guys or whatever. But they're just losers."

"Guns can turn cowards into heroes," Mrs. Eldridge murmured. "Make little boys think they're real men."

"Oh, Richie wouldn't know anything about that," Angela said coolly. "I guess you've heard what happened at Sonny's last night."

"That wasn't –"

"All right, now," the librarian said. She lifted the corner of the frail drawing. "You know there could be nothing in this space at all. It could be that it's just an empty hole."

"No," I said. "I don't think so."

We apologized to Mrs. Eldridge once more and thanked her for her hospitality. She was gracious to Angela, but the gaze she cast my way told me she thought I was back to sullying her hallowed rooms with my bawdy behavior. Though she let herself unbend long enough to warn us to be careful.

"Bad things can happen in small towns," she whispered at the door. "And that includes hometowns."

The rain had slowed to more of a mist. Angela was quiet for the first minute of the drive back to her house. Then she laughed and said, "I think she wanted to stick you in a corner until you learned to behave."

"Wouldn't be the first time I got sent to one of her corners," I said.

"Oh, no?" She looked at me, saw my smirk, and took her foot off the gas. "Oh, my God. Did you... You didn't... Did you have sex with someone in our town library?"

"I engaged in some lewd acts," I admitted. "But I was a mere lad."

"With who?"

"I think it's 'whom.' Candy Marelli, for one."

She shook her head dolefully.

"Hey, I wasn't the only one. Your brother –"

"Please, I don't want to know," she said. "Anyway, I think we have more important matters to deal with here."

I agreed, though getting lost in that one silly memory had been a small respite. We rolled to a stop at the corner of Fourth Street and I said, "You're just mad because you never did anything like that."

"How do you know?" she said, and drove on.

She made coffee and we spent some time tending to our own thoughts. Presently, she drained her cup, rose from the table, and went upstairs, leaving me alone.

Whatever she was thinking, in my mind it came to this: Joey was dead because he had discovered something so dangerous that he had to be silenced. What I didn't know was what grave secrets a rustic little burg like Wyanossing would have to hide.

Leo and Louie had made the same case in their own weird ways and I had dismissed both of them, Leo because of his history of paranoid rants and Louie because his mind was gone. Crystal had dropped a little trail of breadcrumbs and I had written her off as a cartoon, a blowsy airhead playing a silly, selfish game. Now it occurred to me that I should have been listening a little closer. Wasn't I the actor, trained to plumb the deepest realities of characters and their motivations? I had failed that test.

I didn't have the luxury of beating myself up, because my next thought was that the guilty party might have figured out that the knot was beginning to unwind. Angela and I being stalked meant that someone knew there was trouble brewing. Other people were in danger, too. Nobody would pay much attention to Louie, but what about Leo and Crystal?

My thoughts made another leap. What if all of them were lying? Or in cahoots? What if they had all conspired in Joey's murder and now I was caught up in their evil web? They would kill and eat me and bury my bones and I'd never see my wife and kids again. My story would be an episode on one of those real-life mystery shows. I would finally make it to network TV in something other than a laxative commercial.

"Hey." Angela was standing in the kitchen doorway. "You okay?"

I blinked. "Yeah, why?"

"You had a weird look on your face."

"I'm just getting a little crazy here."

"I don't blame you." She sat down. "So, what do you think, Richie? You think the answer to who murdered my brother and why is in that cellar?"

"I think something's down there. And it's a piece of the puzzle."

She said, "Do you suspect Dewitt in all this?"

"I do," I said. "He's been turning up at these odd moments since the day I got to town. He lurks, you know what I mean? He's got the cop stuff going on. And then there's the little soap opera with Crystal." I shifted in my chair. "She was here."

"Who was where?"

"Crystal. Was here. In your kitchen."

"When?"

"This morning. After you left." I described the knock on the back door and Crystal coming inside, dripping wet – Angela rolled her eyes at that – and her whispers about the dangers hovering about.

Angela said, "Has it ever occurred to you to stop admiring her tits long enough to ask her just what the hell she's talking about? All she's giving you is smoke."

I said, "You know, I can play her, too."

"So far you haven't done a very good job." She smiled. "Maybe you're just not as charming as you used to be."

"I am too," I said. "I'm just a little rusty."

"Is that what they call it?"

This time the banter felt a little hollow and I moved on. "I'll take care of Crystal. She wants my help, she'll have to tell me whatever she knows."

"When?"

I shifted my gaze to the gray day outside. "Before tonight," I said.

"Why? What's tonight?"

"Tonight is when I go back to that barn."

She considered for a few seconds and then said, "You mean we."

There was other business closer at hand. I told Angela I wanted to talk to Leo and find Louie. Leo would be no problem. She said she needed to make a run to the store and would cruise around and see if she spotted Louie wandering the streets. In the meantime, I would drive to his little shack in the railroad yard. She didn't want to have any direct knowledge of that domicile.

As she went out the door, she said, "And don't forget to call your girlfriend."

Before I dialed the number on the card Crystal had given me, I dug out the local phone book. I found several "Nash" listings, but no "Crystal," nor any entries with an initial "C."

The phone rang four times with an odd electronic buzz and then I heard her recorded voice, sounding spry and inviting. Without leaving my name, I muttered a message about something important to discuss with her, the sooner the better.

Next I called Leo and asked him if he had seen Louie. "No, why?"

"I'm a little worried that he could be in some trouble here."

"What kind of trouble?"

"The kind we've been talking about," I said.

Leo said, "Fuck, man. I knew it. I was right, wasn't I? He was right."

"I'm not sure. But I'd like to know that he's safe, okay?"

"Okay, well, if I see him I'll get him off the street."

"You too, Leo."

"Me too, what?

"Just watch your back."

"I always do, bro."

I left it at that. The less he knew, the better, too.

I ducked out to the rental car and did the winding route through town again. That I didn't detect anyone tailing me was little comfort. For all I knew, Officer Dewitt had a network of spies all over Wyanossing watching for my car to pass by their windows. It seemed like just the kind of subterfuge that would engage him and his pals.

I thought I might catch sight of Louie bouncing his ball in the rain, but no luck. I arrived at the bottom of Seventh Street and parked the car beneath a heavy elm tree. It was a long and exposed walk across River Street and through the yard to his shack. There was no other way.

I moved along at a good clip and when I got close, started calling his name. "Louie? Hey, Louie!" His little house was silent in the mist. "Louie! You home?"

The ragged curtain was hanging over the window, so I couldn't see inside. I called his name again. I was too exposed just standing out there like that, and getting wet to boot, so I walked to the back.

Just as I turned the corner, I heard the front door slap on the jamb. I hurried back around to find it open a few inches and swinging in the dancing gusts of wind.

Putting my face to the space, I called again. "Louie? It's Richie." I pushed the door wide and stepped inside.

Some kind of a fracas had disheveled that small space. Louie's armchair was upended and his coffee table had been broken apart. The floor was a-skitter with magazines, newspapers, and some of his LPs. The one lamp was smashed. When I pulled back the curtain for more light, I saw splatters of blood on the floor, the couch, and even up the walls. I stalked around, feeling my heart drumming. I remembered not to touch anything, just in case.

With a last look, I backed outside. As I ducked my head to start my trek to the street, I noticed that the gravel was torn up with divots and gouges that told me the fight had continued outside. The scrapes stopped after few feet and with the ground so wet, following footprints was hopeless.

I hurried across River Street, jumped into the car and called Angela on her cell phone. She picked up on the first ring.

I said, "Did you find Louie?"

"No," she said. "And no one I talked to has seen him." She told me that she had called the halfway house on the off chance that he had shown up there, without luck.

I related my foray to his shack and described what I found there. She didn't say a word when I finished. "I hope I didn't get him killed," I said.

"Why would anyone want to hurt him? He's so out of it. Nobody'd believe anything he said."

"I would."

"Yes," she said. "I think I would, too."

I told her I was going to report what I had found to Tim Raines. She wasn't sure that this was a good idea. "You know he might be sharing everything you've told him so far with Dewitt."

"I know, but I haven't told him very much. I just think he needs to know about this. Louie could be lying out somewhere, hurt."

"I guess that's true," she said.

I told her I was going to run by the police station and see if he was there. Then I'd head back to her house.

She said, "Have you heard from Crystal?"

"Not yet."

She told me she had a couple stops to make and then would be going home.

After we rang off, I sat for a few minutes, staring across the street at the lonely little shack, fearing that I had started something that had landed on poor Louie Zag. Maybe they had decided that, as crazy as he was, it was just smarter to shut him up. That thought sent me racing through the rain to the police station.

Tim wasn't in his office. The girl at the desk explained that he had gone out to work a traffic accident. She raised him on the radio and he gave instructions for me to come find him at the accident site on Wheaton Avenue where it crossed Route 12, just inside the borough limits.

When I arrived at the scene, I saw a truck on its side and a sedan at an angle with the rear wheels in a drainage ditch, the front end bashed. An ambulance and two wreckers sat idling. The weather had cut down on rubberneckers and the neighbors observed the excitement from the shelter of their front porches.

Tim was standing in his raincoat and Smokey the Bear hat, taking a statement from the driver of the truck. The guy was waving his hands, overdoing it, and Tim looked around, getting bored. I caught his eye and he tilted his head toward his cruiser.

I walked to the car and waited. He finished with the driver and joined me. Eyeing the chapeau I had snatched at Angela's, he said, "Nice hat."

"Everyone's wearing them in New York." He looked at the hat again, looked at me. "Never mind," I said.

"What can I do for you?"

"I went to look for Louie at that shack he stays in. You know about that?" Tim nodded. "He wasn't there. The place is all busted up. And there's blood around, on the floor and the furniture and some on the walls. Something happened, Tim. I'm a little worried about him."

"You went there why?" Tim said, an odd question at that point in the conversation. I was ready for it, though.

"I just wanted to make sure I saw him before I left. I figured it would take me a few tries to catch up with him."

"You know he's supposed to stay at a halfway house," he said.

"Angela checked there. They haven't seen him." I watched Tim watch the cleanup of the accident. He wasn't displaying much concern for Louie's welfare. "You have any idea what could have happened?"

"I really can't say until I go by," he said. "It might have to do with drugs, though." His eyes flicked at me for a second, then went away. "I assume he has himself a stash wherever he stays. Someone could have gone after it." His faint smile returned. "I think Louie would fight for his stash."

"He wouldn't fight for anything, except maybe his life." Now Tim gave me a curious look. I didn't care; even after my long absence, I knew Louie Zag better than he ever would.

Either way, we weren't going to discuss it. "I'll have my people keep an eye out for him," he said. "But I don't think there's anything to worry about. Louie gets into things and gets out of things. He could have just hurt himself over there, cut himself or something, and went off to get some help." He drew a pen from his pocket. "Don't worry, we'll find him. But thanks for the information." He started writing on his pad. "So when are you heading back?"

"Soon," I said. "Monday."

"After your hearing."

"That's right."

"Well, it was good seeing you." With a nod, he walked off to do some more law enforcing.

I hadn't expected him to jump in his car and rush off to the train yard with the siren screaming, and so I wasn't disappointed. He didn't think it was any big deal. I wondered how many bizarre episodes had featured Louie over the years.

I climbed back into the rental car and drove the streets for a while longer. I circled Seventh Street School twice. No Louie. I had just started back to Angela's when my cell phone chirped. It went flying when I fumbled it out of my pocket and I almost destroyed another car trying to snatch it.

When I finally managed to push the talk button, I heard Crystal say, "Richard, I got your –"

"Have you seen Louie Zag?"

"Louie Zag? The crazy guy?"

"Yeah, him. Who else?"

"I haven't seen him in weeks, why?"

"I need to find him."

"Why?"

"I think he might have been hurt."

"Sometimes he goes down to the railroad yard."

"I went there. And the school. I didn't see him. Nobody's seen him."

"He wanders around a lot."

"I know he does, Crystal," I said. "Jesus Christ."

"Don't snap at me." She sounded like a wounded child.

I took a breath. "Listen. You know something about what's been going on here, don't you?" When she didn't answer, I said, "Crystal?"

"I'm here." It was a slow, low whisper.

"Joey's dead," I said. "I had a car trashed. Someone took a shot at Angela and me. And there's a –"

"Who took a shot at you?"

"Never mind that. The point is there's something wrong. I want you to tell me everything you know. Or you can tell Tim Raines. Or somebody."

"Tim Raines?" She came up with a cold laugh. "I'm not telling him anything."

I let that be. I didn't want to get into her problems with the local police chief on top of everything else.

"All right, then don't tell him. Tell Angela. She's a lawyer. If you know anything, you can tell her."

"I know enough."

"You keep saying that, but I haven't heard a goddamn thing. Do you have anything or don't you?"

She paused again. "Are you really going to help me?" she said.

I bit down on my anger. "What did I say this morning? You come to New York and I'll help you. What I can't do is offer you a career in show business. You have to do that on your own. And it's a rough ride."

"I know that. But I'm assuming it would be better than sucking cock in Wyanossing, PA, right?"

I recovered from my surprise and said, "That's for you to judge."

For a moment, I was afraid she was going to hang up. She didn't though; she let out a dark little laugh laden with meaning that I couldn't begin to guess. Anyway, we needed to move things along.

"I need whatever you know about what happened to Joey," I said. "That means no games. No holding back. I want all of it. That's the deal."

She paused for a few seconds, then said, "Where will you be tonight?"

"Wherever you want."

"I'll come to Angela's house. Through the alley. Like I did this morning."

"What time?"

"After dark. Seven-thirty."

"All right."

"All right." Her voice sounded oddly sad, as if she was giving something away. "I'll see you tonight." The phone went dead.

Angela and I sat at the kitchen table. I told her about my conversation with Crystal.

She said, "You think she'll show?"

"I wouldn't lay money on it."

"Me, neither."

"So what's your best guess here, counselor?" I said. "What's going down in your humble little borough?"

"I think Joey found out about something dirty," she said. "Someone got scared about it and cornered him up on Nock Hill and pushed him off Council Rock." She stopped to steady herself, then went on more deliberately. "Whatever it was is somehow connected to that barn out on the ridge. I think Roy Dewitt is involved. Maybe he said something to Crystal. Pillow talk or whatever. Now she has the goods on him. If that's the case, she's in the middle of it. And she's playing angles of her own."

"I don't care what she's doing," I said. "I just want whatever she knows."

We sat without speaking for a few moments.

"So who shot at us up on the tower?" she said.

"Dewitt. John Miller. Some other fool. Everybody out here has guns, right?"

"Pretty much, yeah."

"Do you?"

"There's a pistol upstairs somewhere," she said. "It's more along the lines of a paperweight. You want it?"

I shook my head. The rain had quieted some and so did my thoughts.

I said, "The problem is we still haven't got anything solid. I mean, we're just guessing, right?"

"Well, there's nothing I could take to court, if that's what you mean. Unless Miss Crystal delivers a bombshell."

I was pondering this when Angela broke into my thoughts. "She really said 'better than sucking cock in Wyanossing, PA'?"

I nodded. "Verbatim."

"She goes from airhead to angel to slut. Maybe she's got some acting talent after all." She eyed me. "Are you really going to help her in New York?"

"If she does her part. I said I would." I waved a hand. "Don't worry, even if she does show up, in a month she'll be running for home. Hey, forget about her. I don't know if *I'm* going to have a career when I get back."

"I hope that's not the case." She stood up. "Do you want something to eat?"

The way she said it was so off-hand, so domestic, that we both stopped for a moment, caught in a sudden might-have-been moment. After a few seconds, she came up with a winsome smile and without another word, walked out of the kitchen.

13.

I hadn't put anything in my stomach since the last bloody mary. I was still too keyed up to eat. I didn't want another drink, either. If I needed liquid courage, it would be better to drop the whole adventure. Also, I felt responsible for my partner in crime and wanted a clear head.

Seven-thirty arrived and Crystal didn't appear or call. At quarter to eight, Angela said, "How much longer?" She had been pacing and fidgeting.

"Another fifteen minutes, then we leave."

It was a nerve-wracking quarter-hour waiting for St. Michael's bells. At the first toll, I stood up. We put on our coats and passed through the kitchen. Angela stopped to reach into a cabinet for a flashlight and we stepped out the back door and into the drizzle without exchanging a word.

I again followed a jagged pattern through town to see if anyone was following. The streets were shrouded in rain, and full of shifting shadows, and as we drove our roundabout route, landmarks appeared from the mist. One little house was still covered in ivy and surrounded by stunted trees and flower bushes, once a fairytale cottage made all the more so by the sad-eyed old couple who had lived there. I remembered solemn whispers about an unnamed tragedy left behind in the old country.

I turned another corner and spied a storefront, now abandoned, and remembered wandering inside on a rainy night just like this one. The proprietor, a thick sack of a bachelor with a glum face, let me huddle at the magazine racks and read for a couple hours, *Mad* and *Car Craft* and *Song Hits*. Not another soul came through the door as the storm passed outside. The newsprint was cheap in my fingers. I recalled the photograph of Big Maybelle in a shimmering dress that showed off a gorge of cleavage. It seemed an odd memory to conjure at that time, but a way to avoid thinking about what might lie ahead.

The moment Angela told me about Joey's fall from Council Rock, I felt a twist in my gut that was more than shock and sorrow, but a sharp sense that something was wrong about it. In the space of five days, as I moved from Manhattan to my hometown, the disquieting notion had grown to a cold certainty that his death had not been an accident. And now one piece of the proof could be waiting in the darkness outside town.

Or maybe the liquid shadows were getting the best of me and the only thing waiting was a soggy path to a dead end. If so, the story would dwindle away to nothing, at least for me. I could not break my promise to go home on Monday. My wife and children were coming to make sure that I would do just that.

"Okay," Angela said, interrupting these musings. Her voice was tense as she watched the mirror. "I don't see anyone."

In another few minutes, we were driving out of town. The streets turned bare, with few houses and fewer porch lights. Angela didn't shift her gaze when we passed Joey's single-wide.

I drove the route I had taken the day before and steered down the service road, pulled to a stop alongside the stack of ties, and shut off the engine. The darkness was a black blanket and save for the light patter of rain on the roof, the night was still. My eyes adjusted until I discerned a twisted tangle of branches and undergrowth that could have been lifted from a page in a Grimm Brothers tale. I told her we needed to wait a few minutes to make sure no one was tracking us or lurking in the trees. She settled back.

In the next silent moments, my thoughts turned down one path and then another and arrived at the long ago nights when she and I had spent in a car parked down some other dark and lonely road. From a far corner of my memory, I conjured her face and body cast in amber dashboard lights, such an ethereal image that it seemed a fragment from a sweet dream.

It wasn't any dream, though; and now I plucked from our erotic history one particular night when we went at it in the back seat of my Valiant with the Slant-6 engine as rain drummed the roof and made a delta of rivulets down the windows.

It seemed that our world began and ended in that lost hour, and when it was over, we curled together, listening to the tympani of raindrops over our heads. Angela started to weep, because she had lain with me again, even though I had another girl, and because in two days, I would be reporting for duty and she feared it was the last she would see of me.

So many years had passed to bring us back to just such a forgotten crook, down an empty trail and hidden from everyone and everything we knew. At that moment, a hollow sadness for what we had lost assailed me and I felt an urge to reach over and touch her. I wanted to hold her face in my hands and kiss her on the mouth and carry the both of us back to a time and place when there were no tomorrows.

I said, "Angela..."

By the way she held my gaze before sighing and looking away, I knew she had been thinking some of the same thoughts.

For the next few seconds, I went adrift with nothing to anchor me. Then the faces of my wife and daughters appeared out of the darkness and I felt my heart crack. How I loved them! How I wanted to see them and smell them and wrap them in my arms. Because the only true way I knew to chase away my fears and sadness was to hide in that embrace.

Some moments passed and I understood that if I lingered there, awash in longing, we'd never move, never finish what we had come for. So I let them go.

I glanced at Angela to find her staring into the night with a faraway expression. "You ready?" She murmured a few words I didn't catch, throwing off something of her own. I said, "What was that?"

"Yeah," she said. "I'm ready."

"It's back through there." I pointed into the trees.

She flexed her hands. "I'm kind of scared."

"Yeah, me, too," I said.

"I'm not chickening out," she said. "But we need to go before I do."

"Right."

She handed me the flashlight and I opened my door.

I waited until we had gone twenty paces into the first stand of trees before pushing the button. Though it was unlikely that anyone in a car passing on the two-lane would pick out the white beam in the darkness, there was no sense in being careless. And the glow of the bulb was a small comfort.

We followed the path that I had taken in the daylight, now even more slowly and with frequent stops so I could get my bearings. When we reached the creek, it was wet, clumsy, too noisy business getting down one bank, across the rocks, and up the other side.

Just as we reached the crest of the bank, Angela hissed at me. "Wait!"

I switched off the flashlight. "What's wrong?"

"I thought I heard something."

"What kind of something?"

"Like somebody moving around."

We stood still. I closed my eyes for a second because the shifting of the branches was too distracting, but it didn't do much good. There were sounds that could have been footfalls or a dozen other forest noises.

"Let's just keep going," I said. "It's not that far."

She said, "Okay," and we moved on.

It would have already occurred to her, as it had to me, that most of the males in that part of the country were hunters and stalked craftier creatures than the two of us through these woods every winter.

This was another issue that put Joey, Leo, Louie, and me at odds with that crowd: we didn't hunt. Leo and I didn't care about the deer one way or the other. We simply couldn't see tramping around in the frigid winter woods. Louie thought it was an insane pursuit – like *golf*, he used to sneer – and would goof about the local "sportsmen" spending thousands of dollars on guns and gear and then attesting earnestly that their families "needed the meat." And Joey claimed it was a blood-lusting, anti-environmental plot to dominate the natural world. Of course, we all enjoyed getting out of school for the first day of deer season.

Those other guys could navigate the woods in the dark. One of them could be tracking us and we wouldn't know it. Creeping on, I thought about Isabel and the girls and wondered what the hell I was doing out there.

It wasn't the time to ponder it. I had put this ball in motion four days earlier, when I told the cab driver to carry me to Avis. So that I could do the right thing and pay my respects to my old friend. That had led me into something far more treacherous. Now we had come too far to bail out.

Joey had been my brother by another mother. The least I could do was make a stab at avenging his death. Well, not *avenging*, exactly; that would be for someone else to handle. We would just lead them to the –

"What did you say?"

I stopped again. "What?"

"You just said something."

"I did?"

"Are you losing your mind?" Her whisper was sharp. "You're talking to yourself."

"I'm fine." I peered up ahead and saw that the tree line ended after another fifty yards. "We're almost there," I said.

She nodded, took a steadying breath and said, "Okay, then."

For someone who had been away from woodlands for so long, I didn't do too badly. We arrived at the clearing less than fifty feet from the stone barn. I pointed the way and we moved through the wheatgrass to a point directly behind the structure. As we stepped from beneath the dripping boughs, I heard Angela hiss something under her breath. I followed her pointing finger to a tiny glimmer of light.

We crept over the soggy earth and tangles of vines toward the glimmer and when we closed within a dozen feet of the foundation, I saw that it was emanating from one of the framed windowpanes. We stepped up and bent down to see thin scratches gouged into the glass. Angela caught another sharp breath. The letters "JS" had been scrawled there, an eerie signature.

I settled on my haunches. So Joey had knelt at that same spot and carved his initials as a sign – or a message. He had marked the page in the plat book and had marked this pane of glass. As if he had known someone would come along behind him.

Angela studied the glass for a long few seconds, then straightened and turned away before I could read her expression. We made our way along the side of the barn, hearing only the wind, the gentle hiss of rain, and the occasional plop of a heavy drop hitting the ground. When we rounded the corner to the front, she went stalking up the incline and through the door opening. I followed her out of the drizzle.

Once inside, I could see tiny pencils of light from below through gaps in the wood. Angela took a step forward. The creak of the floorboard sounded like a gunshot in that quiet space and we both jumped.

As I backed up, motioning for her to follow me, I saw her staring over my shoulder. She said, "We've got company."

From the darkness, I heard a voice mutter, "What you got is a world of trouble."

I turned around to see John Miller and three other men emerge from the darkness and walk slowly up the slope, spreading out at event intervals. All four were wearing camouflage fatigues and brandishing weapons. John was toting a nasty-looking chrome .45 and the other three held AK-47s. Though rain-dappled, their fatigues were still starched tight, so that they resembled kids playing Army. It was such a weird sight that I barked out a stunted laugh.

The man on the left, the youngest of the group, raised the barrel of his weapon a few inches. “Something funny about this?” he said.

He was one of those from John’s table the night before. Angela recognized him, too. “You’re Darlene Yarnell’s son,” she said. “You went to school with my son. I know your mother. I did her will.” She looked him up and down. ”Does she know you’re out here with these clowns?”

Yarnell blinked and shifted his gaze away, his chin stiffening. Angela turned her glare on John and said, “What are you going to do, John? Shoot us?”

He stared back at her and said, “Maybe.”

Angela hooted, honestly amused. “Somehow I don’t think you will.”

“Then you don’t know nothing about me,” John said, snapping the words with such bile that I felt a first spike of nerves. Who knew how crazy he had grown over the years? Or what he was liable to do to prove himself? He’d already been shamed once.

Angela was simply perturbed. “You dumb shit. Put those goddamn things away. Unless this is your property, you have no rights.”

“Zip it, counselor.” John waved the pistol in a menacing fashion. He spoke in a low voice and took a few more steps forward. I noticed that he was wincing and wondered if I had cracked one of his ribs. I hoped so.

Even with the pain, he was enjoying this rude little scene. I caught a shade of the same cruel and greedy smile he had worn when we were kids and he had the most candy. And John always had the most candy.

But if his show of force was meant to scare us, it wasn’t working. Angela stood shaking her head in derision. For my part, I could make the jump from John Miller, the nasty but mostly harmless kid, to this buffoon and his band of pretend soldiers. At the same time, the posturing made a kind of sick sense. Lacking the wits to keep up with a world in flux, such characters were secure only in the cockeyed universe at the margins. And God help anyone who tried to take that shrinking bit of turf away from them.

So having all the hardware trained on us was no joke.

Seeing he wasn't getting our respect, John tightened his jaw and said, "Okay, *move*, you two."

We stayed put. Angela said, "Do you have any idea what you're doing? You're making a deadly threat."

"Fucking right, he is," one of his minions said.

Angela cut her eyes at him. "That's a felony, you stupid asshole."

"I told you to shut up," John said. His tone shifted to cold and brisk, the man in charge. "And move."

I was ready to stand my ground and see what they'd do. At the same time, I wanted to find out what they were up to and what occupied the space under the barn. I looked at Angela and we shared an eye-rolling glance of victims playing along with a practical joke. We took our time letting them escort us back down the incline and around the side of the barn.

John led the way with one man on either side and one behind us. Halfway along the side, he turned and said something I didn't hear and the Yarnell kid stepped to the slope of earth that edged the foundation and bent down. He jerked his arm and a hurricane door flapped open, casting a swath of white light into the rainy night. Dirt and sparse grass clung to the door in an odd way and I realized that these materials had somehow been affixed there so as to conceal it. These guys were taking their act seriously.

John said, "All right. Down you go."

We were standing at the top of concrete steps that led into the basement below. Angela stopped and turned around and I could see from the look on her face that she'd had enough. She waited until John said, "Did you hear me?" before descending underground one grudging step at a time. John managed the stairs with difficulty, huffing and cursing. He saw me glance at him and said, "What?"

The hurricane doors closed behind us with a bang and we stood gazing at a bizarre spectacle. Within the basement walls of stacked stone was a maze of partitions holding gun racks and a selection of military charts, along with metal shelves stacked full of ordnance and other equipment. Two RPG launchers leaned in a corner next to two fifty-five-gallon drums. A storage room had been framed into the back wall, six feet square with a thick door that was closed. Next to this enclosure, three long tables were draped with tarps. With all the olive drab, I experienced an odd flashback to my Army days, when that color had dominated my world.

Along with all this hardware, the partitions were festooned at regular intervals with posters, placards, and framed documents conveying various screeds about resistance and rebellion, with blacks, Jews, and Mexicans displayed as targets. I had seen such matter in documentaries about hate groups. It was something else to encounter it for real. I felt a flutter in my gut; I didn't like the looks of this at all. Angela peered about, pursed her lips, and said something rude.

John and his three pals stepped around and into my line of sight as we perused this display, keeping their distance from Angela and me as they fanned out in a semicircle.

Angela didn't seem a bit daunted as she again fixed her cold eyes on him. "Are you out of your fucking mind or what?" He answered with a sneer and she said, "Well? Are you going to shoot us now or later?" Her tone was impatient, as if she was tired of a stupid game.

John didn't take the bait. Neither he nor any of his men spoke or moved, and I got the sense they were waiting for something.

Maybe I was too stupid to be frightened, but I couldn't believe these characters thought they could get away with doing us harm. Even if they were willing to commit the violence, too many people knew of our suspicions. I had told Leo, Tim Raines, Mrs. Eldridge, and Isabel more than enough. Angela and I disappearing or turning up dead would be impossible to cover.

John had to know this. But what if he and his crew of fools were too far gone into their militia madness to care? A colder thought came to me: what if they were the ones who had murdered Joey? It would be too late for them to go squeamish. I pushed down a second dark rush of nerves that we might be in real danger. It was something I had learned to do a long time ago as part of the craft of drama.

In the tense pause that followed, the seconds expanded and the frame shifted back into the realm of the ludicrous. Angela had it right. Who were these idiots playing soldier? They were weak, unimportant men who thought uniforms and loaded weapons meant they were powerful.

True or not, this did not calm my nerves. I knew that people driven by fear were liable to go off, all the more so when deep into a rabid cause. Slavish drones, they served a master monster or some horrific idea that gave their lives direction and meaning. It was an old story, steeped in centuries of blood. Now Angela and I were encountering a small piece of it firsthand, stage-managed by John Miller, whom I'd known since the first grade.

Whispers passed back and forth and on his orders, we were herded to the empty back corner. Though neither or us looked down, Angela had to be as aware as I was of the plastic sheeting duct-taped to the floor and up the walls. As if someone was getting ready for a mess.

Her gaze flicked this way and that and settled for a long moment on the draped tables. Then she turned on John. "You need to stop this shit right now," she said. "You have no idea what you're doing. I'll ruin your lives, goddamnit."

"How many times I got to tell you to shut up?" John looked over at Yarnell and shook his head. "You believe this bitch? Making threats?"

He started to chortle, then stopped when Angela turned to taunting him. "You wouldn't call me that if you weren't holding that popgun. Would you, you fucking pussy?"

The men in the basement gaped in awe at her gall and her language, me included. John's mouth flapped and his face went pink. She had called him out for the second time in two nights, but whatever his reaction, whether he slapped her or shot her, she was still a woman. The only thing that could have saved him was some retort just as cutting, but he didn't have the brains. He had never been that bright. So he stood there with his eyes bugging and his face flushing crimson.

"All right, now what?" she demanded in the same withering tone, as if she had assumed charge and wanted answers.

John said, "You don't fucking worry about *what*." I heard the breathless tremble in his voice as he choked on his rage. "You'll find out *what* soon enough." At this, the others recovered, trading surly grins. John produced a mean man's smile and called out, "All right, we're ready here."

In the rough silence that followed, my senses perked and I became aware of a shuffle of noise from inside the room on the opposite corner. Angela heard it, too, and turned, her eyes narrowing. The door swung wide and two figures emerged from the shadows inside. The first one didn't surprise me: Roy Dewitt, sporting the clothes he had worn that morning, and offering the same flat expression that gave away nothing.

When the second man stepped into the light, Angela hissed and said, "Goddamn. You."

Tim Raines was wearing cargo pants and a sweatshirt under a thermal vest. A baseball cap was pulled low over his forehead and a nickel-plated .45 hung at his hip. His badge was not in sight. He barely glanced at Angela as he stepped into the cone of light. His blank blue eyes settled on me and he frowned with a vague annoyance. He said, "You should have let this be, Richie. Let us be."

I was still in a daze at seeing him and all I could manage was, "What the hell? What are you doing, Tim?"

He treated me to a steady look. "You need to be asking yourself that question," he said. "Why didn't you stay in Jew York where you belong?" He stopped for a long moment, as if weighing his words. Then he said, "You people. You don't get it, do you?"

"Get what?" Angela snapped back. When he didn't answer instantly, she took a half step forward and said, "Get what, Tim?"

He drew himself up, all righteous, and took on a lecturing tone. "This country is in real danger," he said. "And it's because of people like you. And the people you support. Those fucking Clintons and Gore and all of them."

Angela gaped at him, appalled at what she was hearing.

"They made us weak," Tim went on. "Left us vulnerable. And you see what happened? We were attacked. Because of –"

"Excuse me." Angela cut him off, her voice spiking. "Do you

remember who was in the White House on September 11th? Who was running the country? Who was supposed to –"

"Clinton!" "John shouted, jerking into sudden animation. "He's the one let it happen! Him and that goddamn bitch wife of his! The both of them!" The words rushed out in a weird infantile squall that would have been funny except for the rattle of the weapon in his hands and the manic glaze in his eyes.

"All right, that's enough," Tim said. "I think they get the idea."

Though my mouth was dry, I managed to say, "You can't be serious."

Tim pursed his lips. "We're dead serious. Don't you get it? This is about the future of America. You can't see that? Even after your city was attacked?" He looked past me. "Being blind is one thing. Working to destroy this country is something else entirely. And helping someone do it is a crime. It's treason."

Angela stared at him and said, "Sonofabitch. You murdered him."

"He was a traitor," John blurted. "He was a –"

"That's not why you did it." Angela snapped. She held still for a cold second. Then, in a motion so sudden that it caught everyone by surprise, she took two steps to her right, grabbed the edge of the tarp covering the closest table and jerked it away, exposing a weird assortment tubes and cans and bottles. Glass and metal clattered.

"You think I haven't seen enough meth labs to know what one looks like?" She tossed the tarp with a rough gesture. "This is how you're financing your fucking crusade?"

Tim almost recovered. "Until the day the citizens of this country wake up, we have to raise the funds for our movement however we can. And if it's –"

"Give me a break." Her black eyes shot blades of venom. "Jesus Christ. Your *movement*? These idiots couldn't take over a bingo game. Even with the guns." "You sick fuck, you!" Her voice swooped up a shrill half-octave and her face paled with anger. "You *murdered* him over this."

Tim jutted his chin as if it was high noon in Dodge City. "We're patriots," he said. "We're going to save this nation from destruction.

I'm not about to let anyone stand in the way of that. And I don't have to make excuses to the likes of you, either."

Angela wasn't listening. In a staccato burst, she said, "He found out about your little business venture and he was going to bust you. Right? That's what happened? Then so long money machine. And your whole fucking life, to boot. He would have buried you."

Tim got snappish. "Your brother had a bad habit of putting his nose where it didn't belong and then shooting off his big mouth," he said. "That was a mistake. He was going to try and stop us. He paid the price."

I listened to this bizarre exchange, my brain still stuck in gear and grappling with the notion that Tim Raines, the three-letter man, senior class president, chief of police, and all-around upright guy, had come to do this evil, murdering Angela's brother, my friend, in order to cover up a drug operation that was being used to finance a militia.

It couldn't be true; and yet I heard the words he spouted and saw the loaded weapons his little band of lunatics had trained on us. I read Angela's mask of broken-hearted rage and wanted to tell her I was sorry for dragging her into this nightmare. I could have left that magic moment when Joey and I crossed a threshold into another place in my memory alone. I could have stayed home. I should have gone home once I had said my final good-bye.

But she was staring at Tim with that same hard gleam in her eye. That she wasn't quailing had thrown him off.

"Yeah, what?" he said.

She said, "Do you think I'm stupid, Tim?"

He shrugged. "I don't think about you one way or another."

She stopped and one of her eyebrows rose in a cool arc. "Oh, we both know *that's* not true."

Now I was watching a scene in a TV drama. The change in Angela startled me more than witnessing the vicious bully emerge from behind Raines's cool lawman front. There was something deep and furious in her gaze and I realized that over the decades, a narrative that had played out in this little town was coming to a grim head.

Thanks to my meddling.

This rolled through my brain in a matter of seconds, something to distract me from the thoughts of my wife and children. I didn't want to come apart now, so I focused on the most mundane details: the swirls of dust in the corners, a spider weaving a web between two rafters, the smell of raw earth from between the old stones.

Tim wouldn't meet Angela's gaze and she went on, picking up speed again. "Here's the thing," she said. "Something you should know before you decide to murder anyone else. I'm smarter than you. Smart runs in our family."

"What are we wait –"

"Shut up, John." She kept her eyes on Tim, holding his attention. "You need to hear this. You know I've lived in this town all my life. And I've always kept my ears open. Over the past twenty years, I've heard all kinds of interesting things. From the various scumbags who came through the justice system."

John said, "Come on, let's get it over with."

Tim ignored him, watching Angela. He said, "Do you have a point?"

"Oh, yeah," she said. "My point is that I've kept notes on the confidential testimonies of these individuals. I have recordings, too. Of people you know. One of them could be in this room right now." She let that settle. "I've collected all kinds of fascinating material. Signed and sealed and locked in a safe deposit box. And not at the Wyanossing Bank, either. Somewhere else."

John said, "You bitch, you didn't – "

"That's all, I said." Tim shifted his position slightly, gauging her. I stood by, the helpless idiot, dazed by her performance, out on a high wire and not backing up an inch.

"Hey, John?" Her eyes did not move away from Tim. "When's the last time someone counted up the drug money? I mean to see how much went to the hardware for your little uprising and how much went elsewhere. I'm just curious."

John started to protest but Tim cut him off with a chopping hand. I stole a glance at Officer Dewitt. He was listening and watching, still showing no reaction at all.

Now Angela's cheeks went pale. "You murdered my big brother. Goddamn you."

Tim shook his head. "I didn't murder anyone. And he dug his own grave."

She looked like she was ready to spit in his face. "And you're digging yours right now." She came up with a chilly smile. "You hear this shit, John? He says he didn't murder anyone. You know what that means? Someone else will take the fall for that. Who do you think it'll be?"

"That's enough!" Tim wouldn't look in John's direction. His face settled into a grim and ugly mask and a memory of he and I had riding bikes together in the sun-dappled glory of childhood in a small town crossed my mind.

But my little pal Timmy Raines had grown and changed into the person who now stood trying to decide what to do with two people who had made a mess of the grand, sick scheme he had devised in that same hometown. I could see from his tense gaze that he was trying to decide if Angela was bluffing. She watched him in turn and in the next moment, I saw her face fall. Something had changed. She glanced over at me for a second before dropping her gaze to the floor.

I felt it in the pit of my stomach: now she had gone too far. Even without the murder, Tim and his band of idiots were screwed. She wouldn't deal on whatever she had on them and he knew it.

John spoke up, all brusque. "Come on, what's –"

This time Tim silenced him with a glance and then shifted his stare between Angela and me, as if he had read our thoughts.

"We're going to have to deal with the both of you. Make you disappear and take our chances after." I caught what sounded like a small shade of regret in his voice. "We really don't have any choice. Not now." He smiled dimly. "The good news is the police department here isn't very skilled when it comes to investigations. But you already know that." He turned to me. "You made a bad damn choice coming back, Richie. You had no business here."

Now I understood more. He didn't think that he and his little platoon of nutcases would be taking chances at all. Along with the other lunacy, he had convinced himself that they were immune in that town and would not have to answer for Angela and me any more than they had answered for Joey.

At this thought, the churning in my gut was shoved aside by a sudden black throb of rage. He was prepared to leave my kids without a father and my wife without a husband. And for what? Some money and a cruel, stupid cause that was doomed to collapse.

In that moment, I decided that I would not cringe in front of these cretins. And I wanted to show Angela that I was with her, no matter what happened next. So I said, "Joey was my business. He was my best friend. So fuck you."

Hearing this, Angela straightened at my side. She looked at the men with the weapons, saving a final glower of contempt for Tim. "Well?" she said. "Go ahead and do it, you sick prick."

Tim took a step back and said, "You heard the lady."

The three underlings tipped up their weapons, tightening their grips to keep the barrels from wobbling. They were more scared that we were. I grabbed onto this in hopes that they wouldn't be willing to go the rest of the way. A rough push in the dark of night was one thing; a firing squad was a whole other matter.

I said, "Do you ever do your own dirty work, Tim?"

Before he could come back at me John took a step forward and said, "I do mine."

I stared him down and the bitter words came out of my mouth. "You fucking cowards," I said. "You ganged up on Joey, too, didn't you?"

John's face turned a darker shade and he began to raise his pistol. He said, "Now I'm going to fix you for the last time."

I had started to blurt, "Goddamn you –" when a voice barked. "No one move!"

In the next second, the six men and one woman in that corner froze in surprise. Officer Dewitt had taken a step back and to the side and was pointing his automatic directly at Tim's head.

Tim looked over his shoulder, frowning, as if he hadn't heard right. "What did you say?"

Dewitt held his pistol hand firm. "I said don't move. And everyone drop your weapons."

Now Tim did a half-turn to gape at him. "What the hell? What are you doing? Have you lost your mind?"

Dewitt slipped his free hand under his sweatshirt to produce a wallet and flip it open. "State Police," he said, then snapped the badge back.

In the next seconds, I stood numbly watching the blood drain from Tim's face. John and his minions stared with their mouths open in variations of stupid shock.

Dewitt said, "Weapons down. I'm not going to say it again."

The three underlings didn't know what to do. They hadn't signed on to tangle with cops, especially one who was armed and ready. Miller was blinking crazily, as if he could not grasp what was transpiring, while Tim's face settled by grim degrees into a hard scowl as it dawned on him that his vicious little party was coming to a dead end.

Dewitt spoke to him in a low voice. Tim held out for a few seconds and then said, "Put them on the floor, gentlemen." His voice was flat. One by one, each man bent and dropped their rifles and pistols.

Dewitt said, "I want every one of you on his knees. Hands behind your heads."

The men did as they were told, deflating as quickly as they had puffed themselves. The Yarnell kid looked like he was going to start crying.

Dewitt let Tim stay on his feet, giving him that much. He backed up two more steps, keeping the pistol at the ready as dug into his pocket for a cell phone. He punched a number, murmured a few words, then snapped it off.

I heard Angela let out a soft moan and realized that my hands were trembling and that my shirt was soaked with sweat. Tim's eyes came around to settle on me and now it was my turn to read his mind: I was the one that had brought this down on him – or Joey and I, to be exact. His gaze was hateful, but the best he could come up with was, "What the fuck are you looking at?"

I don't remember doing it and still don't know why. Maybe because of the blank revulsion in his eyes, the sneer of those who presume superiority with no questions asked or allowed. Maybe it was all the Tim Raineses and John Millers of the world, men who made bullying a way of life. But it was mostly what he had done to Joey and what he had been ready to do to Angela and me, and the awful tragedy he would have visited on my children and my wife.

I didn't realize that I had bolted forward and slammed into his chest, toppling him, until I heard his breath whoosh as we hit the floor together, with me sprawled on top.

From above me, I heard Dewitt yell, "Mr. Zaleski! Freeze!"

It was too late. The adrenaline had dulled my aching muscles and bones and we were grappling as we had on the school playground long ago. Then and now, Tim was stronger, and he got one arm around my neck in a chokehold while the other worked its way south toward my crotch.

I guess it didn't occur to him that I'd have anything for him. I relaxed as if giving up and when I felt his grip loosen, I pulled away enough to get my right arm free and whip the point of my elbow into his Adam's apple. He gagged and coughed and I came back with the same elbow under the tip of his nose. Blood blossomed from both nostrils and his eyes bulged in shock and pain. I jerked my shoulders hard, breaking what was left of his grip, and scrabbled away, kicking blindly.

Dewitt shouted again. "I said, freeze, goddamnit!"

Tim pushed to his feet, his vest soaked red. His hand grasped at his beltline and in the next dull second I realized that he hadn't been going for my scrotum, but for the small pistol tucked in his waistband. He whipped it out and drew down on me and I heard Angela shriek, "Richie!"

The shot cracked like wicked lightning and Tim stumbled as if he had been chopped by a tackler and crumpled to the floor. His hands came up to grasp at the air. He wheezed out two heavy breaths, shuddered once, and flopped back.

I'd seen death played on the stage, and they weren't anything like the real thing. It wasn't pretty. He was soaked in blood from his chest to his thighs and his dead, lidded gaze was fixed on the rafters.

I rose on shaking legs. Angela was weeping, one hand over her mouth and the other held out to me. We came together, clutching desperately at each other as the first sirens wailed on Line Road. It was an embrace stronger than love and yet the whole time I could think only of my wife and children.

The rest of the night began as a ragged jumble and eventually settled into a strange calm, the aftermath of a storm. Angela and I were carried to the borough police station in an unmarked SUV, sequestered in a meeting room, and questioned at length by senior agents from the state police and the state attorney's criminal division. We took turns walking them through what had transpired over the past week, leading up to the scene in the cellar of the stone barn.

Ninety minutes into the session, two FBI agents from the office in Williamsport appeared. They were content to listen and take notes.

Ronald Dewitt was in the room through these long hours, leaning in silence against the wall with his arms crossed. Now and then, I would mention a twist in the story and the agents would nod in a perfunctory way, as if they already had this information in hand. When that happened, I shifted my gaze to Dewitt, but could read nothing in his face. He appeared placid for a man who had just shot another to death and I don't think it was a front. Either he had done it before or he really was that stone cold.

We finished a little before three a.m. and were ushered to the lobby to discover that the press had landed, with a half dozen cars and TV trucks from stations in Scranton and Harrisburg crowding the front parking lot. A small mob of townspeople had assembled as the word spread. To avoid all this, we were led out a back entrance where Leo's niece Kelly was waiting in what turned out to be her own car. She carried us to Angela's house under the cover of darkness.

The rain had stopped and the moon hung hazy white in the sky. Kelly had alerted her uncle Leo and he showed up with Brenda – the same Brenda who hungered for big city scandal. We sat at the kitchen table and replayed the night as the two of them sat there speechless. As I listened to Angela's voice and then my own, I couldn't shake the feeling that it had all happened to someone else, scenes from a movie I had seen somewhere.

It was only after Leo and Brenda had left that I felt steady enough to call Isabel. Though it was now almost five, she answered on the second ring and said, "Richard?"

I almost wept at the sound of her voice, sweet and low. "What's wrong?"

"It's all over here," I said.

"What's over? What happened?"

"I'll tell you later," I said. "I just want you to know..." I was having trouble getting the words out. "That I'm all right."

She sensed that something horrendous had gone down. Her throat cleared and her tone climbed a frantic notch. "Richard, what hap –"

"It's okay," I said "I'm okay. Just please get the girls up and go get the rental car and get on the road. As soon as you can. Please."

"Oh, my God. What happened?"

"It's all right," I said. "I'm safe. I'll explain it all when you get here."

"Okay, okay." She caught a breath and I could all but hear her heart pounding. "I'll call you when we get on the road, okay?"

"Okay," I said. "I want to come home."

Angela was rocking in a gentle sway and gazing at her yard, now cast in the soft gray light of the pre-dawn. A silk shawl embroidered with peacocks on flower branches was draped over her shoulders. She looked up when I stepped through the door and something about my expression caused her to stop her motion and stare at me.

"You okay?"

"I called Isabel and I started coming apart," I said. "It's like it's just dawning on me what happened. That we were that close to –"

"I know," she said. "I think I'm still in shock."

"It was the real deal. We could have died out there." She paused. "And Tim's dead."

She closed her eyes for a second and shuddered as if she had a chill. I reached out and drew the shawl over her shoulders before I sat down. The chair creaked softly.

I stopped to regard her in wonder. "I can't believe the way you got up in his face like that."

She opened her eyes and laughed a little. "I was out of my mind. I don't know what I was thinking. It wasn't happening. I felt like I was in a movie." She looked at me. "Is that what it's like? You leave your body?"

I began to reply and felt the words go dry in my mouth. What did I know about real acting?

"You jumped him," she said.

"I know. It was insane." I put my face in my hands and saw a jumble of wild images race by once again. Had it really gone down like that?

Angela spoke up, chasing the crazy pictures away. "Hey, Joey would have been proud of you."

Hearing this, I felt a sob rise to my throat. But then Angela said, "So what's going on with Isabel?" and it went away.

I dropped my hands and raised my head. "She's coming out today. And bringing the girls."

"That'll be nice."

"But we'll go back in the afternoon. Can you fix it for Monday?"

"After all this?" she said. "Yeah, I can fix it."

"Because I need to get out of here."

I saw a glint of light in her eyes. She smiled her sweet, sly smile and said, "Yes, I think you've caused quite enough trouble for one week."

14.

On that final Sunday, we sat on Angela's back porch and watched my girls explore her yard. So much nature so close at hand was a marvel to them. They were oblivious to the two state police cars parked across from the house. Special Agent Dewitt had been kind enough to arrange for our privacy.

I knew the media would eventually get around the official wall of silence over the arrests. Once the story got out, they'd track me down in New York. What was a tawdry little tragedy would be turned into a twisted melodrama. Let them come; I was determined that I would not garner fame by way of being caught in the middle of a nightmare.

For this morning, we still had some peace. Isabel and Angela rocked in the chairs while I sat in the sun on the top step with my back against a post. Leo showed up after dragging himself out of bed to drive all the way to the Polish bakery in Shamokin for *paczkis*. I was touched by this gesture, and took it upon myself to make the coffee and wait on everyone, including the cops outside. Isabel, Angela, and Leo were kind enough to pretend not to notice when my trembling hands rattled the china or my voice shook when I tried to speak.

I had provided my wife with a minimum of detail. The way I related it, a group of local men had set up a meth lab in a place where they thought no one would look and were using the money to finance a pathetic little military group. John Miller stood as the commander, but Tim Raines was its true leader. They had done a good job of keeping the darker side of it under wraps until Joey came snooping around. Between his forays into the fields and his research at the library, he had deduced the scheme. There was no doubt about what he'd do with the information. So they cornered him on Nock Hill and pushed him off Council Rock and to his death.

Angela and I had stumbled through the puzzle to end up at the barn. I told her that in the midst of a confrontation, Raines had gone for a pistol and Dewitt had been forced to fire, killing him. The other men were taken into custody.

She listened without saying a word, instead choosing to stare at me for long periods in silence. I could see the battle going on behind her eyes, flashes of glaring anger over me getting into such lethal danger doing battle with relief that her girls still had a father and she a husband. I sat there and took my medicine. I owed her that.

She was right, of course. Still, she didn't grasp that once it started there was nothing we could do but see it through. She couldn't understand because she hadn't known Joey. I sat with her until she settled into a calm relief.

Angela needed some time to herself and slipped inside. Leo joined the girls, lecturing at length on the varieties of butterflies, which I'm sure he knew nothing about.

After a few moments watching them, Isabel said, "Angela's some woman, isn't she?"

I said, "She is, yeah. You should have seen her in that barn. They couldn't stand up to her. She's a..."

Something about the tone of my voice caught my wife's ear and she said, "She's a what?"

I considered for a few moments. "There were these times in my life when I happened on incredible women. I had these encounters that I never forgot. I remember this one time, I was hitchhiking and a family picked me up. The father, sister, and brother, all in the front seat of this big old car. The girl kept turning around to look at me, the weird creature in the back seat. I can still see her. It wasn't that she was beautiful, but her face was full of light. It was just stunning."

Isabel was watching me carefully, wondering where I was going.

"And another time, I stopped at a gas station in this little town and a girl got out of a car, and she was so graceful and lovely. I don't mean like a model. She was just something rare. I wanted to say, 'Don't ever lose that look.'"

"And so?"

"And so maybe once every couple years, something like that would happen to me, a woman like that would cross my path. Sometimes it was just for a few seconds. Sometimes I got to know them. To be with them. And every time it happened, I would think, is this the one? Is she my angel?" I inclined my head toward the house. "Angela was the first."

Isabel's brow furrowed. "Why are you telling me this?"

"Because I want you to know that after all that, I finally found the one. And I know that every time I look at you and our girls."

Sudden tears welled in her eyes and her voice cracked a little when she said, "That right there will get you out of trouble for the next ten years."

After we ate lunch, Juliette and Annabelle hurried back to their exploration of the yard. We were clearing the table when the doorbell rang. Angela went out to the front room and returned with Ronald Dewitt.

She offered him something to drink. He said, "Just water, thank you."

She handed him a bottle from the refrigerator. He explained that he had come by to share some information about the case. I saw his eyes land on Isabel and Leo.

I said, "I'd like my wife to stay, if that's all right. And Leo, too."

He said, "All right, sir."

"You can call me Richard. Or Richie."

Dewitt nodded. "Yes, sir." He didn't do either, but at least he acknowledged the offer.

He explained the state police and criminal division of the attorney general's office had been working undercover in Wyanossing as part of a broad investigation into the increased activity by right wing groups in the wake of 9/11.

He said, "These individuals blamed what happened on certain people putting the nation at risk."

"Yes, we had that discussion," Angela remarked in a dry voice.

"Well, they got busy," he continued. "We became concerned that they were going to mount an attack of their own. Possibly as a response. Possibly as a way to show that the nation was still vulnerable."

Angela said, "Because of people like us."

"Yes, ma'am, something like that," Dewitt said. "We planned only to observe and report. When Mr. Sesto died, it changed the game. We didn't have enough to move on indictments." He paused to regard me. "And then you showed up, sir."

"Richard."

"Yes, sir. You kicked over some rocks and the subjects we were surveilling got nervous. They were reacting. I reported this to my superiors and they decided to wait and see where it went."

"You put Angela and my husband in danger," Isabel said. Her voice was thick.

Dewitt nodded slowly. "That was an unfortunate outcome, yes, ma'am. Your husband and Ms. Sesto took advantage of the weather to escape our surveillance last night. When they showed up at the barn, I had no choice but to make a move."

I said, "He saved our lives, Isabel."

She gave me a look that caused me to stare down at the floor.

Dewitt got me off the hot seat. "In any case, everyone's relieved that no one else suffered any injuries."

"Or worse," Isabel said. She was not about to be placated.

Dewitt said, "Yes, ma'am. Or worse."

I wanted to get off the subject. And I had questions gnawing at me. "Who's Crystal?"

Dewitt looked at me, considering. "All I can tell you is that she's one of ours. I can't say any more, sir."

I was astonished; the girl had zinged it right by me. How much was an act and how much was real? I might never find out. "So she's gone?"

"Yes, sir. And that's really all I can say. Sorry."

I shook my head in numb wonder. Angela and Leo both stared, incredulous, though Leo also displayed a crooked smile and said, "God damn."

"So who trashed my rental car?" I said.

Dewitt gave me an off-hand shrug but a steady look that contained the answer. I moved before Isabel caught on to the idea that her husband had been kept around as bait. "What about Louie Zag?"

Dewitt surprised me by smiling slightly. "Mr. Zagarelli is fine. You'll be pleased to know that he sent one of the members of Mr. Raines's group to the emergency room. From what we understand, this individual was sent to assault him as a warning. The man got a surprise."

Leo laughed over that.

"But what about..." I put a finger to my forehead.

The agent said, "That. Yes, sir. It appears that at some point, he was treated to a hot shot. Do you know what that is?"

Unfortunately, I did.

"What is it?" Isabel said.

"Drugs that are either very pure or mixed with something lethal," Dewitt said. "The intent is to kill the victim by way of overdose. In this case, Mr. Zagarelli survived. But there was brain damage."

I spent a moment digesting that. *Brain damage* meant never coming back. I understood it rationally, but it still made my heart ache for poor Louie. Leo sighed and shook his head.

I said, "So what happens to Miller and those other characters?"

"Various capital charges," Dewitt said. "That will all be sorted out by the state attorney general's office."

Isabel said, "Will there be a trial?"

"Only if they don't plea bargain," Angela said.

"And if there is, will Richard have to testify?"

"It's possible," Angela said. "But it will be a while before that happens. If it does."

I looked at my friends, then at the agent. I said, "I guarantee there are other people living around here who still support those guys."

Dewitt said, "I'm sure there are, yes, sir."

"So how do you protect Angela and Leo now?"

Leo said, "Shit, man. I don't need no protecting."

Dewitt didn't offer any comment.

Isabel said, "You can't, can you?"

The agent said, "That'll be a matter for the local police."

"Let's hope they're better than the last crew," Angela said.

Ronald Dewitt (not his real name) and I shook hands and he made his exit. I understood that he would now disappear into undercover. I wondered if he and Crystal Nash (not her real name) would work together again. I wanted to ask him that and a couple dozen other questions. What *were* their real names? Where did they live? How did they end up as undercover gunslingers? These and more. I knew he wouldn't answer any of them.

A few minutes after he left, Leo and I walked down to the street to stand by his car. He said, "Oh, yeah. The white Sable? It belongs to that Yarnell kid. Actually, his mom."

"Another mystery solved."

He nodded wisely. "Life's full of them, Richie."

I gave him a hug, feeling a thump in my chest. "You watch yourself," I said.

He laughed and patted me on the shoulder. "Nobody's going to fuck with me, man. They wouldn't dare. I got justice on my side. We always did, right?" I gave him a dubious look and he said, "Okay, most of the time."

"You guys take care of Louie," I said.

"We will. Don't worry." He stood back. "Let me know when you're back in town, okay?" With a wink and a wave, he climbed into the station wagon and drove off.

Inside, I found Isabel readying for the trip home.

She said, "Tell the girls to thank Angela and send them in so they can use the bathroom before we go."

"Okay."

"We'll leave you two alone so you can kiss her good-bye."

"Do what?"

"Kiss her good-bye. She'll want you to. And you should." She eyed me. "Just keep it clean, mister."

When I joined them, Angela was telling Juliette and Annabelle about all the different birds that perched and nested around her yard in the spring and summer. She said she got daily visits from wild rabbits. The clincher was the whispered word that now and then a family of black bears would wander into town.

My daughters performed a duet. "Daddy, can we come back? *Please?*"

I told them, yes, absolutely. They gave Angela hugs, thanked her sweetly, and ran into the house to find their mom.

Angela and I traded some idle chatter for a minute. It felt good to drop all the weight and talk about nothing.

"What will you do now?" I said.

"Stay here. Take care of business." She paused and said, "But I've been thinking that I need to get out some more. See some things. Meet some people. Travel a little bit."

I got it; her brush with mortality had changed things. For me, too. "Any trips to New York in there?"

Her mouth dipped in a wry smile. "I was thinking more along the lines of Italy or Germany. I've always wanted to visit Thailand. Australia, too. But I can be in New York anytime." She raised a finger. "I'll tell you what, you get a part in a play, I'll come in."

"I don't know when that will be."

"Whenever it is. Just don't make me wait too long, okay?"

We smiled at each other. It was quiet there, serene. I could have stayed a little longer. But my wife and daughters were waiting for me to carry them back to our lives. So I kissed her good-bye.

Before we left town, I had Isabel drive to the cemetery. She and the girls waited in the car while I walked through the spring grass to Joey's plot. I dropped to my knees and spent a few minutes with the stone that bore his name. And I found myself able to say a farewell that felt like the real thing.

I called Sonia when we got to the interstate. She was surprised; I rarely bothered her over the weekend. I told her I wanted to see her on Monday to talk about cutting back on my commercial work. Because there were other things I wanted to do. She sounded puzzled, but she agreed.

We had just passed the Berwick exit when the voice on the radio said something about a request from a caller in Wyanossing. I heard a familiar rumble of drums and reached to crank the volume on the radio and "She Loves You" rocked the car as we rolled down I-80, heading for home.

A large word of thanks to my band of angels…

Anna Foote, Barbara Saunders, Barbara Sechrist, Bea Fulmer,
Bob Fulmer, Dirk Detweiler, Doug Robinson, Duane Taffe,
Flora Fulmer, Frank Holden, George Weinstein,
Helen Schurz-Rogers, Ilene Dyer, Jack Dyer, James Taylor,
Jane Ravert, Janet Clark, Janice Loehrer, Jennifer Hewitt,
Joanne Mei, Karen Mertz, Karin Koser, Katie Bourne,
Kevin Moreau, Lynn Taylor, Marene Holden,
Martha Woodham, Melissa Stephenson,
Michael Reeves, Scott Armstrong, Shannon Clute,
Sonny McCord, Steve Loehrer, Sterling Fulmer, Susan Archie,
Tara Coyt, Thurston Fulmer, Trudel Leonhardt …
and Sansanee Sermprungsuk, who has saved me once again.

About the designer...

Susan Archie is a Grammy-award winning art director based in Atlanta. She has been nominated for 4 Grammys and received an "Alex" (Steinweiss) Award for Creative Excellence in Multimedia Packaging. Her work has been featured in Print and I.D. magazines, and has been praised in periodicals ranging from The New Yorker to Rolling Stone.

LaVergne, TN USA
05 March 2010

175060LV00001B/2/P